The keeper Of LoSt Things

Also by the Author:

A Hairy Tail

Another Hairy Tail

All The Pretty Ghosts

Ashes to Ashes

A World Without Angels

Fairy Tales Retold

Fashion Fraud

Gifted

Dark Eyes: Cursed

Songbird

Tainted Magic

Ten Thousand Wishes

The Project Integrate Series

The Starkissed series

Trouble

Two Beating Hearts

The Keeper Of Lost Things

Jamie Campbell

ISBN: 197 982 7095
ISBN-13: 978-1979827096

"The way to love anything is to realize that it may be lost."

-   Gilbert K. Chesterton

Chapter 1

Leave.

Go.

Now.

The words screamed in my head as I urged them toward the couple sitting on the picnic table. They were wrapped up in a conversation, completely forgetting about the tube of lip gloss that had been used and then placed on the table.

They were ready to leave, it was written in their body language. One held the straps of her handbag tightly, ready to grab it before going. The other, a male, had planted both his feet on the ground so he could stand.

Go.

The suspense was too much. I silently willed them to leave so I could grab it. I needed it. There was something yearning deep within my belly that said I had to have it.

I would give it a home.

I wouldn't let it be discarded into the trash where

nobody would ever love it again.

It wasn't going to fall into the dirt and be caked with mud, rolling into the storm drain in the next rainfall. It would be safe, it wouldn't be forgotten, it would be mine.

The pair liked to talk, their smiles broad as they clumsily forgot about the lip gloss. They were careless, just like all the others. Nobody else cared about what happened to all the items left behind.

But I did.

Lost items were no more valueless just because they were lost. They had worth, they existed in this world for a purpose, they should never have been lost in the first place.

Just like me.

The male stood, putting his feet to good purpose. The girl followed, hitching her handbag onto her shoulder. They walked off without a second look back at the table.

The lip gloss was left behind.

It sat on the table watching its owner walk away from it forever. It would no longer touch her lips, no longer make her face prettier, her lips softer. It would never again know what it was like to live in her handbag.

Now.

Now was my chance.

I darted across the courtyard, my focus solely on the small round tube. I would rescue it, stop it from suffering the fate of something left behind. I would give it a new home, let it know how valuable it was to this world.

With one swift swoop of my hand, I grabbed the lip gloss and slipped it into my bag.

It was no longer lost.

I would keep it forever, far longer than the girl would wonder where she had left it. It would be a fleeting thought in her mind, but to me the memory would last a lifetime.

I always remembered where they had come from.

Nothing was lost to me.

As I turned to get to class, someone caught my attention. It was a boy, standing on the side of the courtyard. His hands were shoved into his pockets, his dark hair so long it flopped over his eyes.

He was watching me.

My heart raced as my breath caught in my throat and threatened to strangle me. I had to push it all away, just like I had done all the times before when my emotions had threatened to make me feel.

He was nothing. So what if he had seen me. I was doing nothing wrong. Taking lost items was not a crime, it was a service, a kindness that the world lacked.

I did not care about this boy.

Not his tall, lanky frame.

Not his messy hair.

Not his eyes that were looking at me.

Not his rosy lips as they formed a slow smile.

He was nothing to me and I needed to get to class. There were far more important things in the world than being watched by a boy who clearly had no manners.

I rushed to class, passing the girl who had lost her lip gloss. She was heading back to the courtyard, did she know about her loss already? Would she be searching for her berry bliss gloss for long?

That wasn't my concern.

She had lost it and it was now mine.

Shame on her.

Taking my seat in English, I listened intently to the words of Mr. Greene. He enjoyed talking, he was a master of creating imagery that placed you in the middle of the action. There were few other teachers that I actually gave the compliment of listening to.

While my gaze scanned the room–searching, always searching–they travelled across the boy from outside. I'd never noticed him before. I doubted I'd even seen him before.

His eyes met mine as I was caught looking. My gaze quickly darted back to Mr. Greene, pretending I had never been staring in the first place.

I kept my face forward for the rest of the class, escaping the monotony of school with the final bell. My house was four blocks from the school, meaning it was just far enough to be a long walk but not far enough for the city to subsidize a bus ride.

The lip gloss was singing to me from inside my bag. It was thanking me, ever so grateful for the opportunity of a second chance. It trusted me to find a place for it, for it to never suffer the indignation of being lost again.

My house came into sight, standing out from all the others. It was the only one with a black façade, the result of a fire many years ago. Nobody bothered to scrub the smoke from the bricks, leaving it there for everyone to remember the tragedy of what had taken place within the walls.

The house was ugly, both inside and out.

But it was home.

It was where I could be found.

"Good afternoon, Em," my neighbor said as I hurried past their pristine white picket fence. It was Mrs. Justice, out watering her roses. She liked to talk. "How was school today?"

"Fine, thank you, Mrs. Justice," I said politely. I couldn't admit that I was in a hurry because of the lip gloss calling to me in my bag.

She wouldn't understand.

Mrs. Justice had never been lost in her life.

"I heard the school carnival is coming up soon. Are you going to go?" she asked with such enthusiasm that a tiny bit of guilt crept into my mind.

"I don't know yet," I lied.

She gave me a kind smile, the same one she used when she was feeling sorry for me. "Well, I hope you decide to go. It looks like it will be lots of fun."

"I'm sure it will be." I smiled too, but mine felt fake. "I'll see you around, Mrs. Justice."

She watched me take the few more steps to my house and go inside. They burned on my back, even when I was through the door and it was closed behind me.

I hurried up the flight of stairs to my room at the end of the corridor. I locked the door behind me as my gaze roamed over everything inside, searching for anything that was out of place.

Sometimes Uncle Marvin came into my room when I wasn't home. I never knew what he did in there, but sometimes things were moved.

I didn't like it when things were moved.

This time, everything looked to be in the right place. All the items stacked on the shelves were right where they were supposed to be, awaiting my return in silence.

Taking the berry blast lip gloss from my bag, I stood in front of the cramped shelves. I knew exactly where it needed to be placed. On the third shelf up, with the other fourteen lip glosses that had been lost by careless people.

I placed the tube at the front, because I liked the smell of it. Berries filled my nostrils even though I had replaced the cap. I had fifteen now. Fifteen little soldiers, so brave and courageous.

It was no longer lost now.

It had a home.

I would keep it safe.

Chapter 2

"Get your butt down here for dinner!" Uncle Marvin bellowed from the kitchen. He never just spoke, he only knew how to bellow. Sometimes I wondered if he was going deaf and nobody realized it.

I knew if he got to a second bellow, I wouldn't be having any dinner that night. I scrambled to get downstairs, almost tripping down the stairs as I did.

"I'm here, Uncle," I said, just to be certain he knew.

"About time."

He laid down the burnt meatloaf on the table, stabbing at it with a knife until it fell into two pieces. He dumped one onto my plate, shoving the ketchup my way.

I drowned the meat with the red, sticky sauce. It was the only way to make anything Uncle Marvin made edible. Every day I was surprised that I hadn't turned red from the excess intake of ketchup. It was a miracle, really.

We ate in silence, the dry meat sticking in my throat

with every bite.

"You got anything to say?" he asked, his voice more of a grunt than a proper enunciation of words. He saved his polite voice for Mrs. Justice and the few others that dared speak with him.

"Um, how was your day?" I knew he didn't care about my day so there was no point in sharing. What Uncle Marvin really wanted was to complain about all the trials of his day, but he wanted an opening first.

"Everyone at work is an idiot," he started, which was how he normally did. Everyone he worked with was an idiot, everyone he encountered was an idiot, everyone in the *world* was an idiot except for him.

I was an idiot too.

He reminded me quite often.

His fork banged on the table, making the ketchup bottle quiver with fear. "Are you even listening to me or are you thinking about those stupid ideas of yours again?"

"No, I'm listening," I lied. I did that a lot. Lie, I mean. The truth rarely escaped my mouth. I'd heard it called a compulsion before, by my school principal.

I called it a necessity.

The truth was ugly, nobody wanted that.

Uncle Marvin continued his tirade against the world while I tuned out again. This time I made sure to nod where appropriate so it looked like I was agreeing with him. He wouldn't catch me thinking thoughts of my own again.

"You have to cook dinner tomorrow night," he changed the subject abruptly, like the thought had only just occurred to him and he needed to say it before he forgot.

"I can't," I replied. "I have recycle club on Wednesdays."

"Recycle club? Who the hell joins a recycle club?" He was bellowing again, his voice so loud it made Matilda, our cat, flee the room. Not even the possibility of getting the meatloaf leftovers was enough to convince her to stay. "You are outstandingly weird, girl."

I chewed on my bottom lip so I didn't say anything I would regret later on. The best way of dealing with Uncle Marvin was to let him do all the talking. It got the conversation over that much faster.

"Your father was smart leaving you," he continued, his eyes crazy and wild while his bushy eyebrows tried their very best to contain them. "If I could run away from you, I would too."

The thing about my Uncle Marvin was that he knew exactly what to say that would shatter me into a million pieces. I should have been immune to his barbs by now. But every time he mentioned my father, it cut me in two.

Then ten.

Then a million.

Until I was nothing but the six year old I was back then, watching my father leave in the middle of the night without looking back to say goodbye.

I blinked away the image, refusing to let it cause tears to fall. It was the truth, after all.

Like I said, the truth was ugly.

Nobody wanted that.

"Yes, Uncle Marvin," I replied dutifully before standing to clear the dishes. I'd had enough of the meatloaf that I could stomach for one night.

He leaned back in his chair and undid the belt straining his huge belly. The moment the leather was free, a mass of flesh bulged over his pants. Uncle Marvin could use a diet but I wouldn't be the one to tell him.

His beady black eyes followed me around the kitchen, inspecting what I did while waiting for an opportunity to criticize. I kept my back to him, going about my chores while keeping my mind blank and unthinking.

Matilda slid through my legs, walking between my ankles and meowing for dinner. I filled the tabby's dish until she was purring with happiness and eating contently. Her fishy cat food looked more appetizing than the meatloaf.

"That cat smells," Uncle Marvin grumbled.

His nose was nowhere near Matilda. He was probably smelling his own body odor.

"I will bathe her tomorrow," I promised. At least, I would run a wet rag over her and tell him she had had a bath. Matilda wasn't the smelly one here.

Uncle Marvin stood, making his chair screech with the movement. "You'd better." He stomped off, his girth barely balancing over his stick legs. Quite frankly I was surprised his body managed to get around at all. It seemed to always be balancing like a spinning top.

I finished cleaning up and gave Matilda a pat. At least someone in the house was pleased I was there. The cat and

I were alike, we had both been abandoned by our parents and adopted by Uncle Marvin.

The memory of finding Matilda when she was lost was still vivid in my memory. I had been searching the area behind a construction site, looking for lost things, when I heard the most pitiful meow on the planet. Her pathetic voice led me right to her.

She weighed less than the tube of lip gloss and was mostly bald. Whatever had happened to her in her short life as a kitten was hard on her. I took her home but she didn't belong on one of my shelves. I cleaned her up, shoveling food into her mouth until she started to gain weight.

Uncle Marvin didn't know about her for three weeks.

I was punished when he did.

Still, I begged and pleaded until he finally allowed me to keep her. I was given a million rules to follow, including making sure he never had to do a thing for her, but she was officially mine.

She was officially found.

He'd been grumbling about her ever since but I didn't care. Matilda was mine and she was the only living being that I never lied to. She was always honest with me in return.

While Uncle Marvin settled himself in front of the television game shows—where he knew all the answers and the contestants were idiots, of course—I took Matilda upstairs to my room.

We curled up on the bed together, having survived

another day.

* * *

My eyes were always scanning.

Looking.

Searching.

For lost things.

It came naturally to me now. I didn't have to undergo any training to spot items that were lost. They spoke to me, calling to me to come and rescue them. I always just followed their cries and there they were.

Someone had left behind a book underneath the tree on the edge of the school grounds. It was sitting there on the grass, crying out for its owner to return and take it away with them.

The owner didn't care.

They hadn't even been missing it.

Collecting the book was going to make me late for class. The bell had already rung, everyone around me hurrying to make it before receiving a tardy note.

I didn't want another tardy note.

But I couldn't leave it behind.

I wouldn't abandon it.

My feet stepped off the path and hurried to get to the book. Perhaps if I ran I would still be able to make it to class on time. I could slip in and pretend I was invisible, pretend I was one of the cool kids who made a point to be fashionably late.

I was almost there, just a few more steps and I would be able to pick up the book and shove it into my backpack for safekeeping. I would add it to my shelves when I returned home later.

Just as my hand was reaching, my knees bending, someone stepped out from behind the tree. It was a male, the same one who had been watching me yesterday.

This time, he spoke. "I wondered if you'd come."

My hand was frozen mid-reach, my knees still bent. It was like someone had switched a freeze frame switch and paused me into place.

"Get away from me," I replied.

"Did you get up on the wrong side of the bed?" Of all the random questions he could ask me, he chose that one? I didn't have time for this… idiot.

"Stop talking."

"You don't want to talk?" His head cocked to the side and I could see all the unspoken questions in his sparkling eyes. I didn't have time to notice sparkling eyes, I needed to get to class.

My body could move again as I picked up the book and shrugged off my backpack so I could stow it away. The boy watched my every movement.

He made me uncomfortable.

He made me curious.

"I left that book there," he said. "I wanted to see if you would take it. I guess I got my answer. Today is the third day I have been watching you and I still can't figure out—"

"Stay away from me," I growled, finally getting the book to safety.

I backed away from him before running to class. I didn't know who he was or who he thought he was, but he needed to leave me alone. I made it one of my rules to stay away from people and found they generally did the same to me.

That boy was breaking the rules.

And I didn't like it.

He also made me receive another tardy note. I added it to the pile in my bag. So far I think I had the record for how many one student could receive in a semester. They should have given me an award.

I slipped into my seat and ignored the looks I received from the others. They were generous, my peers, with their judgements. They threw them at me without knowing one little thing about me. I would have been surprised if they knew my name.

Emmeline Grace Gabrielle.

That was what my parents had named me.

Before they left.

I hated it.

"We have a new student with us today. Let's get to know a little more about Francis Bolero," old Mrs. Thompson said with a smile. I wasn't really paying attention until the kid from outside stood up.

He shuffled to the front of the class, not an inch of embarrassment to him. "Hey, I'm Frankie. Just moved here from somewhere else. Looking forward to rocking it out." He raised his fist to the air which made some of the girls giggle.

Not me.

I had a name now to add to my list of people I needed to keep away from.

Frankie Bolero.

Even his name was annoying. It dimpled like his cheek, all round and sharp at the same time. He was someone I needed to avoid, someone that would serve no purpose to me.

At least I now knew why I hadn't seen him before. He would soon enough make friends that would find him interesting because he was new to the school. They'd lose interest after a while, like they always did. By then someone else would have started that they could move onto.

Then Frankie would be one of the lost.

Or maybe he wouldn't. Judging by the amount of girls hanging on his every word as he introduced himself without saying anything real about his life, he wouldn't be lonely. I wouldn't have to add him to my shelves.

I suffered all through the double History class until lunchtime. Any break in the curriculum was prime time for rescuing lost things. People forgot about their things when they were having a good time, wrapped up in conversations and gossip.

My lunch tray was full when I took it outside to sit in the corner. If I sat with my back against the wall, I could watch. I could see it all and search for those items that were in danger of being lost. They needed me and I couldn't abandon them.

Not when they needed me the most.

Just as I was munching away through my jello cup, someone stood in front of me and blocked my view. I was staring at their legs before my gaze travelled up the black skinny jeans, the T-shirt that was supposed to be funny, and then settled on the face.

It was *him*.

Frankie.

"I thought I told you to leave me alone," I said in the bluntest and emotionless voice I had.

He sat cross legged on the ground in front of me. Still blocking my view. I was going to miss something if he didn't move soon. "Oh, you did. But I decided that it wasn't something I wanted to do."

I dragged my gaze from the lawn to him until our eyes were peering into one another. They were blue, like the ocean on a cloudy day. Blue and deep and sparkling.

"Why don't you find someone else to bother, *Frankie*." I liked the way his name sounded, like it was angry when the K caught on my tongue. Like it could hook there and refuse to move, much like the boy himself.

"I didn't realize I was bothering you."

"Well, you are. And now you know, so you can go away. Please."

His lips quirked up into a smile, one which I'm sure he thought was charming. It probably worked on all the other girls. "I was hoping we could get to know each other. You seem… interesting."

I had been called many names before, but interesting was not one of them. *Freak* was the normal term of endearment for me. It was usually muttered just a moment before the person walked away from me.

Not all people appreciated their lost things being found. By me.

Especially when I didn't give them back.

It was time for a lie. It had been at least fifteen minutes since I'd used one. "My friends will be here in a moment and we don't like dealing with the new kid. So please go away."

Frankie didn't look away, he accepted my lie like it was the truth. Of course, he didn't know me very well. He nodded solemnly, his head bobbing until his messy hair fell in front of his eyes. Then he stood up and left, taking his tray with him.

As the boy walked away from me, something hurt inside. I felt sorry for him, regretful that I had lied so casually and he had taken my words as golden.

Maybe I shouldn't have been so mean to him.

But I had to remember my rules.

They protected me.

I ate the rest of my lunch watching everyone else and not being a part of their world. If Frankie watched me again, I didn't see him. Although, something told me he wouldn't be far away.

Just watching.

He would know I was lying by now.

Chapter 3

Someone was following me. I'd become aware of them when I left Geography and they were still there as I turned down the corridor to reach my locker.

I could tell they were female from the sound of their footsteps. She didn't try to disguise the fact she was following me, she simply was and that was all I needed to know.

My heart raced as I wondered why.

I would get my answer soon enough.

Without warning, the girl grabbed my backpack and pulled me backwards. I lost my footing and slammed into the bank of lockers. My vision swam for a moment before everything settled back into place.

"What are you doing?" I asked, angry now. Nobody had the right to touch me, especially this girl.

She leaned in close until I could feel her hot breath against my cheek. I wanted to blink but I didn't. "You stole my book."

I pushed her away, refusing to be scared by this girl who was as skinny as a model. She didn't scare me, she barely made me shudder under her accusing glare.

"You *lost* your book. Therefore it no longer belongs to you. When you walked away from it in the courtyard, you lost all rights to that book."

Her face was red now, blazingly angry at not getting her own way. She crossed her arms over her chest, the discontent written in each of the lines across her face.

"It's *my* book. Jennie said she saw you take it and I want it back. It's a library book, they're going to charge me forty bucks to replace it," the girl continued, as if her words would have any bearing on the outcome.

I shrugged. That was not my concern. She shouldn't have abandoned her book yesterday and left it to fend for itself like she didn't care about it. She was the one in the wrong here, not me.

Now she was even angrier. "I know what you do, *Emmeline*. You steal everything you can get your grubby little hands on. Now give me back my book or I will hurt you."

"Em. My name is Em."

"Give me back my book, Emmeline."

"Don't call me that," I warned.

"Then give me my book."

"No."

"Give it to me."

"I don't have it," I lied.

"Yes, you do."

"Nope."

She growled out a cry of frustration before shoving me into the lockers. "You're going to regret this, Emmeline," she sneered before stomping down the hallway.

I really hated it when they thought they had a claim to their lost item. Nobody ever realized that their things were better off in my care. At least they were safe there, they were protected. The book would suffer a far worse fate if returned to the girl.

The corridor started to fill with people as they left their final class of the day. I stood tall again and readjusted the straps of my backpack. Smoothing my hair, I hurried to leave the school grounds.

I was going to be late for Recycle Club.

Ignoring all the school-designated bus lines, I walked the block for a public bus and hopped on the 43. It took me downtown to the Lakeside Mega Mall where the club gathered once a week.

I was the only member of the Recycle Club.

I was the founder, president, secretary, and treasurer.

It wasn't a real club.

The Lakeside Mega Mall was a breeding ground for lost things. No matter when I went there, lost things screamed for me to rescue them. I went once a week, compulsively searching for the lost.

Uncle Marvin didn't know about my lie. He had been excusing me from cooking dinner on Wednesday nights for over a year. He never came to the mall so he would never know of my deceit.

I started with the food court, slowly filling with students from the surrounding schools as they munched on high-sugared treats and sipped on drinks they thought made them look cool.

As the noise levels grew and echoed around the open area, my blood pulsed quicker. There were lost things around, I knew there had to be, I just had to locate them before I could make the rescue. My nerves were sitting on edge until I found them.

The anticipation grew until my palms were sweaty. The lost things needed me, I had to find them. I spied a pair of boys, boasting about their sporting prowess on the football field while their table was splayed with food, drinks, and their belongings. They were at high risk of losing something.

My profiles were rarely wrong.

Girls in groups tended to forget about small items they took out of their handbag. Boys in pairs often forgot their phones after taking them from their pockets and dumping them on the table while they ate determinedly.

People with children were one of the worst offenders. The smaller the child, the more likely they were to lose things. It was easy for a baby to throw an item out of their stroller and their parents never noticing until later when they were searching for it. A pacifier, a single shoe, a toy, they all were lost over the side of a stroller.

Baby things were always sad to add to my shelf. They were always so cute and pastel, yearning to fulfil their purpose with a baby and instead ending up on a shelf in my room for the rest of their lives.

Still, a lost thing was a lost thing and they were treated equally by me. I rescued them all like they were the most important item in the world and I had to make sure they were safe.

There were no families in the food court that afternoon. Only teenagers and bored senior citizens who couldn't hear the ruckus of their younger counterparts. The elderly quite often left behind newspapers, maybe for someone else to read after them. Unless someone was quicker than me, I took those too. The newspapers were added to the found pile.

My eyes remained on the boys, getting ready to leave now. They didn't bother putting their trash in the can, just walked away and made it someone else's problem.

I searched the table with my gaze as I sat nearby, looking–always looking–for their lost items. Their table was scattered with their litter, but nothing seemed to be lost. What a waste of time.

My profiling had let me down.

The lost things called to me, screamed that they were in the food court somewhere. I had to find them before they were doomed to forever waste away in the trash or the mall's Lost and Found department.

Even lost things deserved better than that.

My gaze flicked to a group of kids a few tables over. It was a mixture of boys and girls, all sitting around eating and laughing happily. It was prime location for at least one of them to lose something.

They became my next obsession.

My eyes fell on one of the boys, the back of his head seemingly familiar. I knew the group was from my school because I'd seen most of them before. But this boy, there was something tugging at the edge of my mind about him.

He turned to speak to the girl next to him when it clicked.

It was Frankie.

He was smiling and talking, the new kid had obviously made some new friends after his introduction at school. It was the first time I'd seen him interacting with others and it seemed out of place. Every one of his facial expressions appeared to be forced, squeezed out of him by social convention.

I was glad his back was to me.

Now it was my turn to spy on him.

The heavy book in my backpack reminded me that I couldn't trust him. That he was capable of setting a trap for me and I needed to be careful. Nobody got close to me for a reason, they would only end up as lost as I was.

I could say a million bad things about Frankie, but I couldn't say anything bad about his hair. It was perfectly messy, a little longer than the other boys, but it looked soft. And shiny. He looked after his hair, if not his manners.

After seventy beats of my heart had passed, the group started to leave. They didn't go all at once, breaking off in pairs and triplets to depart from their group.

As Frankie stood to leave–alone, a singular–he saw me.

I wasn't quick enough to avert my gaze before he caught my eyes and held them there.

One second.

Two seconds.

Three and four seconds before he would release me. I felt exhausted from that one stare, like an hour had passed in the time it took us to lock eyes.

I didn't know what that meant.

I didn't *want* to know what that meant.

The lost things were my concern, not the boy known as Frankie who came from somewhere. Once they were all gone, I took a walk to the trash can, using it as an excuse to get a better look at the table.

Only half of the group had cleaned up after themselves. The students in this town needed to learn better manners as well as how not to lose things. They were pigs, messy and unkempt.

Out of control.

It was no wonder so many items found themselves lost.

Someone had left their cell phone on the table. It was haphazardly resting underneath a burger wrapper. Whoever lost it was seriously going to regret it later on.

I swooped in and picked up the phone, placing it in my bag carefully. Phones were a hassle, they always rang frantically as its owner tried to reclaim it. When they ran out of battery it was always a relief knowing they would now remain silent.

The phone was the only lost item. It was a good catch for a long afternoon in Recycle Club. It was starting to get dark outside, the large skylights hanging over the food court showing the grey clouds as they started to swirl over the town.

It was time to get home.

I grabbed a burger and some fries to eat on the bus ride home. I had to sit in the back and tuck the greasy paper bag into my backpack so I didn't get caught. Bus drivers hated it when you ate on their bus. It wasn't because it was against the rules–which it was–but because the smell made them hungry.

The bus rolled along the streets, groaning around the corners, and complaining every time the brakes were tapped. The town needed a bunch of new buses but the mayor said it wasn't feasible. He'd gambled all the town's money away when he didn't think anyone would look. He'd been covering it up ever since.

How did I know?

Mayor Hay had lost his notebook at the cinema one night.

I read it cover to cover, seeing all his lazy scrawl spell out his troubles. His debts grew over the pages until they were too large he started underlining the numbers in red pen.

At least he kept good records.

His notebook was currently sitting on my shelves.

Safe and found.

I didn't need to wonder what Uncle Marvin had for dinner when I arrived home. The house was in darkness except for the living room television. The soap opera was casting out its rays in all different colors, leaving the room illuminated in a kind of blue hue.

Uncle Marvin was passed out, a bottle of whiskey on the floor next to him. His mouth was open while he snored, a line of drool running down his chin.

My uncle had indulged in a liquid dinner.

He somehow managed to look just as mean and dispirited unconscious as he did while awake. Still, I covered him with a blanket and left him there. He probably wouldn't move until the morning, depending on how much he'd actually drunk.

I took the stairs to my room, opening the door and making sure he hadn't disturbed anything of mine. If Uncle Marvin did go snooping today, he didn't leave any traces.

The phone was starting to sing, the screen displaying the same number repeatedly. It was probably the owner, trying to find the person who picked up his lost phone.

A picture of a dog was his screen background. It was cute.

The former owner deserved his panic now. He should be worried enough to search for his lost item. He would never get it back and maybe that would teach him a valuable lesson to take through his life.

Everything had value.

Everything was precious.

Nothing deserved to be lost.

If only it was that easy to educate people. Humans were inertly reckless, they acted without thought or care. Hurting others came naturally, so why shouldn't it extend to their things? They would never really learn.

I placed the phone with the other two I already had on my shelf. It was getting cramped in my room. The lost things were spilling over, having to be shoved together just to remain on the shelves. There were too many for them to be comfortable.

I needed more space.

My collection had started more years ago than I could remember. The first item was a keyring with a single key dangling from it. From then onwards I noticed lost things everywhere I went. I started picking them up from that day forwards.

Assessing my rows and rows of shelves, I was proud of my accomplishment. I had saved so many things from being lost that I deserved a medal. If not for me, all those items would have ended up in the trash or ruined forever. I gave them a home and a second chance.

No item was going to feel lost.

Not on my watch.

People weren't going to stop losing things, and I wasn't going to stop rescuing them. Unless I wanted to end up like one of those people on *Hoarders*, I needed to expand my shelf space. I wasn't going to be found buried under a six foot high mountain of lost things one day.

That wouldn't be me.

I made a mental note to solve the problem another day. Right now I was exhausted and needed to rest. If Uncle Marvin was passed out for the night, that meant I could be too.

After taking a nice, hot shower I fell into bed, only faintly aware of the new cell phone still chirping away with missed calls and messages.

Everything was silent when I awoke in the morning. I was awake before my alarm started buzzing, it took a few bleary moments to remember that something else had pulled me from my sleep.

Knock knock knock.

The hard beats were coming from downstairs, someone was knocking on our front door. They tapped incessantly, demanding my attention and forcing me to get out of bed.

I had to hurry. If Uncle Marvin hadn't answered the door, that meant he was still asleep. He was worse than an angry bear when awoken earlier than he needed to be.

Slipping on a robe, I raced down the stairs barefoot and hurried to reach the door to silence the noise. One glance to my right confirmed my suspicions that Uncle Marvin was indeed still asleep in the chair in the living room.

I pulled open the door just a crack, stopping the person mid-knock.

The last person I expected to see was Frankie Bolero.

Chapter 4

"What are you doing here?" I demanded as Frankie's hand recoiled from his knocking. He was wearing jeans with a black button-down shirt. He looked too perfectly put together for so early in the morning.

"I'm here to get my phone back," he replied, flashing me a smile that tried to endear me toward him.

It only kinda, sorta worked.

"What makes you think I have it?"

"Because I lost it on purpose. I wanted to know where you lived and I tracked it here using an app." He sounded proud about it, like he hadn't just *stalked* me.

"Well I don't have it," I lied. I told you I was a liar. About anything and everything. The truth rarely had a place in my life to be spoken.

"Yeah, you do. See?" He held up an electronic notebook with a map on the screen. There was a blinking dot over my address in the street. It was as red as a siren, blaring that it was here, come and get me.

"It's wrong." I shrugged, like I couldn't care less in the world about his app and the blinking dot.

"Can I come in?"

"No, why would you do that?"

"Because I've come all this way and you have my phone," Frankie said, taking a step closer to the doorway. Mrs. Justice was already out in her garden, only paying half of her attention to her roses, the rest to me.

I stepped back from the door. "Fine. But you're not staying and you have to whisper."

Seeing Frankie in my house was wrong. Every voice in my head screamed to get rid of him. They just didn't tell me *how* to get rid of him, otherwise I would have done it immediately.

His eyes roamed everywhere, looking at everything in the shabby excuse for a house. There was only one painting on the wall and it was of a sad, lonely horse. It had been here when I moved in and I couldn't imagine Uncle Marvin purchasing artwork so I always assumed it was here when he bought the place.

I didn't want him seeing my world. This house wasn't much but it was my piece of the world, the shelf I had been placed on when I was lost. I didn't need Frankie judging me for our lack of money or comfort.

My weight shifted from foot to foot as I stood awkwardly. "You should go. I told you to leave me alone. If you lost your phone then that's your fault. I can't help you."

Frankie dragged his gaze back to me. "I'm sorry if I made you uncomfortable but I thought we could be friends. If you give me my phone back, I'll leave."

"I told you, I don't have it."

"I really need it."

"Then you shouldn't have lost it," I pointed out. People were always so regretful when they lost something. If they cared about something so much in the first place they never would have lost it. I had no sympathy for them.

"I didn't lose it, I left it there for you to find," Frankie replied.

"Then aren't you silly."

"Please? It's the only way my parents can contact me."

"You don't live with them?"

"Yeah, I do. But they always need me to work or pick up my sisters, or groceries. Whatever. Please, can I have my phone back?"

"I've already said a million times that I don't have it." I crossed my arms over my chest, reminding myself that I was still only wearing a thin nightgown over my even thinner pajamas. Uncle Marvin was stirring. I held the door open for him. "You need to leave. Now."

His beautiful blue eyes pleaded silently with me. They reached down into my soul and spoke directly to it. But there was nothing I could do. I had never returned a lost thing to its original owner.

It was impossible.

Unheard of.

Against the rules.

My rules existed for a reason and he wanted me to break every single one of them. I couldn't do it, no matter how much I wanted to change those sad eyes. If I flaunted the rules, then what would happen? Something bad, surely.

"Go, please," I said.

Frankie looked from me toward the door and then back again. His feet started moving. I watched him leave without saying another word. The silence hung between us like a wet blanket, smothering everything in its path.

When he was at the bottom of the steps, I closed the door. Uncle Marvin was starting to waken so I quickly ran upstairs and got ready for the day. Properly this time, not having to hurry to get to the door.

I wasn't quick enough to escape the house before Uncle Marvin barked at me to make him breakfast. "Eggs or cereal?" I asked politely, gritting my teeth together so I didn't say something I would instantly regret.

"Eggs, idiot."

Of course.

I flew around the kitchen, throwing everything into the pan and then willing it to cook faster. The eggs were only slightly runny when I served them.

There was no time to stop for Mrs. Justice outside. I threw a 'good morning' her way without slowing down. I was going to be late–again. Just once it would have been nice to show up to class on time. It would probably astound the teacher more than myself.

When my butt hit the seat in Geography class eight minutes after the bell rang, Mr. Brisinger only had a stern expression for me. "Miss Gabrielle, so nice of you to join us." His forced smile was filled with crooked teeth.

"Sorry, sir."

"Don't get too comfortable, you're off to the principal's office."

"But I—"

"Now, Miss Gabrielle." He pointed to the door, just in case I had trouble finding it. I dropped my books back into my backpack and stood, feeling every pair of eyes in the room on me.

As I walked down the empty corridor I wondered what the punishment was for dozens of tardy notes. Surely they wouldn't expel me just for being late occasionally? Or repeatedly? Constantly? The thought of having Principal Moore calling Uncle Marvin was phenomenally terrifying.

Uncle Marvin would kill me.

He told me once his only rule was "Stay out of trouble and out of my way". I was good at the latter and only slightly better at the former. I really did *try* to stay out of trouble but surely being late wasn't considered trouble?

I was stuffed.

I was going to have to come up with some good lies to tell Moore. I'd already used one about my house burning down, my Uncle Marvin needing to be taken to the hospital, my cat swallowing a coin, and nearly every other excuse I could think of. This one was going to have to be good.

When I reached reception, Moore's assistant was typing like her life depended on it. She didn't look up when I stood in front of her. "Um, excuse me. Mr. Brisinger told me to see Principal Moore."

She flicked her eyes to me once, making sure I was a person and not a recorded voice before replying. "Go on in, he's waiting for you."

Mr. Brisinger worked fast if he'd already told Moore to expect me. They probably started doing that after the time I was ordered to the Principal's office and then disappeared for half a day. I started Recycle Club early that day.

I knocked on the door before hearing the terse "Come in" boom from inside. It was going to take some fast talking to get out of the office alive.

It was best to go on the offensive. "I'm really sorry for being late, Mr. Moore. My Uncle Marvin choked on his breakfast sausage and I had to call an ambulance. They said he was lucky to be alive and he told me to come to school even though he was shaken and—"

"Sit down, Miss Gabrielle," Moore barked, completely interrupting my apology.

It was then that I noticed we weren't alone. The girl from the corridor the day before was sitting down already. Her arms were crossed over her chest and her cheeks were pink. She purposefully wasn't looking at me.

I somehow doubted this was about being late.

It was worse.

I sat down and waited, trying to look younger than my sixteen years and more innocent than I was. In other words, I tried to lie without using words.

Moore got down to the point quickly. "Miss Clark came

to me this morning with an allegation against you. She said you stole her textbook. What do you say to that?"

"I honestly have no idea what she is talking about," I replied, thinking back to the Science textbook sitting on my shelves. It was perched on the second one from the top, on the far left hand side. It had a few others to keep it company.

"She's lying!" the girl erupted. "I saw her take it."

"Where did this happen?" Moore, ever the master detective. Was he going to fingerprint the scene of the crime too? The thought almost made me smile.

"Out in the courtyard. I had it out at lunchtime, revising for our quiz and then it was gone."

"And you're sure it was Miss Gabrielle?"

"Jennie said she saw her."

"Was there anyone else around to witness this?"

"That new kid, Frankie. He was there, he saw the whole thing. I know he did." The girl sat back in her chair, as if to say 'case closed'.

Moore pressed a button on his phone. "Callie, please asked Francis Bolero to come to my office immediately."

Damn it.

Frankie was going to be a problem.

I knew he was going to cause me trouble sooner or later. He'd seen too much, been too interested in what I was doing. And now he was going to ruin everything.

As we waited, Moore's forehead scrunched into lines of wrinkles. "Are you sure there is nothing further you want to say about this Miss Gabrielle? Something you'd like to confess before Mr. Bolero gets here?"

"Nope. I told you, I have no idea what she is talking about," I replied. He didn't scare me, even though he kind of did. I'd talked myself out of a lot of situations before, this one was no different. I just needed to think of an excuse to counteract whatever Frankie was going to say.

I could tell them I found the book and handed it in to the library.

I could tell them I wasn't even in the courtyard that day.

I could tell them the girl had stolen my textbook and I was only taking it back.

There had to be a way out of the situation. The last thing I wanted to do was admit my guilt. They would make me pay for the textbook and I didn't have that kind of money. God knew Uncle Marvin would never give it to me.

Frankie knocked on the door before he peered inside. There were no more chairs left so he had to stand at the side of the room, awkwardly looking down at us.

"Mr. Bolero," Moore started. "Miss Clarke here has misplaced her textbook. She said you witnessed Miss Gabrielle taking her textbook from the courtyard two days ago. Do you remember seeing this?"

"It was lunchtime," the girl added helpfully.

I held my breath while I waited for Frankie to speak. I needed to know what he was going to say so I could develop the appropriate lie to counteract it. It would probably be best to cast doubt on his witnessing ability, considering he was new and didn't know any of us. How could he recognize one new face out of many?

Yeah, that was going to be the way to play it.

Dispute everything Frankie said.

"Mr. Bolero?" Moore prompted.

Frankie's hands were stuffed into his pockets as his eyes flicked between the three of us. If he was anything like me, he was wondering who best to make happy that would lead to the most favorable outcome for himself.

Eventually, he took his hands out of his pockets and let them fall limply at his sides. "I don't remember Em being in the courtyard that lunchtime, sorry."

I clamped my teeth together so my mouth didn't drop open. I wasn't the only liar in the room.

"Are you sure?"

"Yes, sir."

"Thank you, Mr. Bolero. You may go." Moore waited until Frankie slipped out before focusing his attention back to us again. "Miss Gabrielle, I highly suspect you did take Miss Clarke's book, but there is no way to prove it."

"But she did take it," the girl protested. She clearly didn't know when to give up. "Jennie saw her. She has it."

"That may be the case, Miss Clarke, but there is no evidence to prove it." Moore pinned me with his gaze. "I suggest, Miss Gabrielle, that you do the right thing and return the textbook. Remember, guilty consciences are heavy burdens to bear."

I shrugged.

Whatever.

My conscience was clear. The guilty one was the girl who shouldn't have lost things in the first place. Maybe this whole episode would teach her a lesson or two about cherishing the things she had.

"You should both return to class," Moore said, finishing the matter. I'd been in his office so many times the room was comfortable and familiar to me. It probably had the direct opposite effect on every other one of his visitors.

The girl was too indignant to leave yet but I didn't have such a concern. I left Moore's office and hurried to return to class. If I ran, I might just be able to incur Mr. Brisinger's wrath just a little more.

I didn't see the guy standing just outside the reception area, almost running straight into him. My gaze travelled upwards to see it was Frankie.

"I get the feeling Mr. Moore doesn't like you," he said.

He was blocking the way. "No kidding. Please move, I have to get to class."

"There's a pop quiz in Geography this morning."

All the bad feelings curdled in my stomach. Trying to complete one of Mr. Brisinger's pop quizzes in half the time was like a medieval torture session. They counted toward the final grade too, just to make them even better.

"I guess it's official, this day can't get any worse," I muttered.

Frankie smiled, one of his cheeks dimpling inwards, making him look even more adorable than I'd ever seen him. "I take it you're not a fan of pop quizzes either?"

"I'd just prefer all the time allotted to complete them."

"Me too."

As I watching him, Frankie stepped backwards two steps. He leaned over casually and pulled the fire alarm with that same smile on his face.

Instantly, the alarm bellowed out its siren. It wailed repeatedly as students started to filter out from classrooms in neat lines. They marched toward the exits.

Frankie grabbed my wrist and pulled me along until we slotted into one of the lines. We fell into step, filing out like all the rest of the students, blending in effortlessly.

We found Mr. Brisinger's group and joined in with the rest of our class for rollcall. He read off our names, ticking them from a sheet attached to his clipboard. When he came to my name, he faltered but said it anyway. "Emmeline Gabrielle."

"Present," I called out, my teeth grinding together. I really wished people wouldn't call me that. My name was Em. It wasn't hard to remember, even shorter to say.

The smile never left Frankie's lips as he stood next to me. It was frustrating that I couldn't work him out. He had every chance to snitch on me in Principal Moore's office. He could have made sure I had detention every day for the rest of my life, maybe even gotten me expelled.

But he didn't.

He lied for me and I didn't know why. Frankie didn't know anything about me except that I stole things. He had trapped me on two occasions now, losing things on purpose just to watch me take them.

Why?

The question echoed around my head like a basketball.

Bouncing off the edges of my skull in perpetual motion. It was a question that would never get an answer, not until I figured out what his game was.

Maybe he was lost too?

The unanswerable question joined the first one, beating a path through my brain to be heard above all the others. It was silly, really, thinking Frankie was anything like me. For all I knew he was perfectly found, his life one that a storybook would be envious of.

Somehow, I got the feeling Frankie would be a riddle that I would never be able to solve.

Chapter 5

Going into the attic had seemed like such a good idea. I couldn't wait to climb the rickety and highly unsafe pull-down ladder into the space.

I was searching for lost space.

Space Uncle Marvin had forgotten about that I could use for my lost treasures. I needed to expand operations from my bedroom and the attic had seemed like the obvious choice.

As I walked through tangled cobwebs and tried not to imagine the spiders that called them home, it didn't seem like as much of a good idea.

The place smelled like the past. If the past smelled like mildew, smoke, and dust, that is. My nose tingled as I stepped over a box and tried to ignore the rat poop littering the floor.

If I could look past the current state of the room, it could definitely work for my collection. There were plenty of walls to attach shelves and Uncle Marvin never came up here—I doubted whether he could even fit through the manhole anymore.

I could fix it up.

It could hold all my lost things.

There were a few stored boxes that I would need to clear, along with all the cobwebs, dust, and poop but that would only be a matter of some heavy duty cleaning. Cleaning was something I was good at.

The flashlight shone on to a box in the corner. It appeared to be newer than the others, it only had a one inch thick dust coating while the others had two. I kneeled next to it and carefully pulled open the lid, half expecting a giant rat to jump out and bite me.

It only had a few things in it.

Things that belonged to my dad.

I pulled out the item on top—a picture of my father holding me when I was only a baby. I knew it was me because of the small birthmark on my arm. It was a red patch in the shape of Africa if you squinted hard enough.

Sometimes I panicked that I had forgotten what my dad looked like. I would try really hard to imagine him in detail. From his dark hair to the lilt of his lips. I would concentrate so hard my head would start to hurt from the effort.

I never really remembered his face. The image that always came to mind was his back as he walked away from me and slapped the front door to our home.

My fingers traced his outline in the frame, creating a clean line through the dust. He was younger in this photo than when I had last seen him. Of course, he didn't leave until I was six. I had a small amount of time with him, just long enough to love him and sear his being into my memory.

Not long enough for a lifetime.

He looked happy in the photograph. He was smiling while he held the baby version of me. Was he truly happy then? Or was he just smiling for the camera? It was so difficult to tell with photos. The person behind the camera always said 'smile' and we all obeyed like good children.

If he was happy then, what had changed in those years that followed? What would make him so sad that he had to lose me? That he had to leave me behind and never look back?

I had lost track of how many times I had asked that question years ago. It was questions like that which made me insane. They burrowed into my brain and repeated themselves on an endless loop.

Why did he leave?

Why didn't he take me with him?

What did I do wrong?

It was the last one that was the real kicker. If I knew what I did wrong, then I would know what I had to change to be better. And maybe, just maybe, he would come back then.

The whole subject was pointless.

Because he was never coming back.

I knew for certain because I had lost hope of that happening a decade ago. It was only that small, tiny voice at the back of my head that refused to give up.

I hated that voice.

It was called hope and it had no place here.

I gently placed the photograph back into the box, memorizing it first. I wished I could replace the image of my dad in my head with the one in the photograph. Even if it only covered it with tape, loosely hanging there for as long as possible.

With my foot, I pushed the boxes into the corner. They were probably lost too, so they could join my collection but only if they sat silently in the corner.

The rest of the place would be filled with shelves. This time when I concentrated, I could see them already. Sun would shine once again through the grimy window, illuminating the lost things and making them feel special again.

It would definitely do nicely.

I climbed down the ladder and popped it back up into the ceiling. Scouting the new space had put me behind schedule and Uncle Marvin would be looking for dinner sooner rather than later. I ran downstairs and put some spaghetti into a pot on the stove.

Right on cue at six o'clock, my uncle heaved his considerable weight onto a chair around the dining table. "I'm hungry."

"Dinner is almost ready," I lied.

"It's late."

"Sorry, it's taking longer to cook than I thought it would." Another lie. I was full of them tonight. I stirred and willed the spaghetti to cook faster. "Maybe you could read the newspaper while you wait?"

"I read the paper after dinner."

"You could switch it up tonight."

"Just hurry up," he grumbled.

I fed Matilda while I waited, at least I could use my time wisely. Uncle Marvin sat staring right up until the moment I placed his plate in front of him.

"About time."

We ate in silence until I found the courage to bring up the topic I needed to talk to him about. It was about the same time his inner monster was quelled with food.

"I went up into the attic today," I said tentatively.

"Why'd you do that for?"

"I'm running out of shelf space in my room. I was wondering if I could use the attic to store my things?" Uncle Marvin didn't know about my cause. All he knew was that I had a crapload of stuff on my shelves.

"I don't care."

"So it's okay?"

"I said I don't care. Are you deaf now too?" He pinned me with his scary face, the one that made me feel like I was two years old again and little more than the size of a pea.

"Thank you," I squeaked back.

Inside I was bouncing with happiness. Expanding my collection into the attic would mean I could rescue as many lost things as possible. Everything would have a home permanently.

Saturday didn't come fast enough as the days dragged

by. At eight o'clock exactly I was standing outside the fence of the aptly named *Tip Shop* as it opened. Located at the entrance to the county trash dump, the Tip Shop rescued anything people threw away if it was sellable.

They were professional Keepers of Discarded Things.

I loved going to the Tip Shop and seeing everything they had rescued. There was everything from chinaware to clothes to building supplies like basins and shower recesses. They cleaned it up and put it on display for purchase. If you ignored the stench of the nearby dump, you could believe you were in an ordinary shop from the high street.

Or, at least, I could.

Someone had thrown away everything there like it was worthless. The Tip Shop had given it all a second chance. It was one of my favorite places to shop. Everyone and everything deserved a second chance.

I was there to find some shelving for my new attic extension. I had walked there with nothing but hope, a few dollars in my purse, and a wheelbarrow to fill.

Hopefully Uncle Marvin wasn't up to any gardening today.

It had been me who found the wheelbarrow anyway. It had fallen from a construction truck along the highway and nobody had bothered to find it. The lost wheelbarrow was covered in a layer of cement but it still worked fine.

I started in the metal section, piled high with all kinds of indistinguishable pieces of twisted steel. For this section, I slipped on a pair of old gardening gloves I kept just for my visits to the shop.

The metal section was dangerous.

I found that out the hard way.

Still, I rifled around until I found some metal brackets that would be perfect for holding up my shelves. I even found a bowl of rusty nails that would go with it. All of them were given the opportunity for a new life with me.

All kinds of wood were stacked up to one side of the tip shop. It was all in various lengths, conditions, and types. I needed something shelf-sized and flat.

My fingers ran over the pieces, listening to their stories as they hummed out the tragedy of being discarded. They were all grateful for the opportunity to live once more and not burn with the rest of the trash at the dump.

I found a few lengths that were perfect for shelves, choosing four and wrangling them into the wheelbarrow. I wheeled the whole thing over to the office to pay.

"Twenty bucks," the man said. He only had one eye, but it was a keen one.

"Eight," I replied. Everything in the Tip Shop was up for bargaining. Nothing actually had a price on it.

"Fifteen."

"Ten."

"Deal." He grinned, showing me he was missing quite a number of teeth too. The man held his hand out for the cash as I handed it over. "You have a good day, Em."

"Thanks, Mr. Adison."

He tipped his old, holey hat to me before I left. I'd probably spent more time with Mr. Adison than I had with

Uncle Marvin. On days when it wasn't busy, he would take me around the shop and point out anything new he had found. He always told me the full story, like 'I found that one under a dead rat. It smelled like a sewer but I cleaned it up real nice. I think it came from one of those posh houses in the hills. I'm gonna sell it for a buck'.

It was busy today, he didn't have time to share stories. But that was okay, because I was busy too. I had shelves to put up before Uncle Marvin returned from the racetrack. He wouldn't like me making so much noise while he was in the house.

The wheelbarrow was heavy to begin with, covered in cement as it was. So when the metal and wood were added to it, my journey home was going to be slow, hot, and possibly painful.

I took it slowly, ignoring all the people that stared at me. They could look all they wanted from their perfect houses with their perfect families that never lost anything. Good for them.

About halfway, someone tried to push me aside to take over the handles of the wheelbarrow. I gripped onto them firmly, not wanting my items stolen. I pushed the person away with my hip.

"Hey, I'm just trying to help."

I stopped, almost dropping the wheelbarrow onto Frankie's foot. "Are you still following me? I told you to leave me alone, what part of the English language don't you understand?"

"I wasn't following you, I swear."

"Yeah, sure. You just happen to be hanging around the road to the dump on a Saturday morning." I crossed my arms over my chest as I faced him. "Do I look stupid? Because only an idiot would believe that."

"My family's store is right over there." Frankie pointed across the street where a small hardware store was open. "I work there sometimes and I saw you coming down the street. I thought I was doing you a favor."

I swallowed down my guilt at the accusations. Perhaps I had flown off the handle just a little too quickly. Still, I wasn't going to tell him that. "I don't need your help."

"I know you don't, but it would be un-gentlemanly of me to let you continue on without offering my assistance."

"You're not a gentleman."

He bowed like a gracious lord. "That is because the lady has not allowed me to be one. Please, M'Lady, may I escort you home and help with your heavy load of…" he looked into the wheelbarrow, "…wood products?"

He was being too nice, he had to want something.

But my arms were hurting and it was still a long way home. Perhaps this one time I could accept his help. Only this time, though. Never again.

"Fine," I sighed.

Frankie's warm smile appeared as he took over the handles of the wheelbarrow. He lifted them and started walking. I kept up beside him.

It was too silent, I had to say something as we walked. "How long has your family been in the hardware business?"

"Not long. Before we moved here they had a small diner."

"Why'd they buy a hardware store then?"

"Everyone needs a change now and then, right?" Frankie looked at me like he expected an answer, someone to agree with him so it would all make sense.

"I guess," I replied, not wanting to disappoint him.

"What's all this wood for?"

He answered my question so I guessed I needed to reciprocate. "I'm building shelves in my attic."

"How come?"

"Does it matter?"

Frankie laughed. "I guess not. Where did you get it? You didn't steal it, did you? I'm not an unwitting accomplice to your crime? Not that I would mind, I would just like to be an informed accomplice."

"I didn't steal it. I *bought* it from the Tip Shop."

"Oh, you saw Mr. Adison? How was he?"

"You know him?" I asked, stopping in my tracks.

"Yeah, he's great. Did he tell you the story about how he lost his eye?" Frankie's eyes were glittering under the sunlight, sparkling with excitement.

"In a sailing accident, walked straight into the boom."

"Exactly! Who would have thought he was a sailor?" Frankie laughed and I couldn't help doing the same thing. His emotions were infectious, taking me over without my permission.

We started walking again, the silence not so unbearable this time. Frankie let go of the wheelbarrow's handles outside my house, reminding me he knew exactly where I lived because he had stalked me.

I needed to be more careful.

Frankie already knew too much now.

"Thanks, I'll take over from here," I said, trying to push him out of the way and reach for the handles.

His hands remained steadfast. "I could help you put up the shelves. I know how, I helped get the store ready for customers. You can only imagine how many shelves that involved."

"No, I can do it. You can't come in."

"I just want to help, Em. I swear, that's all I'm trying to do. Is it so hard having someone be nice to you?" His head tilted to the side like a puppy might do when he was trying to figure something out.

I didn't want Frankie figuring me out.

But for some reason I also didn't want him to go.

He had successfully managed to turn my world upside down.

I sighed. "Fine, you can help. But then you have to leave."

He picked up the handles again. "Wouldn't dream of doing anything else, Em."

Chapter 6

Getting the wood up through the attic manhole would have been extremely difficult alone, I realized later. With Frankie's help, it was actually bearable. He handed it up to me while I accepted it crouched next to the hole in the ceiling.

We got it all up before I had to help Frankie climb up too. He stood in the middle of the attic, making it seem much smaller than it did before.

"It's nice, if not dusty," he declared after he looked around.

"I'm going to clean it up."

"I'm sure you will." He sniffed. "How come it smells like smoke?"

"There was a house fire once. I'll get rid of the smell too."

"I've got no doubts you will."

Frankie smiled too much, nobody could be that happy.

His motives would become apparent soon, I was certain of it. In the meantime, I needed to get the shelves up so I could start my lost things expansion.

"Where do you want the shelves?" he asked as we got down to the serious business of home improvement. I showed him the walls I had planned on covering with shelves and we got to work.

I held things in place while Frankie drilled and levelled. We worked mainly in silence, the occasional sneeze breaking the stillness of the air.

The box containing my father's things sat in the corner staring at me. It teased me with its contents, begging me to open the lid and delve inside.

I wasn't going to do it.

I would ignore that box forever.

"What are you planning on putting up here?" Frankie asked. It had been at least ten minutes since he asked me a question, that had to be a record.

"Stuff."

"What kind of stuff?" He was persistent.

"Just stuff, okay?" I said, harsher than I had intended. I didn't like people asking questions. That led them to knowing things and I didn't want anyone knowing my business.

"Stuff, got it."

He went back to hammering and I continued to hold things in place for him. We worked around the room until all the pieces of wood I had purchased found a home against the wall.

The sun was starting to go down outside, shadows dancing around the room as we moved. I didn't realize it was so late. Uncle Marvin would be home any minute now and I couldn't let him meet Frankie.

"You need to leave now," I said.

"Okay, I'm almost done."

I stood impatiently awaiting him to finish with the last few nails. As he finished, I was ready to push him out the door. My insides were screaming at me to get rid of him. I couldn't let Uncle Marvin see him, it would be disastrous.

"Let's go." I led him down the rickety ladder and through the house. The whole time I expected to hear the rattle of Uncle Marvin's old car pulling into the driveway. The only option then would be to make Frankie leave over the back fence.

I doubted he would agree to that.

We reached the front door with no signs of the rattle. "Thank you for your help today. Please don't tell anyone where I live."

"I won't. And you're welcome. It was kind of fun actually. I haven't—"

"Please go."

Frankie paused with his words still on his lips. He thought twice about letting them free and closed his mouth instead. "I'll see you at school."

"I suppose you will," I replied, closing the door behind him.

I leaned against the old wood and closed my eyes for a moment. Frankie had been very nice to me and given up his Saturday to build my shelves. I should have been nicer to him.

But the consequences of him lingering long enough to meet Uncle Marvin would have been much, much worse. My uncle hated anyone coming into the house–unless they were his friends. He would have been so angry.

When Uncle Marvin was angry, you ran.

Frankie didn't need to see that.

I stepped into the living room and switched on the television, knowing that would be my uncle's first destination when he returned home.

The news was on and I left it on his favorite channel. Just as I was about to leave, I heard the news reporter speak a familiar name.

Marshall Gabrielle.

My father.

I raced back to the television and kneeled on the floor to watch the report. The woman was so professional as she announced my worst nightmare. "Marshall Gabrielle, the father of two, was reported missing by his wife Samantha Gabrielle earlier today. His credit cards and bank account have been left untouched since he disappeared three days ago. Grave fears are held for his wellbeing. If you have any information about his whereabouts, please contact the Lakeside Police Department immediately."

My father was missing?

He was still living in Lakeside?

I hadn't seen him for so long and I always imagined he was living somewhere far, far away. Beyond the enchanted forest, through the looking glass, and beyond.

But he was still in the same city I was.

The pain of knowing he was so close and hadn't done anything to contact me was just as bad as knowing he was missing. The news reporter said so many things I didn't know.

I didn't know he was married.

I didn't know his wife was named Samantha.

I didn't know he had *two* children.

I didn't know where he was.

I didn't know why he had vanished.

I didn't know anything about my father.

The list continued on into infinity. It stung and it hurt but it only bounced off the armor I had built around myself. My father could do nothing to hurt me anymore. I had blocked him from my pain many years ago.

I stared at the television screen but they moved onto another story about a squirrel attack. While my mind was still trying to process everything I heard, I headed to the kitchen and made dinner. It was nothing more than eggs and bacon, it would have to do.

Uncle Marvin must have smelled the dinner because he arrived home just as they were ready. He plonked down on the chair while it groaned under his weight.

The plate was immediately placed in front of him while I sat opposite. I only let him have one bite before I asked the question I had been dying to. "Do you know my father is missing?"

He made a *humph* sound.

That was usually a yes.

"What happened to him? Do you think he's in trouble?"

Uncle Marvin pointed his fork at me, a piece of bacon still clung to the prongs. "Don't spend any time worrying about your daddy. Whatever he did, he deserved it."

"But he might—"

"Don't say another word about it," he warned.

I zipped my mouth, knowing anything further would only infuriate him. When Uncle Marvin was angry, bad things happened.

We ate in silence, the only noise the whistle from my uncle's nose as he breathed. I cleaned up afterwards and fed Matilda. I asked her about my father and she only meowed.

It seemed Matilda was as in the dark as I was.

I admired my new shelves once more before I went to bed that night. I ran my fingers along the new wood and imagined all the lost things that would find their home there.

It cheered me, somewhat.

The next day was Sunday, a day I normally spent outside the house because it was also Uncle Marvin's day off. He would watch sports on television or mow the lawn with a machine too loud to be healthy.

I set off for the mall, hoping I would be able to find many lost things today. It was amazing how many people were so irresponsible with their things.

Unfortunately, I didn't reach the mall. My traitorous feet led me to a residential neighborhood. It was lined on both sides with nice houses, all mirror images of each other.

Earlier that morning I had gone online.

I had found my father's address.

His house was one of those I now looked at. It was number twenty-three and was on the right hand side. I could see it from the end, it had a large tree in the yard.

It looked like a nice family lived there.

Neat and pristine.

The opposite of my house with Uncle Marvin and his temper.

While I was watching, the front door opened. A woman and a little girl came out and got into the car parked in the driveway. They left in the opposite direction of my location.

The woman had to be my father's new wife. The girl must be his new daughter. He had replaced my family quite well, apparently. To think I was related to them was surreal. The little girl had the same hair color as I did, shining under the glint of the sun like mine occasionally did.

I wanted to hate them. They had my father while I was lost to him. They had been careless enough to lose my father. He was just another lost thing that belonged on my shelf now.

Thanks to Frankie I now had room for him.

He belonged in the attic with the box of his possessions.

The sudden urge to talk about everything overwhelmed me. I wanted someone to tell me that I wasn't crazy, that it was okay to stand outside my father's house and feel the way I was.

I needed someone to keep me sane.

The edge of the precipice was slippery.

My feet were moving before I could stop myself. They seemed to know the destination better than my brain did. I had no choice except to let them go wherever they were going.

I was surprised to be standing outside Frankie's house twenty minutes and a bus ride later.

The moment I got there I wanted to turn away and go someplace else. Just because Frankie helped me to put up shelves all day and he'd walked my heavy wheelbarrow seven blocks, didn't mean we were friends or anything.

I told my feet to move.

They took me to his front door.

My hand knocked.

The door opened a few minutes later with the head of a little girl peering out at me. She was older than the girl I had seen at my father's house, but only just.

"Who are you?" she asked, not unkindly.

"Sorry, I have the wrong house," I stammered out, stumbling over my words like an idiot. It was a bad idea coming here, one that would ensure I never trusted my feet's opinion again.

I turned around and started walking, leaving the little girl's eyes on my back. They drilled two identical holes into me, searing through my shirt to reach my skin. All of me flushed with embarrassment.

Why had I gone to Frankie's house?

He wasn't my friend.

I didn't have any friends.

"Em! Wait up!"

I walked faster, increasing my pace to outrun the voice and the boy it belonged to. Frankie's little sister must have told him there was a strange girl at the door. He had instantly pulled my image into his mind.

"Em! Stop!"

I didn't walk fast enough. Frankie caught up with me, a little breathless but otherwise fine. He fell into step beside me, regaining strength into his ragged breath.

"Go away," I said.

"You came to visit me," he replied.

"It was a mistake."

"I'm glad you did. Will you just stop for a moment, please?" He grabbed my arm and I instantly yanked it from his grip. I did, however, stop. "I'm happy to see you."

"Was that your sister at the door?" I asked, because it was the only thing I could think of that wouldn't require me to blurt out everything inside my head.

"Yeah, that's Lillian. She's ten and has this thing where she likes to answer the door and pretend she's opened the door to another world or something. I don't know, I don't really understand her sometimes."

Would I understand *my* little sister?

Would she play silly games that didn't make sense?

I shook the thoughts away. "You look like her."

"But better, right?" His eyes sparkled with cheekiness. Maybe it wasn't such a mistake going to him. I was feeling a little less panicked. "Why did you come over? Do you want to hang out or something?"

"My father is missing," I blurted out.

"That's terrible. What happened?"

"I don't know. But he has this whole other family I didn't know about and he stayed in the city without telling me. I haven't seen him in ten years and he replaced me. And now he's missing."

"Woah, slow down. You haven't seen your dad in ten years?" I nodded. "That is totally his loss. I bet if he really knew you he would have told you everything."

"I highly doubt that." The thought was ludicrous, but sweet of him to say.

"What do you know about his new family?" Frankie asked, his expression curious and sympathetic at the same time. He had the most honest face of anyone I had ever met.

"They live at 23 Huxton Street. He has a wife and a daughter. They look like they have the perfect life. Except for my father being missing, anyway."

"Have you gone there? Did you speak with them?" Always so many questions, always making my head spin trying to answer them.

"I went there but I didn't go in."

"Do you want to?"

Did I?

They wouldn't know me.

"Maybe."

Frankie smiled and it felt like maybe things would be

okay. "How about we grab a milkshake and talk about it some more? There's no way we can make decisions like that on an empty stomach."

I allowed myself to nod and then followed Frankie as he took my hand. He seemed to know his neighborhood well, even though he hadn't lived here for very long.

He took me directly to a small diner where we slid into the booth. A waitress hurried over to us, white teeth all showing in her smile. "Frankie, good to see you again. Do you want the usual?"

He looked from her to me. "Chocolate okay?"

"Yes."

"Make it two, please, Diana."

"Coming right up," she said happily. How could someone be so happy when they were spending their Sunday morning bringing strangers food and beverages?

Frankie was opening his mouth, ready to ask another million questions. I got in first, cutting him off. "Where did you live before Lakeside?"

"A tiny little town called Belmont. It had a population of two hundred and thirteen people," he said, almost as happily as the waitress.

Maybe they slipped antidepressants into the food here. That would explain it.

"Why did you move here?"

"We had a small family business but it burned down. My parents took it as a sign that it was time to move on. We've lived in twelve places since I was four years old."

"That's almost a difference place every year."

"Yep. We move around a lot."

Diana delivered our milkshakes at that moment, hushing our conversation abruptly. We waited until she left again before speaking once more.

"Why do you move so much?" I asked, reeled into this boy and all his mysteries. I was starting to understand why he asked so many questions.

Frankie shrugged one shoulder. "Just do."

He was hiding something.

I wasn't the only one with secrets.

Now wasn't the time to press for answers but I would get them eventually. The more I knew about Frankie, the more I suspected that he was lost.

Just like me.

His past was a puzzle that I would find all the pieces for and then join together. It was only a matter of time before I discovered everything about him.

"Do you live with your mom?" Frankie asked. "I mean, if you don't live with your dad, you must live with someone."

"My mother is dead."

"Oh. Sorry."

"She died when I was a baby so I never knew her. My Uncle Marvin said she was beautiful and too good for my father."

"Is that who you live with, your Uncle Marvin?"

"Yes."

"What's he like?"

"He hates everyone."

Frankie made a face before taking a long sip of his milkshake. I didn't want to answer any more questions about me. He knew enough already, more than his fair share, really.

We drank our milkshakes in silence before leaving the diner. It was a nice place, I liked it. Even with Perky Diana and her too-smiley mouth.

Frankie insisted on walking me home. I left him at the door, thanking him for his time and assuring him I didn't need him to accompany me all the way inside.

Not even to check the shelves.

Or check for burglars.

The excuses he came up with to come inside were laughable but none of them worked. I hurried inside alone and closed the door securely behind me.

Right before running straight into Uncle Marvin.

And he wasn't happy.

Chapter 7

"Who was that boy?" Uncle Marvin demanded. Both his hands were poised on his hips, making him seem ten times bigger than he normally did.

He almost managed to suck in his big belly.

"He's just a boy from school," I replied, eager to get away from the conversation. There was a reason I didn't want my worlds colliding and this was a prime example of how it started.

"Is he your boyfriend?"

"No. Absolutely not."

"But he wants to be." I shrugged, indifferent. I couldn't speak on behalf of Frankie. "You need to stay away from him and all the other boys. Especially the ones that walk you home."

"Why? I'm sure he's not planning on hurting me," I replied. Even for Uncle Marvin he seemed to be blowing the whole thing out of proportion.

"Boys are bad and they'll do horrible things to you. They are nothing but trouble and will get you caught up in their trouble. Do you understand?"

"He's a nice person."

"So you think. There is no such thing as a nice teenage boy. Stay away from him or you'll be thrown out of here so fast your head will spin and your butt will be sore for days. Now, do you understand?"

"Yes, Uncle Marvin."

"Good. Now make me lunch, I'm hungry."

I made him a baloney sandwich.

I spent time with my lost things.

I checked the news for updates on my father.

I went to bed.

The next morning was Monday, the beginning of the school week and yet another morning when I had to get up and pretend like I wasn't the liar I was.

On the way in through the school gates I checked the lawn and courtyard for lost things. They were both clear. Either someone else was doing my job or people were getting better at not losing things.

My usual desk was occupied in English class. That probably should have been the clue that today wasn't going to be a good one. Just as the teacher started the class, someone knocked on the door and then opened it.

Two policemen whispered something to the teacher before looking at me. Instantly I thought of all the lost things, and that girl's accusation that I'd stolen her book, and I thought for sure they knew what I did.

I wasn't doing anything wrong.

I *rescued* lost things so they weren't lost anymore.

Some people didn't see it that way.

The police were one of them.

"Miss Gabrielle, please step outside. These police officers would like a word with you," the teacher said, ever so politely with the fuzz watching his every move.

Every pair of eyes in the chairs followed me out of the room. One of the policemen was really tall, the other extra short. They made for a mismatched pair.

We assembled in the corridor, a row of lockers on one side and doors on the other. I blinked at them, waiting expectantly for them to raise the problem. Then, and only then, would I be able to think up a plausible lie to solve it.

"Miss Gabrielle," Tall Cop said. "We are here to discuss your father, Marshall Gabrielle."

Oh.

So this wasn't about me, but my absent father.

"I know he's missing. I saw it on the news." And thanks for informing his daughter of that fact *prior* to having to hear it on the six o'clock news. Well done, boys in blue.

"Very well then, so you know his wife has reported him missing and is very concerned about his wellbeing. When was the last time you spoke with Mr. Gabrielle?" It was Short Cop this time, holding a pad with a stubbed pencil in his little fat fingers.

"Ten years ago," I replied flatly. I wasn't going to show any emotion, this was just routine. They didn't care about my problems and wouldn't be able to solve any of them anyway.

"You haven't had any contact with him since then?"

"Nope. Father of the Year, huh?"

Short Cop wrote something in his notepad and I couldn't read it no matter how hard I tried. "So you wouldn't know anything about his current whereabouts or if he had any enemies?"

"Nope." I let the word pop on my lips. "Have *you* discovered anything about his disappearance?"

They exchanged a glance, one that asked the other if they should say anything. Tall Cop spoke next. "We believe he might have gotten into something he shouldn't have. Some business deals gone wrong, if you know what I mean."

"Do you think he's dead?"

He scrambled for an answer. "We can't rule anything out at the moment. But rest assured we are doing everything we can to locate your father. Thank you for your time, Miss Gabrielle."

As they were walking away, I blurted out something I was supposed to keep locked inside. "What are they like? His new family?"

They stopped and spun around slowly, almost like they were trying to move in slow motion to buy themselves some more time. It only made me more impatient.

While I waited for an answer my heart hammered in my chest and my breath caught in my throat. I was at risk of having a major coronary.

"They seem very nice," Tall Cop said. "They are very

eager to get Mr. Gabrielle back and have been most cooperative."

Nice.

Eager.

Cooperative.

No wonder my father left me to shack up with them. They were everything I wasn't.

I nodded so the cops didn't have to stand there awkwardly any longer. They were starting to feel sympathetic toward me and I just didn't need it.

They started walking again and this time I let them go.

I wasn't going to cry.

I returned to my desk in class, ignoring all the eyes on me that were drilling little holes into my skin. It didn't matter what the others thought. Maybe I would tell them a lie, say they were here to arrest me and I went all 'I want a lawyer' on them and dodged the charges.

Anything but the truth.

Class was torture after that little encounter. Even the teacher seemed to be interested in the reason for my police visit. I found him staring at me curiously on more than one occasion.

Unfortunately, it was a double period.

I sat there until lunchtime.

The bell was my savior, making me want to scream 'Hallelujah' at the top of my lungs when it finally came. I grabbed my stuff and got out of there as fast as humanly possible.

I moved so fast I was almost at the front of the cafeteria

line. I grabbed my lunch and found an empty table. Hopefully it would remain that way for the full forty-five minutes allocated to enjoying the midday meal.

Two girls from my English class passed by my table. They were the blonde kind, full of giggles and hair advice. "Did you make bail, Emmeline?" one threw at me as she passed. Her friend giggled.

"I hear orange is a very fetching color," the other replied, once her fake giggles were under control. "You'll be a hit with all the other criminals."

I ignored them.

They would get the karma coming back to them.

I would just help it along a little. The blonde one on the right had lost her cell phone a couple of weeks ago. She left it on the shelf above the sink in the girls' bathroom.

There were a bunch of things I could use it for.

Revenge would be sweet.

Much sweeter than they were.

A smile spread over my lips, perhaps it wasn't the worst day ever.

I started scanning the room like I always did at lunchtime, looking for things that might be lost. The cafeteria was always a good place.. Kids would be too distracted with all the food to care about what happened to their possessions.

It was only early so everything still seemed to be with their owner. By the end of the break there would be at least something left behind, it was almost guaranteed.

Frankie sat across from me, placing his tray on the table

like he had permission to sit with me. "Hey, Em. How's it going?"

My eyebrows arched in question. "What are you doing?"

"Eating lunch. What are *you* doing?" He grinned, thinking we were playing some game.

We weren't.

"My Uncle Marvin said I can't talk to you anymore."

"That's because he hasn't met me. If he did, he would know how awesome I was and be fine with it."

"He doesn't acknowledge the word 'awesome'."

Frankie shrugged and picked up his burger with both hands, shoving it into his mouth to take a bite. He chewed with his mouth closed, at least he had manners.

"You're not going to leave, are you?" The realization was hitting me. Nothing I could do or say would make Frankie leave me alone. It should have angered me.

It didn't.

And he was going to get me into trouble one day.

"We're friends, why would I want to leave and eat with people I don't know?" He took another bite of the burger, dipping it in ketchup first.

I wasn't going to argue with him anymore. Instead, I was going to change to a topic that made me even more uncomfortable. "I'm going to my father's house after school today. Will you come with me?"

"Of course. Is he still missing?"

"Yes. The police asked me where he was today."

"They sound like they're thorough. That's a good

thing."

I guessed it was.

I wondered how they had come to know of my existence. Was it through government records detailing my birth and forever linking me with the missing man? Or did the stepmother I never knew existed tell the police my name?

It would be interesting to find out.

"Are you going to go up to the house today and talk to the people inside? Or are we purely on a staring mission?" Frankie asked with a smile. I suddenly wished I hadn't told him about my first visit to the house.

"I want to talk to them."

"Sounds like a plan."

Yes, it certainly did.

Chapter 8

My hand was shaking when I knocked on the door of 23 Huxton Street. Every part of me was saying it was a bad idea. I didn't know these people and they didn't know me.

I stood in silence with Frankie while I held my breath and counted to ten repeatedly. My feet wanted to run, my brain agreed. If she didn't answer the door when I reached nine in my next count, I was going to leave.

Unfortunately, she answered on eight.

The door swung open to reveal a woman in her forties, brown hair that was obviously dyed, eyes too wide open, and clothes that were probably designer knock-offs.

She stared at us.

We stared at her.

"Can I help you?" she asked.

Frankie nudged me while I tried to gather some courage. "Are you married to Marshall Gabrielle?"

"Yes." Her eyebrows narrowed as she squinted. "Wait

a minute. Are you Emmeline?"

"I go by Em." Wait for awkward pause. "This is Frankie."

"Hey." Frankie waved and smiled.

Her face relaxed into a smile. "I'm Samantha. Come in, please. It's so lovely to finally meet you." She stood back from the door and gestured inside like a gameshow model.

Against all my better judgement, I followed her deeper into the house until we reached a pleasant living room. I tried to find a reason to hate it but I couldn't. The house was actually quite lovely.

"Can I get you something? Are you hungry, thirsty? I've just baked some cookies."

"No, thanks."

"Cookies would be great," Frankie said. I shot him a disapproving look. Did he learn nothing from fairytales? You don't except food from what could be a wicked witch.

If she threw us in the oven to eat later, I was going to kill Frankie.

The woman—I couldn't think of her as my stepmother–fetched some cookies and milk and laid them out on the coffee table in front of us. Frankie immediately helped himself.

She sat across from us. "Your father talked about you a lot. He would call you his little Emmeline."

"I'm surprised he remembered I existed."

"He loved you, Em." Turned out I wasn't the only liar. "I always hoped we'd meet one day. You look so much like him. I just wish it was under better circumstances. I take it you are here because of his disappearance?"

"I saw it on the news."

"The police are working very hard but I fear they don't have any leads that have proven helpful." She seemed sincere but I wasn't going to be lulled into a safe place where I could trust her.

"Do you know what happened to him?" I asked, watching her carefully and searching for clues that she was lying. I would work out her telling trademarks soon. Then I would always know when she wasn't being honest.

Samantha shook her head. "No, I don't. I thought everything was fine and then he just didn't come home one night. He had been stressed in the days beforehand but that was nothing new. Your father was an uptight kind of person."

"Please stop calling him that. You can use his name, Marshall. He hasn't been my father in a very long time."

She shifted with discomfort. "Sure, honey."

I almost said 'Don't call me that' but stopped myself just in time. I wanted information from Samantha, not to make her hate me within the first ten minutes of meeting me.

"He really did talk about you a lot," she continued. "He wanted to reunite with you but feared too much time had passed. He said you were happy with your uncle. He didn't want to interrupt that."

"He was thinking about that for ten years? Because that's how long he had to forget about me."

An awkward silence followed, only broken by Frankie's

jaw as it chewed on the cookie he'd stuffed in his mouth. I was trying really hard to be nice to Samantha but it was difficult lying to her. For once in my life I was actually telling the truth.

Go figure.

Footsteps padded somewhere else in the house before a little girl appeared at the living room entrance. She stared at us, quiet and wary of the new people in her home.

The kid was about eight, if I had to guess. Her hair was the same dark brown as mine, cut at a similar length halfway down her back. But it was the eyes that got me.

They were exactly the same as our fathers.

I should know, I had the same ones.

"Come here, baby," Samantha said, cooing to her daughter. "I'd like you to meet someone very special." The girl warily skipped over to her mother and curled up next to her. "This is your sister Emmeline."

"Em."

"Sorry. This is your sister Em. Em, this is April."

"Hi," the kid said.

"Hi," I replied.

What was I supposed to say to this miniature human that was related to me but spent all her life never knowing of my existence? I doubted Marshall would have informed her of the daughter he had lost.

Frankie sat forward on the plush lounge suite. "April is a really pretty name. Do you get lots of attention in the month of April? Everyone would be saying your name all the time."

The kid giggled. At least one of us knew how to wrangle one of those creatures.

"Do you go to school?" he asked.

"I'm in fourth grade. I like it when we have art and I get to draw with paint."

"An artist, hey? You'll have to paint something for Em one day. I bet she'd like something to hang on her wall."

They all stared at me while I got that deer-in-the-headlights expression. Diving out the window was looking like a safe option to escape this place.

"I, uh, yeah. That would be nice," I lied. She was hardly going to be Picasso.

"April, honey, why don't you take a cookie and run along? We've got some things to talk about," Samantha said. April nodded and waved a goodbye before she left.

So that was my half-sister.

I wasn't sure if I liked having names to match with the faces I'd seen on the news. I couldn't just pretend it was a serial drama and not real life.

Samantha smiled at us once the kid was gone. "April takes a while to warm up to people. Once she knows you, it will be impossible to get her to shut up."

"Kind of like Em," Frankie laughed, bumping shoulders with me. I was so glad he was there. If he wasn't we'd just be staring at each other across the coffee table.

Literally just staring.

Like it was a competition.

Enough of the family bonding. It was time to get down to business. "What do you think happened to Marshall?"

Samantha sighed, buying herself some time. "I don't know how much I should say."

"Tell me everything."

She was still conflicted, her Botox-laden forehead trying hard to frown. "Your father, I mean Marshall, he took on a job a few months ago. It wasn't his usual thing, he normally accepted contracts from little old ladies and working parents. But this client worked for someone else and he would never say who."

There was a special kind of sting in knowing I didn't even know what my father's occupation was. "What did he do for a living?"

"He worked in IT, fixed computers and networks and such. Most of his business came from referrals, people so happy with the work he did that they told their friends who then came to him."

"Was the new contract for fixing computers?"

"Marshall never went into specifics. All I knew was that he was turning down other work for a few months in order to fulfil this new contract. He worked day and night, I was so worried about him." A few daring wrinkles managed to break through on her forehead. "My gut is telling me his disappearance has to do with that contract, I just can't think of anything else."

"Was he acting weird or anything that day?" I asked, a theory of my own starting to curl up in my brain.

"He was just exhausted. I know it sounds silly, but it felt like something was wrong that morning. When he kissed me goodbye–he always does that when he leaves for work–

he held me extra tight. When he didn't come home for dinner I knew my intuition was right."

A psychic stepmom.

Great.

I suddenly stood, I'd had enough. "Thank you for the cookies but we have to go."

Frankie and Samantha both shot me a curious look before standing. My stepmother hurried to a desk by the corner and rifled around in the drawer for a few moments before pulling something out.

She returned and held it up for me to take.

It was a picture of my father.

Not from ages ago like the one pulsing with a heartbeat in my attic, but from recently. "You should have this, it was taken only last Christmas."

Marshall Gabrielle, the man biologically my father, was smiling like he didn't have a care in the world. It was a different grin from the photo in my attic. This one had seen more of the world, took problems onto his back until it weighed him down, and yet refused to be negative.

My father was handsome.

His eyes hadn't changed. Still blue as the sky and catching the light until they looked like two pools in the middle of his face. I should have been able to look at the photo and feel nothing, it had been ten years since he lost me.

Still…

He was one half of the only family I had ever known. And when the other half was Uncle Marvin, it was important to feel something besides contempt.

A sharp pang of regret rushed through me, slicing me in two like a cleaver. I had a father that lived only a few bus rides from my own home. For all these years we had been so close and yet a world away from one another.

And now he was gone.

My opportunity to know him, to get answers about why he did what he did, and maybe include him in my life was gone. Vanished. Kaput.

"Thank you," I muttered, remembering the others around me.

"Can I have your phone number? You know, just in case I need to contact you."

"Um, yeah, okay." I reeled off my number while Samantha programmed it into her phone.

I thanked her again before leaving with Frankie. The moment I stepped outside I felt like I could breathe again. Being in a house with so many ghosts of the past was uncomfortable. I didn't even know Samantha and April existed until the other day.

I had to get out.

The story seemed all too familiar.

My father had been exhausted and working all the time in the weeks leading up to his disappearance from my life, too. He had insisted he was going to work on the night he walked out and never came back.

What if he did the same to his new family?

April was only a little older than I was. Perhaps his new family weren't living up to his expectations and he decided to lose them, too?

I wasn't prepared to dismiss the theory.

We started walking in silence toward the bus stop.

"She seemed nice," Frankie said.

"Nice enough."

"The kid was cute."

"Cute enough," I replied.

We reached the bus stop and paused to wait for the number 17. As we did, Frankie did something completely unexpected and terrifying.

He hugged me.

Chapter 9

Nobody had hugged me since I was lost. Just imagining Uncle Marvin's arms around me was funny enough. Matilda was the only other creature that would cuddle me.

But Frankie's arms had wrapped around my body and he had hugged me.

Hugged *me*.

Hugged me.

I didn't know what to do so I just patted his back, hoping that would be socially acceptable to him and the people watching while they waited for a bus.

One woman smiled at me.

It was a bizarre day.

When Frankie took his arms back, I was colder without them. I had enjoyed the hug. Already I wanted another but I would have to settle for just one.

"What was that for?" I asked. Every part of my body felt wrong now, like I was too angular and sharp. I wanted to be soft and gooey, have a reason for people to hug me spontaneously.

Frankie shrugged, shoving his hands into his pockets. "I figured you needed it."

I did.

I needed someone to find me.

The bus arrived and broke our silence. Frankie wanted to ride all the way to my house but I managed to talk him out of it. If Uncle Marvin saw Frankie at the house again he'd have a screaming fit.

I didn't feel like dealing with his tantrums today.

We said goodbye when his stop came on the route. I only had another few before reaching my house. I gave Mrs. Justice a wave as she watched me arrive home through her kitchen window.

Hugging.

Waving.

What was wrong with me?

Uncle Marvin was in the kitchen when I walked inside. It was his night to cook, which meant we were probably having macaroni and cheese. Either that or canned soup.

I went straight upstairs to my room, needing a few moments to myself to gather my thoughts. Melancholy was settling over me as I thought about my father.

If he spoke about me like Samantha said, why didn't he ever come to visit me? Uncle Marvin never moved, he knew the address. He'd lived in this house, he could probably find it blindfolded.

My fingers dragged across the shelves of lost things. I

had rescued so many items and they were each as precious as the next. They were all beautiful in their own right.

I stopped when I reached the huddle of cell phones I had rescued. I didn't intend on finding the original owners of any of them, even though it wouldn't be hard. All I had to do was call one of the numbers and find out who it belonged to.

Frankie's phone was the newest. I placed it gently in my palm and held onto it for a few moments. It was warm when I slid it into my backpack.

Perhaps I would break my rules just once.

The next cell phone once belonged to Gina, otherwise known as the blonde who had taunted me at lunchtime while I innocently sat in the cafeteria.

I pressed the power button and the screen lit up. She was smart enough to have a password protect the phone, but she wasn't smart enough to use a word other than her actual name.

Typing in her super clever and secret password, her boyfriend's face blinked up at me as her wallpaper. She was sickeningly a walking stereotype.

My thumb waved over the photos file and I flicked through everything she deemed worthy enough of taking a picture of.

About ninety-nine percent of them were selfies.

Gina in her car.

Gina in her bathroom mirror in a bikini.

Gina pretending to smooch her boyfriend.

And on and on until I wanted to get the past few

minutes of my life back from the endless void I'd fallen into. It was clear Gina loved herself.

Which would have been fine.

If she wasn't a bitch.

I stopped flicking when a photo of her in the tiniest bikini possible flashed onto the screen. I tapped it to copy and then went to her text messages.

I started a new one, sending it to every one of her saved contacts. Attaching the photo, I sent a lovely little message gloating of my awesomeness—as Gina, of course.

That would get their attention.

I then went down her friends list and sent snarky little comments to everyone I recognized from school. They weren't that bad, just little remarks about how Gina was so much better than everyone around her.

Then I turned the phone off and replaced it on the shelf.

Gina shouldn't have made me so mad.

I took revenge.

The doorbell rang downstairs, snatching my attention from the shelves. I tiptoed down the stairs until I could see and hear what was happening at the door.

Uncle Marvin was talking to the police. They were the same officers that had spoken to me at school. Tall Cop and Short Cop, here to save the day. I bet they never saw Uncle 'the brick wall' Marvin coming.

I sat just out of sight and listened in. Uncle Marvin was midway through one of his rants. "I don't know what happened to him and I don't care either. He probably ran off again like the idiot he is. That man can't stick around, it's not in his nature."

"So you don't know of his whereabouts?" Tall Cop, ever so optimistic. If they'd come to my uncle they really must be desperate for leads.

"I just told you I didn't. Do you have cotton wool in your ears or are you just deaf?"

"No need to get worked up, Mr. Gabrielle, we're just doing our job. When was the last time you saw your brother?"

"Years ago when he left me with that lump of a daughter."

Don't feel bad for me.

His comments just rolled straight off my back by now.

Tall Cop was persistent. "And you have no idea where he could have gone?"

"I hope he went to hell. Now bugger off."

Uncle Marvin stepped back from the door, one hand on the handle. He gave them a few seconds to shuffle backwards before he closed it in their faces.

He stomped off back to the kitchen, mumbling to himself. The cat ran in the opposite direction to reach me. She rubbed her sweet little face against my legs before I pulled her onto my lap.

"Where do you think he went, huh Matilda?" She purred in a language I didn't speak.

Still, I petted her and cradled her warm little body against mine. She didn't reveal all the secrets of the universe but I didn't expect her to either. Matilda was just here for the cuddles.

Now I knew why.

They were nice.

"Em! Dinner!" Uncle Marvin bellowed, making the windows shake. I hurried down and placed Matilda on the floor next to her dish. We may as well all dine together.

We ate macaroni and cheese.

It was nice.

Uncle Marvin dropped a spoonful on his shirt, swearing while he scooped it back up again. "Stupid noodles, won't stay on the spoon."

"You could use a fork," I pointed out, holding up mine speared with pieces of macaroni.

"Don't get smart with me, girl."

Wouldn't dream of it, of course.

"I saw the police leaving today. Did you speak with them about Dad?"

"Stupid idiot cops. They must let anyone into the force these days. Even shaved monkeys. Idiots."

"Do you think he ran away again?"

"Probably," my uncle replied, shoving a new spoonful into his mouth. He spoke with his mouth full of food. "It's not like he hasn't done it before. I said as much to the police. If they start bothering you, don't say a word. They'll only twist everything you tell them."

"Okay," I said, not daring to mention they'd already spoken with me. It was easier when he didn't know things. "What was he like? My father, that is."

Uncle Marvin stared at me like I wasn't speaking

English. Then he replied. "He was always trouble, from the moment he was born. I had to share a room with him growing up, he was always taking my things and ruining them. I begged our mother to take him back to the hospital and get a new one. She never did."

I tried to imagine what a little Marvin would look like. All I kept coming up with was a chubby baby with a beer belly and beard stubble. It wasn't a pretty image.

"What was he like with my mom? Were they in love?"

"I guess. They had you, didn't they? Had to like each other enough to produce you."

"He worked with computers, right?" I continued to prod. I was doing better extracting information than the police had but it was still like torture.

"Yeah. He was always pulling them apart and sticking them back together again. I told him he should just leave them alone, then he wouldn't have to put them together again. Idiot."

I wasn't going to get much more from Uncle Marvin. He was already shoving artificially colored macaroni into his mouth and chewing noisily. One more question could have tipped him over the edge and made him grumpy.

We ate in silence for the rest of the meal.

The next day I vowed not to get one more tardy note for being late to class. I was out the door before Uncle Marvin stirred, eager to stick to my word.

When I opened the front door and rushed down the steps to the street, I almost ran into Frankie. He was leaning against Mrs. Justice's fence, his clothes wrinkled but matching his blue eyes.

"What are you doing here?" I demanded. "I told you my Uncle Marvin doesn't want me to see you anymore."

"That's why I'm standing here and not knocking on your front door." Frankie grinned, like that would explain everything and get him out of trouble.

Maybe my uncle was right and boys were just trouble.

This one certainly was.

I sighed and started walking toward school, Frankie fell into step beside me. "If you're going to insist on doing stupid things like this, you're going to have to get better at hiding," I said.

"Noted."

My backpack swung around and hung on one shoulder while I rifled through it. My hands grasped around Frankie's lost cell phone before I tugged it free.

I held the phone out for him.

He took it. "Thank you."

Frankie made me break my rule of never returning things.

"Don't lose anything else, okay? You might not get it back next time."

He shoved the phone into his pocket. "I won't, I promise."

Frankie could have made a big deal out of getting his phone back. He could have made a big deal out of me taking it in the first place and then lying about having it.

He didn't.

Which made me smile.

As we walked, Frankie told me all about his sister's birthday party that was held the previous night. She was turning eight and their mother cooked a big meal for their dinner. They all ate two pieces of birthday cake for dessert.

Frankie talked a lot.

I liked the way I didn't have to say much to contribute to the conversation.

We reached the school yard before I knew it. My eyes still scanned the area for lost things. Walking with Frankie or not, I still had to be vigilant in my search. Someone had to rescue the lost things, I couldn't let them be lost forever.

The grounds were clear as we entered the building. We passed by the blonde girls who had hassled me at lunch. They were standing with their friends, talking loudly.

"I swear I didn't send those messages," Gina said. Her voice was pleading, regretful?

"You're not my real friend," the other blonde girl replied. Her voice was angry. "I knew you were always jealous of me and that message just proves it. I can't even stand to look at you anymore."

"I lost my phone, remember? They must have hacked into it and sent the messages. And the picture!"

"Yeah, right. How can you lie to me?"

"I'm not!"

It was absolutely impossible to remove the smile from my face. I had to cover it with my hand, just so I didn't look like a complete fool in front of everyone.

I reached my locker and opened it. Frankie did the same, just three down from mine. "What are you grinning about?" he asked.

"Nothing."

"Something's going on in your head. What is it?"

I shook my head.

Nobody was going to find out my secret.

The bell rang and I ran down the corridor to make sure I was on time. Another visit to Principal Moore might result in a call to Uncle Marvin and that would not end well.

For all of us.

Uncle Marvin would have to leave work early.

He would call Principal Moore an idiot.

Principal Moore would suspend or expel me.

I would have to find a new school.

Being on time to class would prevent the complete meltdown of my world. So that was what I was going to do.

I slid into my chair before most people walked in. I repeated that same behavior for every single one of my classes throughout the day. I didn't get one tardy note.

It was a miracle.

Someone call the pope.

The final bell rang for the day, releasing us from our educational requirements and took us closer to the end of the semester. Only a few more weeks and it would be summer break.

More people lost things in summer than in any other season.

This was a fact I discovered for myself. My new shelves

would be packed full within a few months. I would have to scour places like the lake and the public pools for lost things. It was a busy season for me.

Just as I stepped out of the building, a boy stood in front of me. He was at least two feet taller than me, his chest a formidable wall of muscle.

I went to step around him but he got in my way again. The kid had a problem. "Excuse me, I need to get by."

"You need to be taught a lesson," he said, barking out the words like a guard dog. I looked up, my eyes travelling over his chest to his thick neck and then finally reaching his scowling face.

"I don't know who you are," I replied, even as my heartbeat started racing I managed to keep my voice level. Surely this idiot had me mistaken for someone else.

"You stole my girlfriend's phone."

"I never stole anything."

"Yes, you did. She wants it back, give it to me." He held out his giant hand, as if I could magically conjure it out of thin air. I may have been a liar, but I wasn't a wizard.

"I don't have it," I lied.

He cracked his knuckles, the popping sound made me grind my teeth together. "I'm going to have to teach you how to be helpful. Unless you want to do this the easy way and hand it over."

"I. Don't. Have. It." I spoke slowly, just in case he was having difficulty with the English language.

The giant buffoon suddenly grabbed my backpack and started shaking it off my back. I jerked back and forth, unable to move away from his clutches.

Something flashed past and the bully was pushed against the wall beside us. I almost toppled over as he released my backpack from his giant hands. It took a moment to work out what had happened.

Frankie had the boy pinned up against the wall, holding him there with an arm pressed against his neck. The buffoon was struggling to get free.

"Frankie!" I yelled. "What do you think you're doing?"

He ignored me, getting closer to the boy and talking directly to him. "You never lay a hand on her again, understand? You need to stay away from her entirely."

"Sure, man. Whatever."

Frankie held him there for a few moments more before he let him go. The boy glared at me before scurrying down the corridor inside.

"You shouldn't have done that," I said.

Frankie smoothed down his clothes after the tussle. "He shouldn't have been touching you. It's not right. You're a little girl and he's... he's..."

"An idiot," I finished for him.

"He's more than that."

I waggled my index finger at him, barely reigning in my rage. "That wasn't your fight. I had everything under control, you shouldn't have interfered."

"He was hurting you," Frankie argued.

"I don't need you protecting me!" I stomped down the pathway, now more keen to get home than before. Frankie had no right fighting my battles for me. I couldn't rely on anyone else besides myself.

He caught up with me, silently walking at my side.

"What are you doing?" I asked.

"Walking. Is there a rule about that too?"

"You're walking beside me."

"Maybe you're walking beside me," he countered with a smirk. I tried to stay angry at him, I really did. But there was something about the way Frankie did things that made me want to forget about fighting with him.

He made me feel warm and fuzzy.

Which was really inconvenient.

"I'm going to my father's workplace," I said, changing the subject.

"What a coincidence, so am I."

Chapter 10

Marshall Gabrielle worked in a small shop in downtown Lakeside. It hadn't been opened since he disappeared four days ago. Samantha didn't know anything about computers and he had no other staff members–according to the news.

The shop was in a row of a dozen, just another bay in darkness. It wasn't the only closed shop, a few others had also taken down their sign and walked away from the lease.

Sandwiched between a law office and a florist, Marshall's Computer Mart was filled with second hand computers and signs that declared his prices to be the lowest.

The door was locked, not budging one inch. I led Frankie around to the back, counting down the number of shops until I found the back of my fathers.

"This one's locked too," Frankie said, his hand jiggling the knob to reiterate his conclusion. I hadn't expected to find the place unlocked, only an idiot would do that.

"Move out of the way." I waited until Frankie moved and then stared into the barrel of the lock. It seemed to be standard issue, I could deal with that.

I pulled a lock pick out of my backpack, something I'd stumbled over a few years back. Mr. Adison had found it at the dump and showed me how to use it. I got it for fifty cents.

Looking around, there was nobody else behind the bank of shops. No witnesses were good, just in case someone decided to be helpful and call the police.

Locks were easy to pick if you knew how and Mr. Adison was a very good teacher. He taught me on all the doors he had rescued, explaining about the different types of locks and how their barrels worked.

The lock on this door was easy. It clicked over within minutes. All I had to do was turn the knob and we were inside. I held open the door for Frankie. "Are you coming in or standing out here all afternoon?"

"You're a very scary person," he said as he followed me. "Can you hotwire a car too?"

"Don't be silly." I could only do that on cars more than twenty years old. Mr. Adison didn't get anything newer at the dump to teach me.

At the rear of the computer shop was my father's work space. Bits and pieces of computers littered every available space. It looked like a giant computer had exploded and its guts landed everywhere. There didn't seem to be any kind of order in the room.

"What are we looking for?" Frankie asked, picking up a

piece of singed motherboard and smelling it. He quickly put it back down again.

"A reason for my father to go missing."

"Can you be more specific?"

I shrugged, not really knowing myself what we were looking for. A note signed Marshall Gabrielle with details of his location and intentions would have been perfect.

Somehow, I doubted it would be here.

"His wife said he was working on a big contract, if we could find that piece of paper it might tell us who he was working for. I guess that might help. Samantha said he was spending a lot of time on it," I replied.

I rifled through a series of boxes stacked against the wall. Copies of invoices and receipts told me they were his accounting records. Marshall Gabrielle wasn't the most organized person in the world.

He was the kind to lose things.

A lot of things.

The boxes made me sneeze as they tickled my nose. I continued on bravely anyway, hoping to find something that would make the three bus trips and a five block walk worthwhile.

Something crashed in the room. I whipped around to see Frankie sheepishly holding onto a piece of computer while the rest was on the ground. "Whoops."

"I don't think my father would even notice," I said. There was already a huge mess, making it a bit more messy wasn't exactly going to change anything.

The last box I checked contained piles of paper. The

white stacks formed two piles. I grabbed the top of one and flipped through the pages. They were service contracts.

Perfect.

"I found his contracts."

Frankie hurried across and looked over my shoulder. "How do we tell which one is the big one?"

Good question. I flicked through a few of them and the words all seemed to be the same. The only items that changed were the customer names, dates, service period, and the monthly fee amount.

"They have a value written in here." I pointed to the line I was looking at. "This one is only fifty dollars. We need to find one worth some serious cash."

We split the stack and flicked through all the contracts, pulling out any that were bigger than the last one. The amounts slowly kept rising until one contract was worth eight thousand dollars a month. I couldn't find any other contracts that came close to that value.

"I have an eight grand contract. Can you beat that?" I asked.

Frankie's eyes bugged out. "Nope. The most I have is two thousand."

The contract sat innoxiously on the counter, keeping all its secrets between the pages until we opened them up and unlocked everything it could tell us.

I almost didn't want to look.

But that would be pointless.

The first page held all the details, neatly written in with

handwriting identical to all the other contracts. I couldn't believe something with so few pages could produce eight thousand dollars a month for my father.

"The name is the most important detail," I said. "If we know the name, we can track them down and find my father. Maybe. I guess."

"Wouldn't the police have already tried doing that?"

I shrugged. "It doesn't look like they've been here, does it? Everything is too... normal. Police would tear the place apart."

Frankie's finger skimmed along the paper until they stopped on the name part of the contract. "This contract is with Withheld."

"Damn it."

"Why wouldn't they want to put their name on a computer service contract? It's not like they were dealing with the FBI or anything," Frankie said, reflecting my own frustration. What was with all the secrecy?

What would my father have to be doing for him that would require his name to be kept a secret? Virus removal and printer installations weren't exactly top secret business.

"Whatever it was, they were paranoid about it," I stated. The only reason I knew why people withheld their names was because they were up to no good.

Mr. Withheld had to be a criminal.

And criminals could easily kidnap someone.

Murder someone.

Blue flashing lights suddenly lit up the front of the store. The cops had pulled up outside and were getting out of the car. "We need to get out of here."

Frankie was on the same wavelength. "Got it."

We headed for the door but it felt wrong leaving with no more information than we started with. My eyes scanned the room, desperate for anything that might make the adventure not a bust.

On the counter was a black hard drive.

It ended up in my pocket.

We hurried outside and closed the door behind us. Then it was every teenager for themselves as we run along the back of the shops to the corner. Then it was a casual stroll as if we had done absolutely nothing wrong.

"At least I have this," I said as I showed Frankie the hard drive.

"You stole that?"

"It wasn't like good old Dad was around to ask his permission. I wonder what's on it." Something, I hoped.

"We can go back to my place and plug it in," Frankie suggested. I couldn't disagree. With Uncle Marvin banning any male person from our house, it was his place or nothing.

"Sure."

My cell phone pinged with a message. I expected an order from my effervescent uncle but instead it was from Samantha. "My father's wife wants me to go to dinner with her sometime."

"That's good, right?"

I didn't know. She was probably just using me, seeing if I knew anything about Marshall's disappearance. She could think I had been in touch with him over the years and we were both lying about it.

Like father, like daughter, right?

Something inside me hoped I was wrong and that Samantha just wanted to get to know me, being my stepmother and all. I couldn't believe that for too long, it just didn't feel natural. People left me, they didn't tend to stick around unless Child Services made them.

"I'll reply to her later," I decided out loud. Why make a decision now when I could do it later? Procrastination at its finest, ladies and gentlemen.

We had to take a few buses to get back to Frankie's home. He used his key to let us into the house and it was immediately apparent that we weren't alone.

Two little kids stared up at us, their eyes wide open and unblinking. Both female with their hair in pigtails. One had a smear of chocolate on her shirt.

"This is Elody and Mary." Frankie pointed to the girl with chocolate first and then the other one. They were so alike they were both carbon copies of each other, even though one stood a little taller than the other. "Say hello to Em, girls."

"Hello, Em," they said in unison.

"Hi." Awkward. What were you supposed to say to little kids? I wasn't good with tiny humans.

"Is this your *girlfriend*?" Elody singsonged. She made Mary giggle.

"Em is my friend. Now go play with your dolls or something." Frankie spoke with an amused sparkle in his eye. His affection for his sisters was apparent, written in every crinkle around his eyes as he smiled.

So this was what a normal family felt like.

Huh.

"We'd better go before they start planning our wedding," Frankie whispered as he grabbed my hand to pull me along. I followed him into his bedroom.

Frankie's room was not what I was expecting.

The walls were covered with photos. Not just a few family pics here and there, but *completely covered*. Like a serial killer would have to remember his kills.

When I looked closer, the photos were completely random. A flower here, a stream, a rabbit, his sisters, what I assumed were his parents, mountains, highways, candles, a book, there was nothing he didn't have a photograph of.

I couldn't help but stare at them all, I wanted to see every single photo but it felt like it would take years to see all of them. They were their own little masterpieces, a window into a time and place that Frankie had thought important or beautiful.

It explained a lot, actually.

Frankie was nuts.

Artfully nuts.

"Did you take all these?" I asked, pointing to the walls at large.

"Yeah. I want to be a photographer one day. What do you think?"

"They're beautiful."

He sat down at a small desk and turned on his laptop.

My eyes fell on one photo just above his pile of shoes by the door.

I was in the photograph.

It was the day I visited the tip shop and he had helped me install the new shelves. I was walking along the street with the wheelbarrow, my hair falling out of my ponytail and struggling with the wooden load.

I'd accused him of stalking me.

I guess I was right.

Seeing the photo made something twinge inside me. Why did he take it and why did he keep it? Photos were little glimpses into the past, a snapshot of a memory that would last until it was destroyed.

"Em?" Frankie's voice cut through my thoughts.

"Hmm?"

"I've got the hard drive open." He pointed to the screen and it took a moment for me to remember what we were supposed to be doing.

I joined him at the desk to go through the files. There was a lot on the drive, plenty of files and folders to keep my mind focused and occupied.

Frankie and I spent the next two hours scouring through all the folders. It was boring, mind-numbing work but it had to be done. With two sets of eyes looking we were able to quickly discard anything that seemed ordinary and useless.

Mr. Withheld made another appearance. "This is for the big contract Dad was working on," I said. Frankie scrolled through it a bit slower.

They were requisition forms, orders with his suppliers for the parts he needed for the job. I was not good at computer-speak so it all looked Dutch to me.

"You use all these to build a network server," Frankie said. When I stared at him in disbelief, he shrugged and continued. "I like computers, okay? It doesn't make me a nerd."

"Yeah, I think it does," I teased.

His cheeks reddened just a tiny little bit. "Your dad was doing regular computer work for Mr. Withheld. It seems pretty standard to me."

"There's an address on the delivery details. Maybe we should look for ourselves?" I jotted down the address on a notepad sitting on the desk and tucked it into my pocket. "I can go after school sometime."

"*We* can go."

"You don't have to."

"I want to see this kickass server," Frankie said, but I suspected it was more than that. He was curious, wondering where this pathway would lead. If it led to my father, then it would all be worth it.

The door to Frankie's room opened and we both jumped, even though we were doing nothing worthy of any guilt. A middle aged woman with Frankie's bright blue eyes poked her head inside. "Dinner is ready, Francis. Your friend is welcome to stay."

Frankie looked at me.

I looked at Frankie.

"I should be getting home," I said, already standing. A

family dinner was not something I wanted to crash. "My uncle will be wondering where I've gotten to."

Mrs. Bolero smiled kindly, she looked like the kind of mom they used in advertisements for baked goods. The kind of mother I used to tell people I had.

I grabbed the hard drive. "Thanks for your help. I'll see you at school."

In less than ten seconds I was out of their house and on my way to the nearest bus stop. I didn't realize it was so late. Uncle Marvin was going to be sitting at the table, wondering where his dinner was. He wouldn't have noticed my absence until then.

The bus rumbled in, spitting exhaust from one end and rattling something at the other. I jumped on board and took my seat, willing it to hurry up.

I looked around at all the empty seats and on the floor. Buses were prime location for lost things. It was amazing how many people got off the bus without something they had got on with. It only took a minute for me to find a lost item.

An umbrella.

It was still wet but someone had loved it enough to fold it so it fit into its plastic slip. I would have to make sure it was completely dry before I placed it on my shelves.

My mind wandered back to Frankie and his family. I now knew he had four sisters, all younger than him. I would bet all my money on the fact he was a great big brother. He was probably the kind that sisters would go to for advice or help with their homework.

I could imagine them all sitting around their dining table, eating home-cooked, wholesome food. They probably kept mac and cheese for comfort food, but never ate it as a meal. Mrs. Bolero would probably gasp at the thought.

Thinking about it made me melancholy but I couldn't dispose of the thoughts. I pulled my cell phone out of my bag and looked at the text message Samantha had sent me.

What would *her* family dinners look like?

There was only one way to really find out. Short of looking through her window and spying, I would have to attend one of them.

I quickly typed a message and sent it before I could think reasonably and change my mind. Once she read the acceptance of her invitation she would expect me to actually go through with it and share dinner with her.

Maybe I just made a huge mistake.

Maybe I didn't.

The bus rumbled to a halt at my stop and I got off, still preoccupied with thoughts of dinners with families. Two offers on one day, that had to be some kind of miracle.

I held the umbrella in my hand the whole way to my house. The moment I was through the front door, I heard Uncle Marvin banging his silverware on the table. "Where's my dinner, girl?"

"Coming, Uncle Marvin," I called out. I left my backpack and the umbrella on the floor and hurried into the kitchen. It was going to be a beans and toast kind of night.

Chapter 11

The umbrella was dry after I left it open for a few hours. Dry enough to be added to the shelves in the attic. It was my first lost thing in the new addition.

As I stared at the pink package, completely alone on the shelf, I wished people would stop losing things. I didn't want to have to be the keeper of all the lost things. I wanted people to cherish what they had so they never lost anything.

It wasn't the umbrella's fault it had been left behind. It had done its job by keeping its owner dry so they could get on the bus. And then they had just left it.

All alone.

Without a thought.

Nobody deserved that, especially the umbrella who had done nothing wrong. It wasn't right but it was continually repeated day after day. Lost things could have ended up anywhere if I didn't rescue them.

I went to bed wondering if things would ever change.

The next morning Frankie wasn't waiting for me, which was a relief. I refused to be disappointed by not seeing him. I shouldn't have expected the kid to be there. Just because he did it once did not mean I should have expected him there.

Mrs. Justice was out in her garden, as predictable as ever. Now *she* was someone that I expected to see. I gave her a wave which she returned with a happy smile. I wondered if Mrs. Justice had ever been lost.

Probably not.

She seemed very nice.

I walked all the way to school, using the time to scan the area for lost items. Sometimes they popped up in the most peculiar of places. Whether they found their way there through the wind or by human intervention, I never knew.

The school grounds came too quickly. I would much rather have walked for longer and given more time to search for items I needed to rescue.

"Hey, Em!" The voice that called out was instantly recognizable as Frankie Bolero. I refused to acknowledge the fact that my heart sped up a beat upon hearing him. He fell into step beside me. "I'm glad I saw you."

"It's school, I am legally obliged to attend every day," I replied, grumpier than I intended. Perhaps I hadn't forgotten the fact he wasn't at my door that morning and the pang of disappointment that I pushed aside.

"Do you want to go and check out the address we

found yesterday?" Frankie asked as he hitched his backpack strap up further on his shoulder. It sat heavily, probably full of books and homework.

"I can't."

"Oh, you sure? It might help us find your dad."

"Of course I'm sure. I'm busy this afternoon and don't have time to chase wild geese."

Frankie's step faltered for just a moment. "Okay. It was just a thought. I guess I'll see you around."

"Yeah. Around," I replied, staring at the path in front of me so I didn't have to see the disappointed look on his face. It was better this way, better that he didn't get too close. This morning had taught me that.

Frankie went one way on the path and I went the other. I shouldn't have told him about my missing father, I shouldn't have dragged him into this mess. He was far better off to stay away from me.

Better now than later.

Much better now than later.

I went to my locker before heading off to class. The only lost item I found was a hairclip, probably fallen from someone's bag as they rushed through the corridors. I slipped it into my pocket for later.

First period was Chemistry. I sat in the middle so I had a better chance of going unseen. Mr. Barbage was a fan of cruel and unusual punishment for his students. If I got in trouble one more time Uncle Marvin was not going to be happy.

Frankie walked in late and was forced to sit in the front

row. He was in prime firing range. His hair was the same color as chocolate and shined in the sunbeam wriggling its way through the window. He always wore an expression like he was telling himself jokes inside his head.

I wanted to be in on the jokes.

But it was a fleeting thought, quickly replaced by far more sensible ones. It would have been nice to be one of the other girls in the class, ones normal and able to have friends and boyfriends. I would never be one of those, not when I was a lost cause.

Frankie would be happier making friends with people that weren't me. He could bring them home to his family and they would know what to do. They would fit in and it wouldn't be awkward.

That's what he deserved.

Not me.

It was better to cut him off now rather than let the friendship grow into something more. The hurt would be far less letting him go now.

My gaze returned to the book in front of me and I tried to listen to Mr. Barbage through the entire morning. It was a double period, making my eyes go blurry with all the reading.

The lunchtime bell was truly a beautiful thing. I quickly packed up my things and slipped out the back door, avoiding any contact with Frankie along the way.

It was raining outside, a persistent dribble setting in coating everything with a layer of cold water. I was forced into the cafeteria, waiting in line for my meal like all the other high school robots.

We shuffled down the line, moving inch by inch closer to the end. I piled my tray full and looked for an empty table. There were none. I couldn't escape outside so it was either the floor, the bathroom, or one of the tables with people already seated at them.

I walked down an aisle, trying to find a table with people that weren't completely horrible. It was tough going. A table holding only one person crept up on my right. I kept going, the person was Frankie.

"Hey, Em, I have a table. Come sit with me," he called out.

I pretended I didn't hear him and kept walking. I didn't want to see the look on his face.

My options were limited after that. It was pathetic to know I had been at school with this class every day for eleven years and could call none of them my friends.

Not even acquaintances.

Finally I decided on a table captured by the nerds. They all shuffled away from me when I sat at the end of their table. Their conversation silenced, carried on by only facial expressions once I was seated.

I ate quickly and went to hang out in the corridors until my next class. The day was only getting worse for me. I managed to avoid Frankie for the rest of the lunch break and headed for English class.

In the last period of the day, my anxiety was growing by the minute. Frankie was in the same class and kept stealing glances my way. As soon as the bell rang, he was going to talk to me again. I was certain of it.

I couldn't let that happen.

My hand shot up in the air. "Yes, Miss Gabrielle?"

"I need to go to the restroom," I said, staring directly at Mrs. Thompson so she wouldn't know I was lying.

She sighed. "Fine. Be quick about it."

I packed up my things and shoved them into my backpack. I took the whole thing with me and bustled out the door. My feet headed into the direction of the restrooms until I was out of sight.

Then I got the hell out of there.

The only way to avoid Frankie was to disappear. He wouldn't break the rules and follow me, he was too well mannered for such delinquent behavior.

Uncle Marvin would never know about it unless I got caught. Hence the running part of my plan. I didn't stop at the bus shelter, instead I kept going until I reached the next stop–a good few blocks away.

My red umbrella bobbed over my head, doing nothing to keep the rain from me. I needed to wrap myself in plastic rather than hold a piece of metal above my head.

The bus was late but it eventually took me to the Lakeside Mega Mall. Today was Recycle Club and I needed it more than ever. The only way to lift my mood was to rescue some lost things and take them to their new home.

Finding my father was not my job. He hadn't tried to find me in all of my sixteen years. The lost things made my world right again, reminded me that even things lost could be found once more. I needed to remember that.

Frankie was just a mistake.

I had to let him go.

The mall was packed when I walked through it. All the stores were having sales and the rain pushed everyone inside. I had to weave my way through the crowds which was difficult when my eyes had to be on the floor and searching.

The idea of personal space went completely out the window during sales times. Elbows found their way to connect with my ribs on several occasions.

I elbowed them back.

They got the point.

It was slow work getting through the mall. I drifted past shops without going in any of them—it was too difficult knowing what was lost and what were products that had merely fallen to the floor. I'd learnt that the hard way and Uncle Marvin would not pick me up from the police station again.

I know because he told me.

Quote.

'You only get one shot, Em. Do it again and I'll let you stay in jail for the rest of your life.'

Unquote.

I gravitated toward the food court where the smell of deep fryers and dripping fat reached my nose. The schools had let out and students were milling around for food.

My search had failed to find anything in need of rescuing but the food court was always a good place to lose things. Shopping bags were forgotten under tables, keys hid under fast food wrappers, and distracted kids dropped toys wherever they went.

It only took one turn around the area before I spotted something.

A set of keys.

Lying on a table.

Completely alone.

I hurried toward them, knowing it wouldn't be long before they found a place to belong once more. I reached for them with eager fingers.

Only to have them snatched out from under me.

My gaze travelled from the hand to the arm to the shoulder and then to the head.

Frankie.

He was holding the keys in his fist, smiling with a proud, satisfied grin. "Beat you to it."

"Give them to me," I replied. I had to remind myself not to look at his beautiful blue eyes. They were as deadly as Medusas.

"I'll give them to you if you answer a question."

"No." Frankie turned to leave, heightening my panic level up five notches. "Fine. One question and then I need the keys."

"Why do you take things?" Frankie asked. His tone was curious rather than vindictive. I doubted he even knew the meaning of the word.

I couldn't tell him why I rescued lost things. I never told *anyone* why I did it. As far as I knew nobody else even knew what I was doing. I was a ghost, a shadow, someone to

114

ignore and forget they existed.

There was no way I could let myself be so exposed.

I was entirely right this morning, I needed to make sure Frankie kept his distance from me. Being nice to him or telling him any more about my life was dangerous.

So I had to do what I did best.

I lied.

"These are my keys, I need them to get into my house. I thought I lost them so I've been looking everywhere for them," I said, as perfectly as if it were the truth.

I told you I was a good liar.

Lying was my specialty.

Frankie looked from the keys in his hand to my face. I don't think he believed me but he was too polite to say that to my face. He merely sighed and held them out for me. I grabbed them before he could change his mind.

"Do you want to hang out? There's a bunch of us from school here," he said, gesturing to the table a dozen feet away. I recognized the faces but I doubted they recognized me.

"No, I'm busy," I replied and instantly regretted my tone. I hadn't meant to be so sharp with him. I wanted Frankie to stay away from me but I didn't want him believing me to be the biggest monster on earth.

Frankie shoved his hands into his pockets and stared at the ground for a moment. "Okay, then. If you change your mind we'll be here for a while. Feel free to join us. I'd like you to be there."

He left me and returned to his friends. I lingered on the

fringe of the food court behind a potted plant. It didn't matter that I looked ridiculous as long as Frankie didn't see me.

The keys burned hot in my hand.

Frankie looked happy with the other kids. He seemed to always be smiling, happy just to be alive and living. I thought back to his home which was filled with his family, his mother was probably preparing dinner right at that moment.

I didn't belong in his world.

It would be a mistake to think otherwise.

Searching didn't sound so appealing after that. I left the mall and took the bus home, determined not to think about the boy again. He was better off without me.

Uncle Marvin was sitting at the table in the kitchen when I arrived home. "Your dinner is in the oven," he grumbled as a greeting.

It's nice to see you, too, Uncle Marvin. How was your day?

Splendid, my dear. And how was yours?

Oh, wonderful, Uncle. I learned so much and my friends were a hoot.

So fantastic to hear. Please join me in this delicious food made with love.

That was never going to happen.

I grabbed my dinner of noodles in some type of cream sauce and sat at the table. It smelled of stale cheese. Tasted kind of like it too. "Sorry I'm late."

"Don't make a habit out of it."

"I won't."

He shoveled some noodles into his mouth and then spoke, spitting tiny pieces out as he did. "Stupid boss changed our routine today. He is such an idiot. Why change something that's worked for twenty years? I told him he didn't know what he was doing and he threatened to fire me. Again. He never will."

I swallowed, trying to reassure myself that bad table manners were not a genetic curse. "What made him change it?"

"God only knows. He probably woke up and thought he was a genius. Thinks he's a big man and all. Ha! Idiot. Luckily he wasn't there when the police showed up."

That got my attention.

"The police were at your workplace today?" I asked.

Uncle Marvin snorted and some more noodles shot out of his mouth. "Yeah. I kept telling them they were wasting their time when they should be out catching murderers. Stupid idiots."

"What did they ask you?" It was only three days since the cops showed up at our door. To hear they were still trying to get answers out of Uncle Marvin was curious.

"They wanted to know where your good-for-nothing father was."

"They think you would know?"

"Nope."

"So they don't think you know?" I asked. My fork stabbed at some noodles as I tried to be nonchalant. If Uncle Marvin knew I wanted all the details, he would make a point of not telling me.

"They think I'm the reason he's missing. The stupid idiots think I did something to him."

That wasn't what I was expecting.

To think my uncle had anything to do with my father's disappearance was almost laughable. The man was so fat he could barely reach over his belly. To do something to another human being–especially a full grown man–would be almost impossible.

Or would it?

Uncle Marvin didn't like my father, he'd made that perfectly clear throughout my years of living with him. The exact reason, I didn't know.

I shook my head, no it was impossible. Making my father disappear would have taken effort and my uncle rarely put effort into anything.

Something clanged behind me, making me jump about a foot high. My head whipped around just in time to see Matilda jumping down from the counter.

"Get that bloody cat out of here," Uncle Marvin bellowed. "That good for nothing tabby is all trouble and no sense. I don't know why you insist on keeping it."

His face was going red as he added a string of curse words to his grumbling. The table would be covered by noodles by the time he finished his tirade.

I grabbed the cat and placed her in the living room, whispering that it was better for her to disappear for a few hours while Uncle Marvin calmed down.

He really did have a temper.

Could he have been that angry at my father?

As I went to wash the dishes, I tried to push all those thoughts aside. It wouldn't make sense for my uncle to attack my father after so many years. If the police thought he had something to do with his vanishing act, they were being misled.

Where were the police when he went missing from my life ten years ago?

That was the real question.

Chapter 12

My father had haunting eyes, that was my conclusion. I sat in the corner of the attic, having opened Pandora's box of his things. I had only gone up to the attic to place the keys carefully on the shelves.

But the box had called to me.

I tried to find something in Marshall Gabrielle's features that I saw in my own face. His haunting eyes, his cupid's bow lips, his slightly crooked nose.

There was nothing familiar about them.

Perhaps he wasn't really my father. Would that have made him leave me all those years ago? I didn't know my mother, perhaps she was playing the field while she was young.

As much as a part of me wanted to believe I might be the milkman's daughter, something deep inside me recognized the man in the picture as my father.

I wondered where in the world he was. I had so many

questions that I always hoped I would get answered one day. Him not being here wasn't conducive to that goal.

Maybe it was only for that reason that I wanted to find him. Because I did, want to find him that is. I may not want Frankie to help me anymore but I did want him located safe and well.

Marshall Gabrielle's photograph was still haunting me the next evening when I was standing on the couch in his home. An eight-year-old was staring at me on the other side of the coffee table. I didn't know what to say to my half-sister.

So we stared.

Awkwardly.

"Dinner's ready," Samantha announced. I had never been more relieved in my life.

We shuffled around the oblong dinner table nestled at the end of the kitchen. My stepmother had gone all out, setting a place for each of us with a cloth placemat and more silverware than I knew what to do with.

She placed a plate in front of us with a flourish, presenting it like it was a prize on a game show. It was some kind of a quiche, I couldn't be sure until I tore into it.

Fancy.

Much fancier than anything Uncle Marvin or myself cooked.

"Dig in, don't let it get cold," Samantha said. She was smiling so widely I thought her face was going to stay that way forever, her jaw would be locked in place.

I smiled back at her before taking a bite of the food. There were vegetables and bacon in the quiche, it was actually really good. As the silence lingered loudly in the air, I had an overwhelming need to say *something*. "Thank you for inviting me over tonight."

"It's our pleasure," she replied, still smiling. "It's long overdue, really. Marshall always said he wanted to bring his family together again."

I almost choked on my mouthful. Somehow, I didn't think my father would have said anything like that. He would have found me otherwise. If he missed me so much he had ten years to find me.

Instead of responding to her ridiculous statement, I changed the subject. "Have you heard anything more about his whereabouts?"

Samantha shook her head sadly. "I speak to the police every day but they never have anything new to tell me. I'm not going to let them forget about him." There were dark circles under her eyes and she looked tired. I would say his disappearance weighed more heavily on her than she admitted.

The ghost of my father in his absence lingered all through the house. It was like he'd just stepped out for a while or was away for a few days. To think he might never return was horrible. Even if I didn't get him to be my father, April shouldn't have to go through the same thing I did.

Nobody should.

Samantha plastered on her smile again. "So how do you

like school, Em? Do you enjoy going?"

"Not really," I replied. I could have lied, I probably should have, but she seemed to be trying to make me feel comfortable and I didn't want to deceive her right then. "The classes are okay, I guess. But I'm looking forward to graduating and getting out of there one day."

"I wasn't much for school either, to be honest. I wasn't one of the popular girls so I didn't have it as easy as some. Still, I stuck in there and saw it out."

My impression of Samantha completely changed in an instant. I assumed she was always the most popular girl in any room. To think she might be more like me changed that image in my head.

"April likes school, though. Don't you, darling." She grinned at her daughter who nodded solemnly.

"What's your favorite subject?" I asked, trying to look interested. We shared the same father, I should know something about the girl.

"I like art," April said, in her little girl voice. She was too young to feel the loss of a parent.

I was too.

Everything kept reminding me of the day when Marshall Gabrielle walked out on me and never came back. I didn't want to keep reliving that memory, I wanted it to be pushed into the dark recesses of my mind so I could lock it up and throw away the key.

It was so much easier said than done.

As long as I kept my lips curled upwards, I could fool them into thinking everything was great. That I didn't feel so betrayed and angry at my father, the man they all *loved*, that I didn't want to scream at him for losing me.

Samantha went all out for dinner, serving up ice cream and chocolate sponge pudding for dessert. All the painful moments of the evening were totally worth it just for the dessert. I wanted to ask for seconds, thirds, and the recipe.

I only gave Uncle Marvin a passing thought as I remembered he would be eating a frozen dinner I left out for him before I departed. He would be having beer for dessert before falling asleep in front of the television. I didn't tell him where I was going, only that I had a study group to attend. He only asked one question: 'will there be boys there?' to which I, of course, said 'no'.

After another round of polite banter, I offered to help Samantha with the dishes but she waved me away. "You are our guest, don't even think about the dishes."

I found myself wanting to hug her.

That wasn't like me.

April tugged on my hand before I could make impulsive actions of affection. "Come see my room, Emmy."

Emmy?

We had nicknames now?

I looked to Samantha for a rescue but she merely smiled encouragingly. I turned to the kid and tried to summon up enough enthusiasm. "Sure."

She didn't let go of my hand until we had walked up all the stairs and entered her room two doors down. April spun around with her hands in the air, giggling to herself. "This is my room. Isn't it pretty?"

The room was pink.

Very pink.

On one side was her bed with a pink canopy that someone had sewn little butterflies of all colors into, creating some kind of fairyland. On the other side was a dollhouse that was taller than April. In the middle were toys littering every available space in front of a chest of drawers and toy box. Fairy lights were strung around the room.

It was everything a little girl could want or need.

It was the room I would have killed for when I was eight years old.

April bounced on the bed cuddling a doll with sleepy eyes. "Do you like my room? You can sit on the bed if you want."

Sitting meant staying and I didn't want to get attached. Still, I guessed just once wouldn't hurt. I sat on the edge, ready to make a hasty exit if I needed to. "It's nice."

"You really think so?" She said it like her entire future hinged on that one question. Like she might just keel over and die if I didn't like her room.

I couldn't help but get caught up in her world. "I really think so. This whole place is really great."

Her face relaxed with relief, her big eyes looking at me without blinking. "Daddy used to talk about you. He said your favorite color is pink."

I was almost ashamed to admit that my favorite color used to be pink. I loved every shade from cotton candy pink to deep hot pink.

Everything was pink, pink, pink.

Then.

Now was another story.

April was still waiting for an answer. It was time to start lying again. "Pink is great. Did he say anything else about me?"

She bit her lip and shook her head. If there were other secrets April knew, she was going to keep them to herself. I would have to worm them out of her slowly. *If* I ever saw her again after tonight.

It was starting to get quiet and awkward again. I pointed at the doll in her arms. "Does she have a name?"

"Molly."

"Is she your favorite?"

The kid nodded with enthusiasm. "Uh-huh. She wants to be a ballerina when she grows up."

"Do you want to be a ballerina too?" There were pink tufts of tutu skirts sticking out of the closet. I could already guess her answer without needing a private investigator.

"Yep. I love ballet."

"It's a good thing Molly does too."

It took her a moment to work that out but when she did, the kid grinned like a Cheshire cat. "Do *you* like ballet?"

"I love it," I lied. All those girls prancing around were not my idea of fun. Give me a pair of ballet flats over pointed shoes any day. I wasn't going to ruin the little girl's dream and tell her how much work went into staying in that kind of shape.

Someone else could crush her dream.

"I always wanted to have a big sister," April said. I instantly felt bad about misleading her. She didn't deserve to have a big sister that wasn't going to really be a big sister. This dinner was probably going to be the first and last one.

I held my tongue instead of lying to her. She could interpret that any way she liked. Samantha could field all the questions about why I wasn't visiting in the future.

April insisted on showing me her entire *My Little Pony* collection, introducing the horses one at a time and telling me their background story.

When it started to get late I excused myself and April followed me downstairs. Samantha was folding laundry, it looked like such a motherly thing to do that I stared at her for a while as the words left my head.

It took a bit of stuttering before I could speak. "I should go, it's getting late. I have school tomorrow and everything."

"Would you like a lift home?" Of course she would ask that question, everything about Samantha screamed that she was an excellent mother.

"There's a bus stop just down the road," I replied, pointing in the general direction.

She waved my words away like she was playing tennis. "Don't be silly. I'm not going to let a teenager walk the streets in the dark. Anything could happen." She grabbed the keys off the hook by the door and was out before I could argue.

We all piled into her minivan–of course–and I gave her directions home. She took me all the way to the door, pulling up on the curb. "Thank you for the lift," I said as I got out.

"Bye, Emmy!" April called out from the backseat.

"See you, April." She held up her doll. "And you too, Molly."

Samantha gave me the parental look, the one that said she was about to say something meaningful and I should listen. "It was a pleasure having you over tonight, Em. If you need anything or just want to stop by, our door is always open. Okay?"

I nodded and thanked her again before closing the car door. Samantha only left when I was inside the house safely, watching my every move until she could no longer see me.

So that was what having a mother felt like.

Protected, loved, wanted, needed, cherished.

All were words that didn't apply to me.

"Em, is that you?" Uncle Marvin called out.

I stepped into his line of sight. "Yeah."

"I heard a car pull away. Who was it?"

"One of the teachers dropped me home after the study group," I said, sounding so convincing I would have believed it myself if I didn't know the truth.

Uncle Marvin just gave an undecipherable grunt in reply. It was his usual dismissal. I went upstairs and tried to get Samantha and April out of my head. If I spent any more time with them it might feel too natural, like I was actually a part of their family.

I wasn't the big sister type.

I wasn't the daughter type.

My place in this world was as a perpetual burden/domestic slave for an uncle that was counting down the days until I was legally not his problem anymore.

That was who Emmeline Grace Gabrielle was.

The piping-hot shower didn't turn around the melancholy coursing around my blood. Nor did the homework that I tried to finish because it was due the next day.

I couldn't sleep. Every time I closed my eyes I saw a montage of my dad, Samantha, April, and Uncle Marvin. They were there, painted on the backs of my eyelids and refusing to budge.

Sleeping definitely wasn't going to be an option.

I crawled out of bed and threw a hoodie on over my pajamas. The house was in complete darkness when I crept down the stairs. Until I reached the living room. Uncle Marvin had gone to sleep in his favorite chair, slumbering in front of the night time infomercials.

Picking up my shoes from beside the door, I slipped out and then put them on my feet. I wasn't sure where I was going or why, but I knew I couldn't continue to stare at the ceiling in my bedroom.

I started walking.

And ended up somewhere completely unexpected.

Chapter 13

Frankie's house was all in darkness. I shouldn't have expected anything else. Real families all went to bed at a reasonable hour, not having horrible problems to mull over.

The stone was in my hand before I realized what I was doing. I launched it at Frankie's window and waited. When he didn't appear, I did it again.

Once more.

His confused face appeared, framed by the white windowpanes. I ducked into the shadows at the side of the entrance steps, my heart thumping out a frantic beat.

What was I doing?

I was supposed to be pushing Frankie away so he didn't get close. And I was throwing pebbles at his window in the middle of the night?

If it wasn't for the overwhelming need to spill all the words held on my tongue, I would have continued to hide there in the dirty corner of the sidewalk.

I crept out again and saw the window empty once more. Another stone left my hand and pinged against his window. This time he appeared quickly, searching the street for the source of the tapping.

Everything told me to hide again but I didn't.

I waved.

Frankie spotted me easily, the crazed lunatic in blue pajamas and a red hoodie was pretty hard to miss. He returned my wave and then pointed downwards before disappearing again. I wasn't up on my sign language but I guessed it meant he was on his way down.

I didn't feel so bad in my getup when Frankie joined me. He was wearing pajamas of his own–Star Wars ones. If there was anyone who could pull off Star Wars pjs, it was Frankie Bolero. His hair was messy on one side and flat at an odd angle on the other, supreme bed head. He looked adorable.

"Nice duds," I said.

"Like you can talk," he replied, a teasing sparkle in his eyes. He sat on the stairs in front of his house and looked out into the street without saying anything further. I sat beside him.

All the reasons I decided to come speak with him just seemed silly now. I should have remained in bed and counted the cracks along the wall instead. It would have been far less embarrassing.

The silence wasn't exactly comfortable. I picked at the skin on my fingers, trying to pretend it was the most interesting thing in the world to do. Like it was normal to be sitting on the street in the dead of the night in our pajamas.

I had to say something.

I had to.

"I'm sorry I was mean to you," I said. Apologizing wasn't something I was used to, but Frankie deserved one. I had been horrible to him and he hadn't done anything wrong. If I had to break the silence, I may as well say something worthwhile.

"It's okay," Frankie replied.

"No, it's not. You didn't deserve to be treated that way when you were just being nice to me."

He shrugged and looked so cute in his pjs that I wanted to snuggle against him like he was a childhood teddy bear. I'd never felt that way about anyone before. I linked my hands together so they didn't do anything they really shouldn't.

"I like being nice to you," he said. "I don't want anything from you, you know. I just want to help."

"I know."

"Can I keep helping you?"

"I'd like that."

Silence again.

Crickets chirped in the few garden beds on the street that refused to die from all the car fumes. They were sturdy and tough, not letting anyone hurt them, kind of like me I guess.

My mouth opened and words tumbled out before I

could stop them. "I went to have dinner with my stepmother and half-sister tonight."

"Yeah? How'd that go?"

"They seem like a nice family."

"And?"

"I don't know how to be a part of a nice family." My gaze flicked up to meet Frankie's. His eyes sparkled even in the moonlight like he was internally have a joke about something. I wished mine didn't seem so flat in response.

"You can learn, you know."

I shook my head. "I'll ruin it. I'll ruin *them*. They are perfectly fine without me."

Frankie's warm hand covered mine on my knee. I stared at his five fingers for a moment, trying to work out if I liked him touching me or not.

I shouldn't have enjoyed it.

I should have pulled my hand away.

But I didn't.

He was changing me and I didn't know if I wanted to be changed yet. It seemed like the world was spinning too fast, making me nauseous and dizzy. I could either beg to be let off or run to catch up with it.

I wasn't sure yet what I should do.

"You aren't going to ruin anything," Frankie said, keeping his hand on mine. I was acutely aware of our skin burning against one another. "It's easy to be part of a family. All you have to do is get along, and that isn't even a requirement sometimes. Just talk to your stepmom and sister."

"Half-sister," I corrected.

"Talk to your *half*-sister. Just be open and ready to let them in. You'll work it out, I know you will."

"I don't share your optimistic view of my future."

He chuckled under his breath. "You can do it, Em. Not everyone is like your Uncle Marvin. Most people are never that grumpy or scary. You might even enjoy being part of a family."

"Do you think they really want to get to know me, or are they just pretending to be kind?" I let the sentence hang in the air, my heart hanging from the end. It could either be crushed or it would fly, either way I wished I could know the outcome. I could prepare for disappointment, I was used to it. I just needed to be able to see it before it happened.

"I bet they are really excited to know you."

"You really think so?"

He nodded kindly. Perhaps *he* was just being nice now. "I really believe it. You're a good person, Em. You just haven't been dealt the lucky cards in life."

I liked the way Frankie put things.

Unlucky cards, that was my hand. My father made sure of that when he lost me and never bothered to look and find me. I stood up and faced Frankie. "Thank you for the conversation."

"Don't worry about it. It's not like sleep is a requirement or anything." For a moment I thought he was angry with me but then his lips curled into a smile. "See you tomorrow, Em. Sleep well."

He started moving toward the front door when I turned and started walking down the street. The way back home didn't seem as long now. I had one person that believed in me, which was one more than I'd ever had before.

Frankie was a miracle.

I didn't deserve his kind words or his friendship but I took them anyway. I would bundle them together with a tight rubber band so they would never escape and leave me.

The front window of my house was still basking in the flickering blue light of the television when I approached. I stopped in the archway and peered in.

Uncle Marvin was still asleep in his favorite chair. I didn't know why he bothered to have a bed when he mostly slept in the living room anyway. I could cut down on my cleaning time by a few minutes if he did away with his bedroom.

He didn't look like a killer while he was asleep. A stream of drool was hanging from his mouth, vicariously close to falling on his grey singlet. He would have a wet patch there by morning.

The police had to be wrong. There was no way Uncle Marvin was involved in my father's disappearance. The only thing he could murder was a dozen donuts.

Which he did.

Often.

The police were looking in the wrong place and that didn't bode well for finding him. If they were too caught up in investigating my uncle they would be too blind to search for the real reason of his disappearance.

I wanted him found.

More than anything.

He had answers for me that I needed. So, so many questions.

I went to bed and tried to pretend I wasn't tired the next day. I didn't speak with Uncle Marvin that morning. Nor for any other morning that week. If he wasn't sleeping on the couch he was working. So much for guardian supervision.

Saturday was a welcome relief from school. I didn't have a reason to visit the Tip Shop but I felt like going there anyway. Seeing the Keeper of Discarded Things always cheered me up and I was hoping for the same result this time.

Lucky for me, Mr. Adison was in a talkative mood. "You have to see what I found," he said, his bushy eyebrows moving up and down like a caterpillar while his one remaining eye sparkled. "You're never going to believe it. I never thought I'd ever find one again."

I followed after him, eager to see what had made him so excited. I'd learned to temper my unbridled anticipation. Past *great finds* had proven to be not so great. Like the time he showed me a left-handed can opener. I didn't have the heart to tell him it looked like every other can opener I'd ever seen.

We had to move to the very back of the shop, past all the dusty aisles and through the thin towel that separated the back from the front. It was a privilege to be admitted to the area past the 'Strictly Staff Only' sign (Mr. Adison found that one underneath a dead rat).

"Hold out your hand," he ordered. "And close your eyes." The excitement and mischief he displayed on his face was enough to make me laugh. I closed my eyes and hoped for the best.

Something heavy was placed on my open palms. It was cold and had the smoothness of metal. I could only imagine what was resting on my hands.

"You can open your eyes now."

I opened one first, peeking at Mr. Adison's grin before I dared to have a good look at what I was holding. Even looking at the object didn't help. It was a round sphere of grey metal. "I give up. What is it?"

"Press the button."

There was a button?

I turned the ball over and around until I found the tiny metal button. I pushed it and the thing came alive. All sides of the ball fell away, cracks that were completely hidden before now opened up to the moving parts.

When it finished moving, the sides of the ball were hanging open like petals on an open flower. In the middle was a dancing pug. I kid you not, it was a *dancing pug*. The tiny metal dog was standing on its hind legs, a tutu around its waist with his front paws in the air forming an arc.

I still had no idea what it was. "You've seen one of these before?"

Mr. Adison nodded. "Nine years, four months, and thirteen days ago. It was sitting in a box of wood scraps. I pulled it out, pressed the button, and voila! Almost gave me a heart attack when it started opening."

"What's it used for?" I asked. I knew everything in this world had a place and purpose. But for the life of me I was having trouble working this one out. It was lucky we had people like the Keeper of Discarded Things to keep things in check.

"It's just a trinket. When I saw the first one I looked it up online, tried to find out what it was all about. The only thing I could work out was that the Higgenbottom Bakery, established 1938, gave them away with a custard tart in the summer of '68."

Call me impressed.

I handed back the dancing pug and Mr. Adison carefully placed all the leaves back in place so it was a ball once more. "It's cool. What did you do with the other one?"

A wide smile cracked his face into two, all his toothless gums showing in all their wonderful glory. "Come on, Em, you know me well enough to know the answer to that."

I did.

He kept it.

If I took two steps to my left in the area he reserved for 'Things I Want to Keep', I would have seen the original sphere. I shook my head and let my own grin take over my lips. "You've got a pair now. I bet not many people can say that."

He elbowed me in the ribs. "Probably only the Higgenbottoms, right?"

"Right."

I watched Mr. Adison as he carefully placed the new ball next to the old. His existing one didn't have any dust or dirt on it, it shone like it would have done when new. He was a good man, he didn't let anything feel unloved.

Including me.

Someone rang the bell on his counter so my oldest friend stepped back into the store to serve them. I followed a few steps back, scanning the shelves and taking in all the newest additions. It was truly amazing what people disposed of. Just because *they* no longer had a use for the item, it didn't mean *nobody* else did either.

"Can you believe this place?" The woman's screechy voice captured my attention. She had already made herself known to my periphery, her expensive clothes seriously out of place in the tip shop. Her sunglasses would have cost more than the entire store put together.

She was accompanied by a stick-thin man. What he lacked in girth he made up for in teeth. When he smiled–or *smirked*–it was like staring into the Tooth Fairy's front yard. He picked up a book and let it drop onto the table again. "It's all junk. They should close this place down. It's a blight, that's all it is."

The woman huffed and pulled her hands together, as if they might touch something and infect her with their dirt if she let them hang loose. "I'm going to have a word with our council representative."

I'd had enough.

"If you don't like it here, you should leave. Now," I said. I pointed to the door just to make sure they didn't waste any time dillydallying on the way out.

They looked like dilly-dalliers.

The woman pouted her lips together, doing a great impression of a fish, as she glared at me. "You'd better mind your manners, young lady."

"Maybe you should take your own advice, old lady."

Mr. Adison stepped next to me, his stance protective at my side. "I think it's best if you leave now."

"Are you seriously evicting us from your trash store?" the man said. "This place is a dump. Literally, we are in a tip. You've got to be kidding me."

"You heard the man," I added for good measure.

They were offended, which made me happier. Mostly I was just angry. These people were the kind to throw everything away. What they didn't lose, anyway. I'd put good money on them being responsible for a lot more trash than what came out of their mouth.

"Come on, Henry. We don't need to be subjected to this kind of treatment." She grabbed her man's hand and they stomped out of the shop. Every footstep caused a little cloud of dust. I hoped their patent leather shoes were covered in dirt by the time they reached their vehicle.

Mr. Adison chucked me on the arm. "Thanks for standing up for this place, kid."

"I hate people like that."

"If it wasn't for people like that I wouldn't have all this great stuff in my shop. Everyone's got their place, Em. We're all cogs in the same giant wheel."

He went back to fussing over his shelves while my eyes

remained trained on the couple. What were they even doing at the city dump in the first place? Their shiny black Mercedes must have been completely lost amongst the trash trucks and the rundown cars of the working class.

I took off shortly afterwards. The couple were still churning themselves over in my head and Mr. Adison was busy so I left him to it. Walking back toward home, I stopped when I realized I was almost at Frankie's family business.

My feet wouldn't keep moving once they realized an opportunity to sit down and rest was at stake. I could do little more than head into the hardware store and feel the rush of air conditioning inside.

But it was a mistake.

I shouldn't have come to Frankie's store, a place I had no business visiting. He was going to think I was a stalker if I kept turning up places where I knew he would be.

"Em?"

Apparently I wasn't fast enough in my escape. I slowly turned around on my heels to face the owner of the voice. "Hey, Frankie. That's right, you work here. I thought it seemed familiar."

He grinned like he knew I was lying. "Yeah, what a coincidence. Can I help with you something? You know, whatever you came here for in the first place?"

The only single thing in my vision was a plastic thing. I grabbed it. "Here it is! I've been looking everywhere for this. You have no idea how many stores I've searched through for this."

"What is it?" Frankie asked.

Of course he had to ask the one question I didn't have an answer for. The yellow plastic thing could have been anything. Nothing on the packaging gave its use away. "Isn't it obvious?" Where was my charade going to end?

An older man decided to step in at that point. It didn't take a degree in sleuthing to work out he was Mr. Bolero, Frankie's father. He was an older, more wrinkled version of his son. If they were the same age I was certain they would look like twins.

"Are you going to introduce us?" Mr. Bolero said. His hands worked their way into the pocket of his overalls. I would have fallen at his feet for saving me from my own lies.

"Dad, this is Em. Em, this my dad."

Simple, but effective.

Mr. Bolero had to take his right hand out of his pocket to shake mine. He had a firm grip, reassuring but not painful. I gave him about nine out of ten for his handshaking ability.

Uncle Marvin was a three. He'd shaken my hand once, when my father showed up at his door and introduced us for the first time. It was only a few hours later that he was guardian.

"It's nice to meet you, sir," I replied, remembering to be polite in all the ways Mrs. Justice had taught me.

"And the same to you. Frankie has told me all about you. You are welcome in our store at any time." He flashed me a smile that looked so much like Frankie's that there would never be a need for a paternity test for the two of them.

Frankie started to take off the apron he was wearing. "I'm going to take a break, Dad. If that's okay?"

"Course it is."

Mr. Bolero stepped away while I placed the yellow plastic thing on its shelf. "I should go."

"You could, if you want to," Frankie said. He was up to something, the little glint in his eye betrayed him. "Or, you could come with me and visit Mr. Withheld."

"You're ready to go now?"

"Why not now?"

Why indeed? He was practically out the door before I finally gave him my answer. We walked some of the way to the address on my father's biggest work contract. The bus filled in the gaps when it could.

Walking with Frankie made me feel invincible. I didn't want it to have the effect on me that it did. But to know he was there, doing this whole thing purely to help me, it made my insides go warm and fuzzy.

I would never tell him that.

I didn't even want myself to know it.

The last bus we took was the longest on our journey. It involved a lot of stops which meant a lot of people moving on and off the bus. My eyes remained constantly scanning for lost things. I hoped today would be the day when nothing was misplaced.

My luck had turned.

And not in a good way.

An elderly lady stepped off the bus without her umbrella. She was long gone before anyone realized her mistake. I stared at the lost thing, my heart pumping and screaming at me to go save it.

But Frankie was with me. I didn't want him to see my compulsion in action any more. I wanted to be normal for him, able to walk away from a lost item and not have to rescue it from a life of being lost.

A bead of sweat started to cover my brow with the sheer frustration of the situation. I couldn't let it stay lost, I had to save it. Every second that passed made my gut ache with need. My eyes couldn't be torn from it, always finding their way back no matter how many times I tried to look away.

I could hear it crying for me.

The umbrella needed me.

But I couldn't. Frankie had seen me take things too many times already. He would never understand why I had to cross over to the other side of the bus and take the umbrella from the floor.

I was going to pass out soon, my heart couldn't take the strain of my indecision.

"You should go grab that," Frankie said, ripping through all my spiraling thoughts with only five words.

"Take someone's umbrella? Why would I want to do that?" I tried to sound flippant, but I hit insane instead. I hit it right on the head.

"Yeah, I think you should. It's got to be lonely over there by itself."

I thought he was joking. For a split second I was certain

he was making fun of me in the worst way and at the worst time. I studied his eyes, flicking between him and the umbrella.

He was being serious.

It was all I needed. I could analyze it later, kick myself for being so compulsive in the privacy of my own bedroom. Right now, I needed to save that umbrella.

As quick as a flash I retrieved it, slipping it into my backpack and closing the zipper. Nobody else riding the bus noticed and Frankie didn't say another word about it.

We sat in silence together while my heart slowed its pace. The sides of the bus pressed outwards again, no longer closing in on me.

All was right once more.

As we started growing closer to our destination, the neighborhood changed. It went from the usual urban sprawl to leafy, tree-lined streets and large houses that seemed far too wasteful for only one family. There was more money in the area than in a bank. More money than I'd probably seen in my lifetime.

Or would ever see.

We passed the houses and then entered a commercial zone. Cafes and chic takeout places lined the streets. To mix things up a bit, there was the occasional boutique full of ironic hipster clothes. Even though they were specifically made to look old and worn, they were twice the price of regular clothes.

The bus stopped right in the heart of it. Frankie followed me off, the umbrella coming with us. It burned hot in my backpack, a telltale heart of my life purpose.

Frankie had a map of the district on his phone, he pointed down a street. "We go down here and then around a corner. The business should be the first one on the right."

It was difficult arguing with the blue dot.

Our feet hit the pavement. It was pristinely clear, tantalizing any graffiti artist to get to work. They probably cleaned it every morning just to make sure no dirt could stick around for too long.

"Fancy place, huh?" Frankie said, verbalizing everything I was thinking.

I shrugged. We'd never had any spare money in our family. The life of the rich and famous always seemed to be wasteful to me. I wasn't ashamed of not having all the newest gadgets. But, for the first time in my life, I worried about what someone would think of my home situation.

Because, really, it was a *situation*.

Neither Uncle Marvin nor I had planned or wanted to live together. It just happened, something we fell into and couldn't get out of.

Like a big hole.

I had been so lost inside my own head I wasn't paying attention to our travels. We were standing in front of the building before I realized it.

It was big.

Little red bricks formed the building that could have been plucked from a children's story book. A terracotta tiled ceiling peaked in the middle, a perfect triangle in proportions. The windows were all surrounded by white shutters, looking more like eyes than glass holes in the walls.

A sign proudly declaring the place 'ICM Partners' in italicized font stood on the front lawn. The grass seemed too green to be real but it was–I checked.

The building also had a sign on the front door that said 'Closed'. "They're not open," I said, clearly stating the obvious. "I guess we should have checked their office trading hours."

"And live without the unexpected?" Frankie waved his hand. "Nah. Where would we be without adventures and long bus rides?" His smile made me feel better.

His smile always made me feel better.

I still didn't want it to.

To avoid the fluttering of tiny wings in my stomach, I went to the front door of the building and peered in. Even with my hands blocking out all the light from outside, I still couldn't see much inside. A reception area, another sign, and some polished wooden floorboards.

I returned to Frankie. "There's nobody inside that I can see. It's all in darkness."

"We should get ice cream," he said.

"Why ice cream?"

"It just seems appropriate."

It kinda did. "I'm not sure what flavors they'll have in this neighborhood."

"Only one way to find out." He was factually incorrect because there were plenty of ways to do research on the ice cream flavors in this neighborhood.

Still, I followed him. We walked the fancy streets in search of the elusive frozen dessert. There were plenty of ice tea cafes, also one with only raw and vegan foods. Hipsters hadn't come out yet to fill the places, leaving them largely empty.

We had to walk six blocks before finding a place that sold ice cream. The flavors were disappointingly normal. I chose chocolate because that was my favorite. Frankie chose chunky monkey. The parlor didn't have any seats, it was takeout only so we took our food down to the edge of the lake only one more block away.

The great lake of Lakeside was quite impressive from this viewpoint. Someone had gone to a lot of trouble in landscaping the edges with grass as thick as carpet and paved paths that meandered through a wobbly course.

We sat on the edge of the lake on a manmade wall, our feet dangling over the edge. The water only reached halfway up, we were at no risk of getting wet.

"Have you had any more thoughts about what might have happened to your dad?" Frankie asked as he took a chunk out of his chunky monkey.

"I think about it all the time but I didn't know him well enough to know what might have happened to him," I admitted. It was difficult saying the words out loud. Especially after seeing how close Frankie was with his father.

"When was the last time you saw him?"

"When I was six."

"That's a long time ago."

"Sure is." Even the thought was depressing. I often wondered how my life would have been different if he had decided to stay that day. Or take me with him. I wasn't sure if it would have been better or worse. It was better to talk about his life, rather than dwelling on my own. "How come your family moves around so much?"

He shrugged, trying to make it seem like it wasn't a big deal but I knew him well enough now to see through his nonchalance. "My parents get bored by staying in one place too long. They always find a reason to move somewhere else because it will be better there."

"That must be hard."

"You get used to it."

I didn't want to voice the fear I had that they would move again.

Away from Lakeside.

"You've got a little," Frankie started, ending his sentence with a gesture that told me I had something on my face. I wiped at my lips with a paper napkin. "It's still there. Here, I'll get it."

Frankie leaned toward me and wiped at my cheek with his thumb. I felt his skin caress mine before he took it away again and wiped it on his pants.

But not before our eyes had locked together.

I blushed, all the blood in my body rushing toward my rosy cheeks. "Thank you."

He looked intently at his ice cream, as if he only just noticed that it was still in his hands. I did the same to mine, trying not to look anywhere else and focusing all my attention on the chocolate ice cream in a waffle cone.

Because if I didn't stop thinking about Frankie, I was going to do something stupid and regret it for a long time afterwards.

I wanted to kiss him.

All I could think about was whether his lips were as soft as his thumb and how it would feel to have them pressed against mine. Would it be like in the movies and my world would rock off its hinges for those seconds?

Would he even *want* to kiss me too?

The taunting questions rolled around in my head, turning over and over on themselves until there was nothing but single letters and exclamation marks swirling inside my mind. To straighten them out and think clearly again would be something that would have to wait until later.

If I continued on my current track I would completely lose my mind all together. I would be as outwardly insane as I felt inwardly. My secret wouldn't remain a secret for very long.

"What are you going to do with the umbrella?"

Or perhaps the secret was already out.

Chapter 14

"What umbrella?" I asked, faking my misunderstanding. Of course I knew exactly what he was referring to. Rescuing umbrellas wasn't something that happened every day. Not lately, anyway.

"The one from the bus." Frankie, playing along with my little charade. I never expected it to be very convincing. I was a skilled liar but the boy seemed to be able to see through my fronts.

My lips clamped together while I concocted an answer. A lie should have come easily, it should have rolled off my tongue and sounded so much like the truth that the listener would believe me.

My lies all seemed to run off without me all at once.

I found I wanted to tell the truth.

That didn't normally happen.

"I'm going to take it home," I started. "I have a collection of lost things in my bedroom, and now the attic, too. I will place it on my new shelves that you helped put up and it will never know the loneliness of being a lost thing ever again."

The truth was out there.

Floating around in the air and being forced into eardrums.

I had never been so scared about telling the truth before. I expected Frankie to call me names, to get up and leave me before telling everyone he knew what a freak I was. I could be prepared for that, console myself with the knowledge that I didn't need friends. Not even if they did make my belly flutter and my lips smile.

What actually happened next was not something I could be prepared for.

"Cool."

"Cool?" I parroted.

Frankie nodded and crunched on his ice cream cone. It was starting to melt a bit, dripping down onto his fingers in the heat of the sun.

When he next spoke, it was with a mouthful of waffle cone. "I get it. That's what I meant by 'cool'. You see things that other people have lost and you feel sorry for them. So you take them home."

"You don't think it's weird?"

"Not at all."

I pinched the flesh between my thumb and fingers, just to make sure I was actually awake and not lost in a daydream. It hurt, but wouldn't it also have hurt if I was in a daydream? What part of the pain is omitted from dreams?

If I fell down in my slumber-induced vision, would it not hurt?

I didn't have time to ponder it in full.

Frankie didn't appear to be joking, nor was it apparent that he was lying. He could have been as adept at lying as I was but it didn't seem that way. Frankie was a good boy, one that was wholeheartedly trusted by his parents and teachers. He'd probably never lied in his life.

Except for me.

I took my gaze away from his deep blue oceans of eyes and looked over the lake instead. Six words kept repeating in my head, over and over again until I could trace the letters with my fingers and write them in the stars.

Frankie didn't think I was weird.

Frankie didn't think *I* was weird.

Frankie didn't think I was *weird.*

If they were lies then they were the sweetest lies I had ever heard. They made everything inside me turn to mush, forced my heart to beat unbearably fast, and all the blood to pool in my cheeks deeper than ever before.

Frankie didn't think I was weird.

There was another human being in this world that understood what I did. He got it. There were no harsh judgements, no laughter, no finger pointing, no straight jacket.

He got it.

He didn't think I was weird.

Somehow, even though it would probably have seemed so insignificant to another person, I felt like my life might never be the same again.

Everything would be different now.

Everything would be—

"Hey, there's my Uncle Marvin," I said, the image of my guardian derailing my train of thought. I pointed to a spot down the lakeside, Frankie followed my finger.

"He doesn't seem very happy," Frankie replied.

"No, he doesn't."

All the jelly of his belly was jiggling in time with his finger pointing. Uncle Marvin was standing with another man, having a very serious conversation, it seemed. His cohort's features were equally as twisted with anger. Their voices carried on the slight breeze but not enough for me to understand what they were saying.

Of course, the yelling helped their voices travel too.

"Do you know the other guy?" Frankie asked. We were both openly staring, probably not something we should have been doing when one of those men had told me never to see a certain boy ever again.

"I don't think I've seen him before."

My sensibilities overrode my curiosity. I stood and tugged on Frankie's hand until he followed me behind a tree. We peered around the edges, hopefully hidden enough to stay out of trouble.

I'd never seen Uncle Marvin so worked up before. He normally didn't have the energy or the passion to fight about anything for too long. When he told me to do something, I did it. There were rarely fights in our small household thanks to this strategy.

I focused in on the other man, the one my uncle seemed so upset with. He was shoving his chubby hand into the man's chest, poking him with every word he yelled. The man replied but he didn't return the physical side of the argument. He was almost bald, with hair so short he shouldn't have bothered with it.

"What do you think they're fighting about?" Frankie was standing close to me out of our necessity to hide. He was too close for me not to notice the warmth of his body.

"I have no idea. I don't even know what he's doing in this neighborhood. He works all the way across town. He's so angry."

The men suddenly stomped off in different directions, climbing into separate cars and speeding off down the road. I slumped against the tree, trying to process everything I'd just witnessed. "Hypothetically speaking, if someone in your life might have done something bad, would you ask them about it? Or would you keep your mouth shut and mind your own business?"

"Hypothetically speaking?" Frankie paused until I nodded my head. "I would probably have to ask them about it. But I'm nosey like that. Hypothetically speaking, if that someone was worried, I would suggest they talk about it without another someone."

"What if they were scared that other someone would think badly of them?"

"Then I would say that other someone wouldn't do such a thing."

I took a deep breath and took in everything he said. It

was a now or never type of thing. "If I tell you something, do you promise you won't repeat it to anyone else?"

Frankie shoved his hands into his pockets. "Of course, I promise."

He was a boy that kept his promises.

I didn't doubt that.

"The police think Uncle Marvin is a suspect in my father's disappearance," I blurted out before I lost my courage. It felt better just to share with someone.

One eyebrow arched upwards over his eye. "What do you think?"

"I don't know. I would never have thought he was capable of hurting anyone. He whines and complains about everything but I never thought he'd do anything to anyone. He always seemed all talk before and no action."

"And now?"

"He *was* pretty angry." I sighed. A part of me wanted to go back to how things were only a few weeks earlier. Back when I didn't know my father lived in the city, back when Uncle Marvin was just Grumpy Uncle Marvin, and back when nobody knew my name at school.

But back before I met Frankie?

Maybe.

Maybe not.

"I don't know if you should keep living with your uncle," Frankie blurted out, like if he didn't say it quickly he wouldn't have said it at all.

"He's not going to hurt me," I replied. If Uncle Marvin was going to hurt me, I was certain he would have done it years earlier.

It would have saved him a lot of money in feeding and clothing me.

Not to mention school fees.

He definitely wouldn't have bothered with the stupid school fees.

"You said yourself how angry he was," Frankie continued, "What about if he turns that anger around onto you? I'm worried about you staying with him."

I waved my hand, batting away all his concerns like they were written between us. "Uncle Marvin won't do anything to me. Who else would cook dinner for him most nights?"

"You cook for him?"

"Yeah, every night apart from Wednesdays." Frankie seemed surprised. "Don't you cook for your parents some days?"

"No. We're kids."

"That doesn't mean you can't cook."

Frankie shrugged and dropped the subject. Uncle Marvin told me all kids cooked for their parents. He'd told me that the day my father left and reminded me at least once a month if I complained about it.

Maybe he was as good at lying as I was.

Maybe I caught it from him.

Whatever. At least I'd never go hungry. My expansive cooking skills taught me how to make a can of beans into a full meal that hit all the good parts of the nutrition tree.

We started to head home after our ice creams were in our bellies. Neither of us said very much but the unspoken words all mingled together and loomed in the air. I couldn't find enough to pluck and use to make conversation.

Frankie got off at the same stop as me. We started walking to my street and got to the corner when I stopped. "You don't have to come any further. I'll see you Monday at school."

"I'll walk you to your door."

"No, really, don't. Uncle Marvin might see you."

"So you *are* scared of him," Frankie said. He stood petulantly still, refusing to go on to his house.

"I'm not scared of him. I just don't want another lecture about how hanging around with boys will ruin my life. I don't need that kind of drama this evening."

"I don't feel right leaving you alone. It's dark." He stared at his feet, suddenly shy. It was utterly adorable and made all my insides go warm and gooey.

"You can stand here and watch until I reach the door, if you want. You should be able to see me the whole time."

"Yeah, I'll do that."

I was suddenly inundated with the urge to hug him goodbye. It was difficult to ignore the feeling but I had to stuff it back into the box it sprung from and proceed without it.

"Okay, bye," I said quickly before leaving him.

He watched me all the way to the door.

And then waved me goodnight.

Mrs. Justice caught me waving back. When she spoke, she scared me half to death. I hadn't seen her. "Oh, he's cute. Is he your boyfriend?"

"No. We're just friends." My cheeks burned as I thought about how much I wanted to kiss him earlier. My fingers touched my lips, keeping the memory of Frankie fresh.

"If you ask me, he doesn't look like just a friend. He's got happy love bubbles all around him."

"Love bubbles?"

Her kind face was wrinkled in a grin. "It's just an expression. He looks happy and is looking at you like you're the prettiest girl in the world."

I wanted to believer her.

But I thought she was probably lying.

"Thanks, Mrs. Justice. Have a good night."

"Goodnight, sweetheart."

I watched her shuffle inside, wondering what had made her appear suddenly after dark. I'd only seen her at night on a handful of occasions. She always went to bed early so she could wake up at dawn and tend to her garden.

Most of the lights were out in the house when I entered. The muffled voices coming from the television set in the living room gave away Uncle Marvin's whereabouts. That would have been the first place I would have looked for him anyway.

"Hey, Uncle Marvin," I said while standing in the doorway of the living room. He briefly glanced up and tore his eyes away from the television.

"You're late. Where have you been?"

"At the library doing homework."

He grumbled under his breath about how school work

was such a waste of time because it didn't give you skills for the real world. It wasn't the first time I'd heard it.

It wasn't even the hundredth time.

"What did you get up to today?" I asked brightly, trying to remain casual and not like I wanted to interrogate him about the argument he'd had. I was pretty certain he hadn't seen me at all at the park.

"Wasted my time with idiots," he replied. I could smell the alcohol lacing his breath. It was a good thing there were no open fires around.

"So you didn't get anywhere, then?"

"No." What followed was a tirade full of swear words I wouldn't like to repeat. He would have made a soldier blush. "Why do you want to know, anyway?"

"I don't know. I guess I'm just interested in your life."

"Nothing interesting about my life."

I begged to differ.

I desperately wanted to ask about the man he'd had an argument with but I didn't dare. Uncle Marvin had never confided in me over anything and I doubted he was about to change now.

"You haven't been hanging around with that boy, have you?" he asked. Once more I tried to suppress the blush rising in my cheeks and failed.

"No, of course not," I lied.

"Something about you is different."

It was easy finding a lie for that one. "I guess I'm just worried about my father and all. They still haven't found him."

"They won't, if you ask me."

"Why's that?"

Uncle Marvin took a long drink from his bottle of beer before he replied. Little flecks of spit sprayed the air. "He's a good for nothing waste of space. Probably took off because he got bored. You don't need to be worrying about him. Your father can look after himself."

"Someone could have kidnapped him," I ventured.

"Why would they bother?" I shrugged. "There's lots you don't know about that piece of shit."

Uncle Marvin turned his attention back to the television and I knew I'd lost him. He was dismissing me so he could drink alone with his good friend the Great American Sitcom.

"Dinner's late," he barked on my way out.

Dinner.

Of course.

Wasn't a fairy godmother meant to come and rescue me sometime?

Stupid unreliable fairies.

Chapter 15

The school hallways were overcrowded with kids all trying to get to class before the bell rang. I was one of them. It was still highly vital for me to stay under the radar of the teachers. Just one more slight on my record and Principal Moore would be sharing space with Uncle Marvin.

My head was down and my feet were beating a steady rhythm to class. I was so close to making it.

Until I saw a lost thing.

Someone had dropped a highlighter pen, left it floundering on the floor near the lockers. I had to get it but that would mean I would also be late for class.

The lost highlighter.

Or avoid a trip to Principal Moore's office.

The decision was agonizing. A stream of kids lay between me and the lost item. I would have to swim through them just to pass over the corridor. It would have been like dancing ballet in wet concrete.

But I couldn't leave it there.

But I couldn't be late for class.

I was frozen in my silent dither dance, torn between my two options and wasting precious time doing nothing. The look of horror was evident on my face.

Then a miracle happened.

Frankie swooped in, appearing from nowhere to pick up the lost highlighter and tuck it into his pocket. He caught me staring, giving me a private wink across the corridor.

I didn't waste any more time, slipping into the classroom and telling my heart it could slow down now. It wasn't like I was trying to win a race or anything.

My bottom hit the seat just before the bell rang. Mr. Barbage closed the door the moment it did. If there was a personal mission Mr. Barbage committed to it was to eradicate tardiness amongst the teenage population.

A second later, Frankie opened the door to join us. "Mr. Bolero," the teacher started, "Congratulations, you just earned yourself a trip to detention."

"I was a second late," Frankie defended.

"So you admit to being late. Good on you for owning up to your shortcomings. Please take a seat before I make it two lunchtime detentions." They had a stare off for only another second before Frankie relented and took the nearest empty seat.

I wanted to thank him for his help but we were a classroom apart. Note passing was not my thing so I had to wait for an opportunity to speak with him.

Which didn't happen until lunchtime.

The moment class finished I went searching for Frankie. He wasn't in the cafeteria so I had to continue looking. Not only did I want to thank him, but I needed to know he still had the highlighter and that it was safe in his possession.

I had walked all around the school before I eventually found him under the bleachers next to the football field. He was picking up trash. "I've been looking everywhere for you."

His head snapped up when he heard me. "I was in detention."

"And now you're taking it out on the trash?" I guessed, even though it was a lame attempt at trying to work out what he was doing.

"Mr. Barbage got bored so he sent me out here on trash duty until lunch is over."

He was being punished because of me. It felt like a kick to my gut. I started picking up trash and placing it in the can, doing everything I could to help.

"You don't have to do that," Frankie said.

"I know. But I want to help."

We cleaned up the filthy area underneath the bleachers until I was convinced the school was just overrun with pigs. But that was probably unfair to the pigs. I'd never actually witnessed a pig littering before.

With just five minutes left of lunchtime, the area looked better than I'd ever seen it before. Frankie and I both stopped at the trash can. He reached into his pocket and pulled out the highlighter. It was neon green. "You should look after this for me. It needs to be saved."

I took it from his hands, it was warm from being in his pocket. It made me highly aware of Frankie's warm skin and the brightness of his smile.

My head shook to get rid of all the imagery.

"Thanks," I finally replied.

"I knew it needed to be rescued."

It was impossible to ignore all the butterflies in my stomach. Nobody had ever done something so nice for me before. So many people yelled at me for rescuing things.

Nobody had ever *helped* me before.

"It means a lot to me. You know, that you did that for me," I stammered out the words like I was typing on a keyboard and I'd forgotten where all the letters were.

"It was nothing. Really, I just thought it shouldn't stay lost." He kicked at a stone on the floor. "You didn't have to help me pick up trash all lunch."

"It was the least I could do."

His eyes flicked up to meet mine and all the words I could remember completely vanished from my head. They were scattered on the floor and I couldn't break eye contact with Frankie to pick them up again.

Time stopped for those few moments we stared at each other. It was like the world didn't exist anymore and it was just us. We stood in a snow globe, protected from everything outside our little bubble.

Our love bubble?

No, that was stupid.

165

Mrs. Justice didn't know what she was talking about. Considering she was about a hundred years old, she could be forgiven.

And then the most incredible thing happened.

Frankie leaned over and kissed me.

It was quick and so sudden that it took a moment for my brain to catch up. His lips–as soft as I'd imagined–were on mine and then they were gone again.

It was my first kiss.

I hoped I remembered it when *I* was a hundred years old.

Two hundred, even.

We both stood there, startled.

Awkward.

Embarrassed.

The butterflies in my stomach were creating a tornado. It was going to sweep me away from the inside before too long. If I continued to stand there it wasn't going to be pretty.

The school bell rang, saving us both.

"See you later," I said, my breath catching in my throat.

"Yeah. Later, Em."

We left in different directions. Even though we were going to the same room.

For the next hour during class I couldn't get the kiss off my mind. I replayed it at least a hundred times, analyzing it from all angles.

Did I do it right?

Should I have done something else?

My gaze purposefully stayed off him during the lesson. I didn't want to be caught staring at him, even though that would mean he was staring at me too.

Did I want him to be staring?

Should I have thanked him for the kiss? Was that something people did?

I'd never wanted a mother, friends, or a female relative more than I did right at that moment. The truth was I had no idea what I was doing and I needed someone to ask. I couldn't speak to Frankie, that would have been all kinds of ridiculously wrong. Uncle Marvin? The thought almost made me laugh out loud.

Uncle Marvin's idea of kissing would be sharing a bottle of beer with a woman. Two lips, one bottle, that counted as far as he was concerned.

"Emmeline?" My name cut into my frantic thoughts. I looked up to see the teacher, Mrs. Keating, staring at me expectantly.

"Em," I automatically corrected.

She didn't seem too pleased with my response. "So sorry for interrupting your daydream. I'm sure it's highly more interesting than algebra. But I would love to know the answer to question 2B of the homework assignment."

I felt every eye in the room staring at me. They were all googly-eyed monsters, ready to laugh at me with any excuse. "It's thirteen hundred and two. May I please go the restroom?"

Mrs. Keating wasn't happy about it, her reluctance found its way into a loud sigh. Still, she couldn't legally deny me my basic rights as a human being.

The right to pee.

It was very important.

"Yes, okay, go on. Be quick," she said.

All the googly eyes followed me to the door. I left them there as I ran down the corridor.

I didn't need to use the restroom, at least not for the purpose it was designed for. I needed to get out of the classroom, away from all prying expressions so I could process the kiss in private.

The stalls were all empty as I entered the female restroom in A block. I hurried into one and closed the lid of the toilet so I could use it as a seat. Locking the door, it was my own private space in the otherwise very public school.

I'd never been kissed before. I guessed that was the last time I would be able to say that. I was now very well kissed, accustomed to the feeling of lips upon my own.

Frankie's lips had been wonderful—warm and tasting a bit like chocolate. When I licked my lips now they had the faint trace of Frankie attached to them.

The one thing I knew for sure was that I would never, ever forget that kiss.

I wanted more.

That single kiss was addictive, making me crave more and more. My cheeks flushed pink with the thought of sharing more kisses with Frankie.

Would he want more with me?

Was he regretting it now?

My stomach was twisted with knots so tight that it was possible they'd stay that way permanently. Only one person could untie them and he was still sitting in class.

I both dreaded and looked forward to seeing him alone again.

My cell phone suddenly pinged in my pocket. I pulled it out to see what had made the noise. It wasn't the usual text message sound or a ringtone.

It was a search alert.

When my father first went missing I had set up an alert for any mentions of his name on the internet. So far all I'd had were a few articles about his initial disappearance. They hadn't told me anything I didn't already know.

With the kiss pushed to the back of my mind momentarily, I followed the link to the site in question. It was a streaming news site, reporting events from all around the world.

My father was mentioned in an article posted only half an hour earlier. It was in connection with a property that had been burned down to the ground last night.

I couldn't see the connection, skimming through the article until I found the details I was looking for. When the fire inspectors were sifting through the rubble and looking for the cause of the inferno, they found an item belonging to one Marshall Gabrielle.

His wallet.

They were positive it was his as his driver's license and credit cards were still in the holders. It wouldn't make sense to belong to anyone else.

I read with more investment into the details now. I scanned the words, trying to find the ones that I didn't want to know. Like whether they found the charred remains of a body in the fire. Or whether they suspected that something shifty was going on in the property.

They mentioned neither.

That was a good thing, right?

If they found remains they would have reported it, right?

My heart was beating faster than it should have. It wasn't for the good reasons now. I was filled with the dread of something horrible happening to my father.

Marshall Gabrielle wasn't just a name to me. He wasn't an inconsequential part of the article about another building that had been burned to the ground because someone fell asleep with a cigarette in their mouth.

He was real.

He was my father.

No matter how many times I had told myself he didn't deserve to be a part of my life, the knowledge underneath it all said that I would have run back into his arms if he opened them for me. I would have turned back into that six-year-old little girl and squealed with delight, never to let him go again.

To stop the panic quickly building, I laid out all the explanations I could think of for his wallet being in that building.

Someone robbed him and then that criminal's house had burned down. He was now walking around without his wallet but with his life.

He had been in the house when it caught fire. He had escaped so quickly he lost his wallet and couldn't go back for it because of all the flames.

He had been in the house when it burned down and he couldn't get out. The police were withholding the details of his body being found.

My father had planted the wallet so people would think he had perished. He could have burned the house down himself to fake his own death.

It was a different man named Marshall Gabrielle who was also missing. It was just a big coincidence that he shared a name with my father.

None of the options seemed more plausible than the others. I just had no idea of what could have happened. The creeping feeling of only one person being able to explain it all washed over me. My father could tell quite the story if he was ever found.

I'd been staring at the article for ten minutes before I remembered where I was and what I was supposed to be doing. I left the restroom and ran back to class, earning myself a dirty look from Mrs. Keating in the process.

I ignored all the snickers coming my way.

A pee shouldn't have taken that long.

Frankie gave me a quizzical look when he caught my eye. I shrugged like there was nothing wrong and backed it up with a nonchalant smile.

I didn't know if Frankie and I still had the same

friendship we did before the kiss. While exceedingly wonderful, it blurred the lines of our relationship now. It was going to be awkward for a while yet.

If he was still talking to me.

Focusing on the class was now all but impossible. I tried to push the fire from my mind but it always pushed its way back in. There was only one thing I could do.

I had to go to the scene of the fire.

Chapter 16

Frankie wasn't in my last class of the day. I managed to survive the afternoon without any impromptu visits to Principal Moore's office. The moment the final bell rang, I was out of there.

The burned ruins weren't far from the house my father shared with his new family. It made the possibility of him being in the house with his wallet all that much more plausible.

If Marshall Gabrielle was taken against his wishes, it could have been someone from the same neighborhood. Didn't they say most murders are committed by someone the victims knew?

I didn't like to think of the possibility of murder.

Or kidnapping.

The most likely reason for my father's disappearance was his decision to run away voluntarily. A large part of my heart suspected that was what had happened.

But this new discovery?

It made me sick to my stomach. My father was good at disappearing. He had proven to me that he was a regular Houdini. One minute he was in my life, the next he wasn't. It was that simple and not a far stretch of the imagination to think he'd done that again.

But he wouldn't have left his wallet.

That was sloppy.

Crews were still recording their pieces for the nightly news when I found the scene of the fire. It was cordoned off with police tape, declared a crime scene until they knew more. The smell of smoke was still lingering heavily in the air.

The whole scene made my stomach bubble with bile and knock on my back teeth with its acidity. The lumpy black items in the area used to be someone's house. They lived there, never imagining it could all be gone in the blink of an eye.

I really hoped there were no bodies.

The property was probably once a house. All its neighbors were, so it would have been out of place to be anything else. A home seemed to make it all that much more devastating.

While the afternoon wore on, I sat in a bus shelter down the road from the site. It was close enough to see what was happening but not close enough to be accused of loitering. The last thing I needed was to end up on the six o'clock news as the devastated daughter.

The site grew quieter as the sun disappeared. By five,

everyone had left–including the police and fire inspectors. I waited a bit longer to be sure before I ducked under the police tape and stepped onto the site.

It could have been my imagination but it instantly felt hot, like the site remembered the blazing heat of the fire and kept replaying the traumatic incident in a loop.

Most of the items were just lumps, indistinguishable from what they once were. I imagined all the items being swept up by a hard machine, dumped at the tip with all the other things that no longer served their purpose.

There would be nothing for the Keeper of Discarded Things to rescue. Once items were charred down to ash they no longer meant anything to anyone. They were the true lost things, forever unable to be found once again.

The whole scene made me blue with melancholy. Fire didn't just burn things, they destroyed their souls. As much as I looked, I didn't find any lost thing that I could rescue.

Either the police or fire department had done a good job in going over the place. They had cleared a path through the lumps, allowing me to wander through the whole area without having to step over things.

I wasn't sure what I was looking for. If my father was in the house he certainly wasn't there now. If there was a body, they had extricated it to the morgue by now and handed it over to the coroner for further inspection.

All I knew was that I had to be there. Something belonging to my father had been lost there. It was something tangible, something he owned and kept on him at all times of the day. It was a link to him that I hadn't had for a very long time.

I wanted to tell Frankie about it. If he were there he would reassure me that everything would be okay. He would come up with some incredible reason for his wallet being here that it would blow my theories out of the water.

Everything was better with Frankie around.

Always.

Everything.

But it was different now. I couldn't hang around him without thinking about the kiss and it agonized me to wonder whether he was having the same thoughts.

Right now I couldn't think of the kiss. My head was filled with thoughts of my father that I couldn't vanquish. He might have been standing exactly where I was now. What was he here for? What was he doing?

The world was filled with questions that never received their corresponding answers. It seemed like mine would jumble with them all and get swallowed up in the giant mass of them.

I walked right to the back of the property where the fire didn't seem to have burned so harshly. Most of the items here were recognizable. I could see a lamp, a chest of drawers, and something looking like a chair. They were all black and charred but maintained their original shapes—even if only half of them were hanging together.

After trying to open the chest of drawers, I only had blackened hands to show for it. After that, I didn't use my hands for anything else. It was my feet that rifled through the rubble now. It didn't matter if my black school shoes got blacker.

I kicked around for a while in the dark. The streetlights worked surprisingly well but they also highlighted my presence on the off-limits site. Trying to explain what I was doing there to the police and Uncle Marvin would be tricky.

My foot moved some burned books and I froze. There was something small underneath them. I bent over to pick it up, examining it in my hands while I tried not to get it black too.

It was a business card.

Either it was shielded from the fire by the books or it was indestructible. I would place my money on the former rather than the latter.

I turned it over in my hand, reading the details until I had them memorized.

I also tucked it into my pocket to add to my shelves.

It was lost, after all.

The business card declared it belonged to Julia Golden Design. There was something familiar about the name but I couldn't connect it to anything.

My mind kept turning it over while I continued my search. The resident of the house must have enjoyed reading because there sure were a bunch of charred books in the remains. It seemed a pity that they would no longer fulfil their purpose and bring entertainment to their reader.

Fires were horrible things.

It was almost six o'clock when I decided I wasn't going to find anything else in the property. It had obviously been combed over with all the good stuff already being discovered by the authorities. Now I was only risking getting caught in a place where I shouldn't have been.

I needed to get home and make dinner for Uncle Marvin. He was already watching me closer after my little interrogation and I didn't really want to alter my schedule.

But I had to know.

The business card gave an address one bus ride away from the property. All I had to do was go there quickly and then race home. It was possible my tardiness wouldn't be noticed.

Unless Uncle Marvin was particularly hungry.

I was so close, I had to risk it. The alternative was to come back tomorrow but I couldn't wait that long. I needed to know what the business was now or it would drive me insane in the meantime.

My feet ran for the bus stop and I caught the next F24 route the moment it arrived. My pulse was racing, urging everything else to go fast around me so I could go home before my uncle started to wonder where his dinner was.

The bus was late.

Of course.

I impatiently tapped my foot on the concrete, willing it to come around the corner and put my panic at ease. Everything was going far too slowly for my needs.

Four minutes and fifty-nine seconds was how long it took to arrive. Three minutes and fifteen seconds late. If I hadn't counted the seconds, I would have driven myself crazy with stress.

There was no point taking a seat on the bus so I stood by the exit doors and waited, scanning the streets for the address the entire time and willing all the cars on the road to get out of our way.

Julia Golden Design came into view and a little spark of hope ignited. When the bus came to an almost-stop I jumped off and ran for the door. If I had taken the steps like a normal person, I would have noticed the place was in darkness sooner.

It was closed.

I was cursed.

It was official.

My fist banged on the door just to make sure nobody was still lurking within. I waited, thinking I saw a flicker of movement but not quite sure.

My nose pressed onto the glass door, hoping beyond hope I wasn't wasting more time. Every day that passed told me it was going to be more difficult to find my father.

If he wanted to be found.

The door suddenly swung open, giving me a heart attack in the process. I needed to concentrate more.

"What is all the banging about?" The middle aged woman stared me down, giving me the impression she wasn't one to be messed with.

Having a plan before I got to this moment would have been handy. Pity I hadn't thought about that earlier.

"Well?" She waited, but not patiently.

"I was looking for a lamp," I blurted out–the first thing that came to mind.

"Well you should have been here during our opening time. Nine a.m. tomorrow morning, that's when our doors will be open." I was losing her. I couldn't let that happen.

"But it's urgent. Please."

She stared at me, rolling back on her heels while she thought about my plea. For a professional liar, I wasn't doing a very good job of it. "You've got two minutes. Hurry up." She stood back from the door to let me through.

I had no use whatsoever for a lamp but I was pretending to search for one anyway. In the meantime, I scrambled for something to say that would help me in my quest. "I've been searching for the perfect lamp everywhere. My computer crashed and I lost all the research I'd done on them."

"You could just do a search online. It's not like they're particularly rare or anything." She was leaning on the doorframe, her arms crossed over her chest.

"But I'd done so much research. I'm sure nobody has as much computer problems as I do." She raised her eyebrows but didn't take the bait. It was time for some prompting. "Do you have a good computer guy?"

"He's alright."

"Would you recommend him?" I asked eagerly.

"He's the same as all the rest. Now, are you going to buy something or not? It's late and I want to go home to my family."

"I guess I'll have to search for a computer guy myself."

"You've got five seconds to buy something or I'm

kicking you out."

Talk about a short fuse.

I ran my hand along the shelves with no intention of buying. "I think I'll keep searching. Thanks all the same."

She gestured toward the door and I slipped through it before she slammed it closed. The twisting of the locks were like a rude way of saying she was glad I was gone from the store.

The visit had been a disaster.

I sat on the steps with the fading light making my shadow long and lean. I just needed a moment to catch my breath before waiting for the next bus going in the opposite direction. Knowing my luck it would probably be early and I would miss it.

But, instead, something even worse happened.

My first thought was 'hey, that car looks familiar'. My second thought was 'hey, it's exactly like Uncle Marvin's car'. My third thought was full of swear words when I recognized the driver as none other than my uncle Marvin.

Of course.

The area where he would never be, especially near dinner time, and he was staring right at me. What had I done to the gods of the world to deserve such bad luck? Did I break a mirror sometime? Walk past a black cat?

He wound down the window of his ancient brown car, the effort of the manual handle making him puff. "What are you doing here, you stupid girl?"

I stood up and trudged toward the car, hoping nobody was watching our pathetic exchange. "I was going to get you a lamp for your birthday. But I guess that surprise is now blown."

"Get in," Uncle Marvin replied. He fixed his gaze forward and didn't look at me again while I climbed into his rust-bucket and secured my seatbelt.

He didn't believe me but he didn't interrogate me any further. Even that was out of my uncle's usual behavior. He was usually nosey when it came to what I was up to.

Perhaps he was also up to no good?

Was he staying quiet because he didn't want *me* asking *him* the same questions he wanted from me?

It was possible. It seemed like my grumpy Uncle Marvin was full of surprises these days. After all, he didn't mention dinner once on the drive home.

I went straight to the kitchen and cooked up some beans on toast for our gourmet dinner. The meal was on the table in under ten minutes, quite the effort on my behalf.

Matilda meowed at me until I fed her too. Kicking up more of a fuss than the grump glaring at me across the table. My whole world was turning upside down.

I had to know why Uncle Marvin was acting so strangely. The last thing I wanted to do was suspect him of having something to do with my father's vanishing act but in all the time I'd known him, he never altered his routine like this.

Something was going on with him.

Really, there was only one option left for me to pursue. I needed information and Uncle Marvin wasn't exactly lining up to offer it to me. It was easier getting money out of him and that was really saying something.

"Would you like some ice cream for dessert?" I said to the quiet room.

Uncle Marvin grumbled something under his breath which I took as a yes. I cleaned up the plates and scooped some chocolate ice cream into a bowl. Before I gave the serving to my uncle, I had one more ingredient to add.

A sedative.

I'd seen him use them before when he claimed the idiot doctor didn't know what had given him the flu and was trying to knock him out instead of fixing him. So I knew they weren't dangerous. I hoped they didn't have much of a taste.

I stirred in the capsules until they melted and then added some sprinkles on top just to be sure they were well and truly disguised. Crossing my fingers, I placed it in front of him.

He guzzled it down in no time.

While I did the dishes, Uncle Marvin retreated to his usual place in front of the television with a beer in hand. He flicked on the news and sighed with all the effort of a long, hard day.

Was it good to mix alcohol with sedatives?

I hoped it would be okay.

My homework had to wait while I discreetly supervised the effects of the prescription drug. A check every five minutes made sure he hadn't stopped breathing.

On the second check, he was fine.

On the seventh check, he was sound asleep.

It was time to go snooping.

Chapter 17

Uncle Marvin's bedroom was like a horrible dentist's office. It wasn't somewhere you really wanted to go but sometimes you just had to.

It had been years since I had cause to enter his personal realm. The last time was when I nine and he confiscated my library book. It wasn't so much that I wanted the book back, more that I didn't want to pay another fine at the public library.

I hadn't got caught the last time and I hoped I wouldn't this time either. Uncle Marvin had seemed out for the count when I last checked on him. He wasn't likely to wake up in the next twenty minutes, at least.

Not unless he'd developed superhuman powers recently.

Because I was forbidden from entering this room, it meant I didn't have to clean it either. Leaving Uncle Marvin to clean anything was always a dangerous game.

There could be any number of deadly bacteria growing all over the place.

Like E.coli lingering under the piles of dirty clothes.

Or cholera hiding in the empty used glasses of water gathering like it's a party on his bedside table.

I didn't even want to think about the stray underwear dotted across the floor.

My feet were planted carefully with every step I took, making sure not to disturb or accidently touch something I didn't want to. The closet was practically a cornucopia of secrets so I carefully made my way there.

The double doors could almost swing all the way open before they caught on some stray clothes. With most of his articles on the floor, it didn't leave many hanging on the racks.

Which worked in my favor.

On the shelf above the hanging racks was a box that was ringed by a layer of dust that hadn't been disturbed in a long time—at first glance.

At second glance, there was a disturbance in the dust. The box had been moved recently, a new layer of dust not having time to settle just yet.

I pulled out the box that was only as big as a shoebox and set it on the floor. It felt like I should be wearing gloves to hide my fingerprints or something but figured Uncle Marvin would never go to those extremes to work out who had been in his room. If he noticed at all—which I was counting on him not doing—he would automatically call me guilty and apply punishment as he deemed fit. There would be no trial by jury, no presumption of innocence. If Uncle Marvin was a Supreme Court judge, there would be nobody left on the outside.

The box was full of personal items, mainly photographs in amongst his birth certificate, old driver's licenses and a… marriage certificate?

When on earth was Uncle Marvin married?

Who would have agreed to that proposal?

I tried to imagine him in love, cavorting with a pretty lady and trying to impress her. The image in my head was wrong, all wrong. Uncle Marvin definitely wasn't the wooing type. I shoved the certificate back in the box and tried to wipe the memory of seeing it all together.

The photographs were safer.

At least *they* didn't conjure up nightmarish scenes.

I flipped through each of them. Some of them were in black and white, pictures of two little boys with cheeky dimples and mischievous minds. Someone had taken the time to handwrite names on the backs of the photographs.

Marvin and Marshall.

Marshall and Marvin.

They were so cute when they were little. The boys were in the playground, in front of the house, riding in the backseat of a car, playing with a shaggy dog. They looked just like perfect little happy kids.

It was sweet to see this side of them. The only Marvin I'd ever known was cynical, never afraid to share his disappointment, and seeing the negative in everything. My father? Well, my greatest memory was watching his back as he left.

These two little boys seemed nothing like them. They had the world at their feet and were excited about every single thing they saw and did.

What happened to them?

One was now raising his niece and the other had vanished into thin air one day.

If their mother was still alive, she probably would have been asking the same question.

I replaced the photographs in the box and secured the lid once more. I took extra care in making sure it was in the exact same position I found it and checked the rest of the closet.

I wasn't even sure what I was actually looking for. A smoking gun, perhaps? Maybe. It was answers I was looking for and they could have taken any form. They certainly weren't in the old pictures kept in the shoebox.

Rifling through his chest of drawers turned up nothing but a messy pile of clothes that I moved around with the pointy end of a wooden backscratcher.

If Uncle Marvin hid all his secrets in the bedroom, I didn't know where. I left the room no further ahead than when I had entered. Except now I felt sadness when I remembered the photographs.

I really hoped he didn't have anything to do with his brother's disappearance. The little boy in the pictures never would have harmed his brother. They were mates, friends, comrades, partners in crime. They wouldn't have dreamed of ever growing apart or being capable of harming one another.

Creeping down the stairs, I checked in on my uncle to make sure he was still breathing–he was. His head was leaning back on the armchair, his mouth wide open while he snored as loud as a sonic boom.

I hoped I hadn't used too much sedative.

Was it possible to die from an overdose of sleeping tablets?

It was best that I kept the poisons hotline on speed dial until he woke up.

I did my homework in the living room, something I never did because Uncle Marvin would tell me I was turning the pages too loudly or my pencil was scratching the paper noisily. He definitely wasn't complaining tonight.

By bedtime he was still in the same position–but still breathing too. I reluctantly went to bed, hoping he would have died by now if the sedative was going to have a harmful effect.

I checked on him several times in the night.

He was alive with every check.

In the morning I was dressed and ready to pretend nothing had happened when I went downstairs. My heart skipped a beat when Uncle Marvin wasn't in the living room. It took a few frantic seconds to find him in the kitchen.

He was nursing a mug of steaming hot coffee, his eyes bloodshot. It was time for my acting to begin. "Good morning," I said happily.

"Nothing good about it," he replied.

"Is everything alright?"

"I'm tired. I didn't sleep at all last night."

My hand covered my slight smile. He may not have *thought* he slept at all but my sleepless night told otherwise. He slept like the dead, it should have been *me* complaining about fatigue.

I had breakfast and got out of there before he started searching for the Berocca (we didn't have any). My night of drug-induced peace had turned up nothing. My trip to the burned down house had turned up zilch. It felt like I was just running around in circles and not getting any closer to finding my dad.

Mrs. Justice was in her garden outside. I gave her a wave as I passed but moved too quickly to stop and chat. At the school gate I did more avoiding as I stayed away from Frankie. I just couldn't deal with the ramifications of the kiss yet, I hadn't properly processed it.

Achieving a personal best of managing to stay away from Frankie for the whole day, I was feeling pretty good about the day by the end of it.

My feet moved to start the walk home.

Until someone tapped me on the shoulder.

I turned around and came face to face with the boy who had kissed me. My face quickly blushed at seeing him again and instantly looking at his lips.

"Hey, I've been looking for you all day," Frankie said jovially, like he hadn't even thought that I might have been avoiding him. He was so sweet and innocent, he had no business being corrupted by me.

"I've been busy," I replied. "Why?"

"Why what?"

"Why were you looking for me?"

Understanding crossed his face. "Oh, I don't know. I just wanted to hang out. I haven't seen you since yesterday. Lunchtime." At that moment, he realized what had happened at lunchtime yesterday.

My cheeks burned deeper.

I needed to change the subject quickly or I was going to burst into flames and instantly combust. "Did you see the news last night?"

"No, I didn't," he said eagerly, relieved at the topic change just as much as I was. Apparently neither of us were equipped with enough emotional intelligence to discuss the kiss.

That epic kiss.

That I had to forget about because clearly it wasn't going to happen again.

"The police found my father's wallet in a house that burned down. I went to the place but didn't really find anything but a business card."

"Was the card for fire safety?"

"No, it was for Julia Golden Designs. It was the name of one of Dad's customers." I waited a moment to let that sink in. "So I went and visited them. Didn't get anywhere."

"What did you say to them?"

I ran over the short conversation between myself and the shop assistant. There was no point glossing over my complete and utter failure to gain any information from the woman.

She still scared me a little.

Even just thinking about her.

"She wouldn't give me any information about her computer guy," I finished. On purpose, I left out details about Uncle Marvin picking me up. That would only make him seem a little bit more shady and I didn't want that.

"What information were you looking for?" Frankie asked. He was full of questions that afternoon. He only needed a spotlight and he would have been able to join the police force as their case closer.

I shrugged. "I don't know. I was kind of hoping she felt either good things or bad things about my dad. If I knew what she thought, then I might be able to tell what kind of connection she had with him. If she loved his services then she probably didn't have anything to do with his vanishing act or the house that burned down."

"You said it's on Conrad Street, right?" I nodded. "Then let's go. You know what bus to take, lead me there."

He was already walking when I replied. "It's a dead end, Frankie. She didn't think much about her computer guy at all, which means it's probably just a coincidence that I found that business card in the house. Maybe someone else was looking for house decorations."

"Perhaps. But it's worth a second shot, right?"

At that moment I wondered what I would do without Frankie. He had bashed into my life completely without fear or judgement and was now the only thing that was keeping me going.

And he had *kissed* me.

I shook my head so the thoughts would loosen and fall out but they were determined to stay lodged in my consciousness. Frankie and I rode the bus together, all the way back to the same place I had stood almost twenty-four hours earlier.

"That's the place?" He pointed to the shop, now proudly displaying an 'Open' sign.

"Yeah. But the woman is really mean, she won't tell you anything."

Frankie just smiled. "She hasn't met Frankie Bolero yet." He confidently strode inside while I hid just down the street. I didn't believe he would be very long, the woman would kick him out the moment she suspected something was off.

The minutes ticked by.

They turned into twenty.

Then thirty.

It was a large crowd of minutes by the time Frankie returned and found me sitting in the gutter. I would have gladly sat on a seat if there were any around.

The gutter seemed appropriate anyway.

Frankie sat beside me, silent.

"Well?" I prompted.

"Nobody can resist the charms of Frankie Bolero," he said triumphantly. "I had a lovely chat with Winnie. She told me her entire life story."

"You're joking."

"Of course not! Winnie is a lovely lady, knows

everything possible about home decor. We shared an ice tea."

I pushed him playfully, unable to believe he had spoken to the same woman I did. There was no way she had given him *something to drink*. "No way."

"Way." He grinned with the smile of a thousand cheeky monkeys. "She said she would love to refer me to her computer guy but she was in the middle of finding a new one. If I pop back in over the next few weeks she'll let me know who she found."

"Did she say what happened to her old computer guy?" Like, my father? The one who was currently missing, possibly under mysterious circumstances?

"Said he wasn't working out. It could have been because her current one is MIA."

I sighed all the air out of my lungs. "She probably heard about the disappearance and knows she isn't going to get Marshall Gabrielle to fix her computers anytime soon. His business calls are probably going unanswered."

"Probably."

I was looking for connections where there weren't any. Just because I'd found the business card in the same place the police found my father's wallet, it didn't mean there was something more to the relationship.

I was grasping at straws and it was only wasting time— both mine and Frankie's. Our time would have been better spent doing homework. At least that would have solved one problem.

My phone beeped with a text message. I retrieved my

cell from my backpack automatically while I continued the conversation. "I can't believe she gave you ice tea."

"She put a slice of lemon in it too."

"Now you're just rubbing it in." My attention momentarily flicked to my cell phone. The text was from Samantha:

Would love to catch up sometime. April misses you. Sam xx.

I showed Frankie the text before my screen went dark. "My stepmother sure is doing her best impression of someone that cares."

"Maybe she genuinely cares," Frankie said. I considered his comment. In my experience people rarely did things because they genuinely cared.

People wanted things.

People tried to get what they wanted.

They didn't actually *care*.

"Hey, isn't there some statistic that says most crimes are done by someone people know?" I threw the thought out there, tried to see if it stuck to anything.

"I guess."

"What about if Samantha has something to do with my father's disappearance? She could be being nice to me to throw me off track."

Frankie tucked a piece of my hair behind my ear, it had escaped with the wind whipping around us. "Or she could just be being nice."

Nah, nobody was nice for no reason.

"I'll keep a close eye on her," I said. There was no point in corrupting Frankie further. One day he would work out the world wasn't full of rainbows and unicorns. Until then, I didn't want to be the person to darken the world for him.

We didn't take the bus home. We walked instead. It was a nice day and we weren't in a particular hurry to get anywhere. As much as I wanted to continue my search, I had no leads. There was little I could think to do that would help.

I *was* thinking about looking into Samantha Gabrielle a little further, though. Movies led me to believe husbands and wives were close, they shared secrets. Maybe she was the holder of my father's secrets too.

Anything was possible.

As we walked, I became aware of a pen laying on the pavement on the upcoming path. It was lost, with nobody around to claim it. I could almost hear it weeping as it thought about a future lost in the drains or never writing something again.

For only a moment I panicked.

Then I remembered Frankie was with me. He had seen me take something before, he understood what I had to do. There was no reason to be worried about saving the lost pen.

We approached it, getting closer and closer until the moment of its rescue was upon us. I bent down to pick it up, slipping the pen into my backpack without missing a beat.

It was the first time I realized Frankie was completely

different to the rest of world.

It was the second time I wanted him to kiss me.

It was the third time I felt my heart skip a beat because his arm was so close to mine they brushed together.

The smile showed all my teeth before I could stop it.

Chapter 18

When Frankie had asked me what I was going to do on the weekend as we walked home from school together on Friday, the first thing that came to mind was a lie.

But the truth slipped out before I could stop it.

I confessed I was going to follow my stepmother and see if she did anything that wasn't entirely normal. I had hoped she would lead me straight to her husband. I would see them meeting clandestinely and know the whole thing was a ruse.

Frankie had insisted on coming with me.

Which I secretly loved.

So far, at eight a.m. on the Saturday, the only thing I had learned was that Samantha Gabrielle enjoyed her sleeping in. There had been no movement at the house she shared with my stepsister and father. The whole thing was completely snooze-worthy.

Thankfully, Frankie brought snacks.

We chomped on chocolate chip cookies for over an hour before anything happened. Buses came and went from the stop where we sat, nobody bothered to ask us why we weren't getting on any of them.

No wonder my father disappeared so easily.

The door to the house opened mid-morning. Samantha and April both went directly to the front gate and started walking. My stepsister was wearing a pink tutu with her hair pulled back into a tight bun on top of her head. There were no prizes for guessing where they were going.

"The eagle is on the move," I said.

"Eagle, really? I'm sure you can come up with something more inventive than that."

I thought for a moment. "The black widow spider is on the move?" It seemed appropriate to me.

"Not bad. How about Stepmonster?"

"Sounds a bit bias."

"And black widow isn't?" Frankie sounded outraged in a playful way. I liked the way we could joke together. I'd never had that before with anyone. Uncle Marvin lost his sense of humor with his waistline.

Frankie and I started trailing after the pair, making sure to leave enough space so she wouldn't spot us. April kept tugging her mother forward, trying to get her to fasten her pace. She was probably excited about her ballet lesson. I probably would have been at her age.

The four of us wound around a few blocks before we stopped. Samantha took April into the dance studio and we waited outside. Hopefully it wouldn't be the kind of dance class that required parental participation.

"Did you ever go to dance classes when you were a kid?" Frankie asked.

I snorted, the very idea was enough to laugh about. "No way. Uncle Marvin considered any kind of after-school activity to be a waste of time because they are all run by idiots for stupid purposes. He thought dancing was pointless."

"My sisters go to jazz classes."

"I hope your family never meets Uncle Marvin."

We waited in silence after that little revelation. Sometimes the truth sounded too sharp when I said it out loud. But what could I do? It didn't seem feasible to lie to Frankie about everything. I had to hope he would simply understand.

Samantha emerged after about ten minutes. She kept going on her walk with us. One of the only good things about Lakeside was the ability to walk most places without needing to be fit enough to run marathons. People rarely used their cars when they found the right neighborhood to settle in.

The next stop on Samantha's day of errands was a pawn shop, of all places. She went inside and straight to the counter. We could see her through the window but had no clue about what she was saying to the male shop attendant.

"You go to a pawn shop when you need quick cash for something, right?" Frankie said. I nodded, that was my understanding too.

Sure, some people went to pawn shops to browse for

items like they would in a department store but those that went directly to the counter weren't after making purchases.

They wanted the cash.

The shop attendant went away for a few minutes while Samantha shuffled from foot to foot and waited. The view through the window wasn't spectacular but I did manage to glimpse her expression when she turned our way a few times.

She looked worried.

But about what?

Hocking things at the pawn shop wasn't illegal, nor was just browsing. There was enough police attention on the industry to make sure the shop attendants weren't dodgy. So what did she have to be concerned about?

For the first time since I met her, I did truly wonder if perhaps Samantha knew more than she let on. She could have been lying to me since that first encounter.

I had believed her.

Every word.

Betrayal was something I was used to, having experienced it since that moment my father walked away from me. I was reminded of it every Mother's Day when everyone else had a mommy except me, on every parent-teacher night when I had to explain why my Uncle Marvin chose not to come, and a million other instances in my life. It should have been something I was immune to.

I wasn't.

It still stung like a bee.

Samantha took a pile of money from the shop attendant and tucked it into her handbag before leaving. She emerged from the shop and immediately crossed the road.

Stop number three for her was an automatic teller machine. Her cash was quickly swallowed up by the machine, she pressed a few buttons, and it spat out a wad of cash. It disappeared inside her handbag too.

"Why does she need so much money all of a sudden?" I asked, never expecting an actual answer to my question. I could think of a hundred reasons why someone needed money.

A gambling problem.

Credit cards were maxed out.

The rent is due before the paycheck comes in.

The list went on into infinity. But the real question was why *Samantha Gabrielle* needed some fast cash. She was a suburban housewife, didn't they all have some secret money tucked away for emergencies?

"Maybe she's running out of money," Frankie offered. "Her husband's business isn't doing anything. She could be finding it difficult to make ends meet without the money coming in."

"That is surprisingly logical."

"I do my best."

Just like that, he had given me the one response that would put my concerns to rest for a while. Samantha's actions were a little odd, but her situation was odd too. If Marshall was the main breadwinner of the family they would seriously be missing his income right about now.

The next stop on Samantha's route was the grocery store. We waited for almost an hour while she was inside. After that she juggled some brown paper bags and went home.

I felt kind of guilty for suspecting her of dastardly deeds.

"What do you want to do now?" Frankie looked eager to move onto more exciting things after our uneventful investigation.

"I don't know," I replied. My weekend usually consisted of searching for lost things and cleaning the house until it sparkled–or at least until Uncle Marvin wouldn't complain about dirt and dust particles. I still needed to do both of those things but they didn't seem as appealing as spending time with Frankie.

"Can you show me your lost things?"

"No," was my automatic response.

"Why not?" Always with the questions, Mr. Frankie Bolero. He should be a cop when he graduated high school. He would be right in his element in the interrogation room.

"Because…" Why not? Because he would think I was a freak? Yes. Because he wouldn't want to hang out any more once he'd seen the size of my collection? Yes.

But before I could try to put my thoughts into words, Frankie linked his arm with me and started walking. "Come on, it will be fun. I really want to see everything." I had no choice except to move with him.

"My Uncle Marvin might be home," I lied. He told me

he would be out late today and to leave his dinner in the fridge. Potentially missing out on his meal was the only reason he enlightened me with the information.

"I'm sure I can talk him into loving me. I've been told I'm very irresistible." I didn't think Frankie was lying. He *was* very irresistible. But Uncle Marvin wasn't the average bag of beans. He didn't like anything.

Most of all, people.

"You don't know my Uncle Marvin," I finally replied. "He hates everyone and everything."

"But he doesn't hate you."

"The jury's out on that one."

Frankie just flashed me one of his irresistible grins and walked a little faster. As much as I didn't want him meeting my uncle, it would have been preferable to have him shoo him away rather than the boy seeing my collection of lost things.

Every step toward home was one closer to the end of our friendship. My mind was too scrambled to think of a more convincing lie. I would have set the house on fire if I thought I could do it without Frankie seeing.

Even Mrs. Justice wasn't in her yard to play interference. The whole world was conspiring against me to allow Frankie into my secret realm.

There were only a few minutes now before our friendship met its inevitable end.

Then just one minute.

And then only seconds.

"This house is really cool," Frankie said as we walked

past the living room. "It's got… character."

"You don't need to give me pity compliments," I replied. "I know this house sucks and it's falling apart. One good gust of wind and it will fold like a house of cards."

"It's not that bad."

"Wait until we get upstairs."

"I've been upstairs, remember? I helped you put your shelves up in the attic."

Oh, right.

So he'd seen the house but that didn't change anything. He hadn't seen my bedroom, which means he hadn't seen my lost things. One look at all those shelves and he would be running home to his mommy.

We moved up the stairs too quickly, bringing us to the moment I dreaded far too fast. The last thing I wanted to see was that look on Frankie's face when he realized what a nut job I was.

Three seconds to go and the door was only a step away.

Two seconds and I held my breath with my hand on the doorknob.

One second and I could feel the rush of blood through my ears.

Frankie walked into my room alone. I stood by the door with my stomach in my throat. There was no way to hide my craziness now, it was laid bare for him to see.

So many shelves.

Each of the items meant something to me. They had a story and I could remember every single one of them. The items were a victory for me, proof that not everything lost had to remain lost. They could find new homes where they could belong forever.

No more hurt.

No more pain.

They were safe now.

Frankie looked at the shelves, walking alongside while taking in each of the objects in his gaze. He was quiet, *very* quiet. I would have given anything to know what was going on inside his head right at that moment.

I never was any good at silence.

"You think I'm weird now, right?" I said. It was better that I said it rather than him. I couldn't bear for Frankie to say those words to me. Not out loud, not when I would be able to replay the sound bite in my head repeatedly.

Frankie stopped and looked at me. "Of course not. I like everything about you, Em. This is your world and I'm thankful you let me see it."

Everything in my body melted into jelly.

I was going to puddle on the floor and seep through the wooden boards.

"Do you really mean that?" My voice was so small I wasn't sure I was actually speaking out loud. A mouse could have done better.

He took a few steps until he was standing directly in front of me. "Of course I mean it. Em, don't you understand?"

"Understand what?"

"Understand how beautifully unique you are."

My brain was a muddle of thoughts, words, and

numbers. They swirled around with no real order, making me completely confused.

For reasons I couldn't fathom, Frankie liked me. He thought I was beautifully unique. It sounded like a compliment.

He thought I was beautiful.

Unique.

Beautifully unique.

There had been plenty of names people had called me before. Liar. Freak. Weirdo. Crazy. But nobody had ever called me beautiful before.

So, of course, I had to go and ruin the moment. "Yeah, right. Because everyone knows collecting things that people have lost is so beautiful."

"Why not? Who else even gives mind to these things? You rescue them, make sure they are safe, I told you I got it. Em, I love everything about you, including your collection."

His eyes were so blue.

They seemed so sincere.

He got it.

He loved me.

I could have lived a thousand lifetimes and I would never have expected anyone to say those words to me.

They were too kind.

Too wonderful.

Surely he had to be talking about someone else.

"Now it's your turn to say something," Frankie said. His eyes briefly went to the floor before they rose to meet mine again. There were no words I could form that would be able to express how much I loved his words.

How much I loved him.

He wasn't just the new kid anymore, the one who wouldn't leave me alone until he discovered my secrets. He was Frankie. *My* Frankie.

"You kissed me," I blurted out. The words had not formed in my mind before I said them. They came out of nowhere with no time for me to recall them.

His shoulders relaxed as a smile lifted his lips slightly. "You kissed back."

"I liked it."

"So did I."

"I think you should do it again." These words were coming out of the most private recesses of my mind. I had no idea how they had managed to escape and make their way into the world.

Why couldn't I shut up?

Where were my lies?

What was it about this boy that made me want to tell him the truth?

My carefully constructed wall I had built around myself was falling apart. The bricks were cracking, making long lines run through the concrete. Just one little huff and it would crumble to the ground.

All the air in my lungs caught in my throat, my heart was swollen and thudding too loudly while I waited for him to do something, to say something more.

It felt like I was dreaming.

Except it wasn't a nightmare this time. It was a fantastic dream, even though I had no idea what to say or do.

"I want to be more than friends with you, Em."

"Are you sure?" I had to check, give him the opportunity to walk away with no hard feelings. That was what I expected. Having people stick around were the surprising ones.

Frankie laughed as his eyes sparkled with amusement. "I'm sure. I've never met anyone like you and I can't imagine my life without you now."

"So I'll be your girlfriend? And you'll be my boyfriend?"

"If that's what you want, too."

I did. I *so* did. "Yes, please. Just…"

"Just?"

"Just stay, okay?"

Frankie leaned over and kissed me on the cheek. I could still feel his lips even when he removed them. My hand cradled my cheek, as if I could hold onto the feel of his kiss and keep it there forever like a tattoo.

Butterflies were set off in my stomach, completely fluttering over the fact that I was falling in love with the boy standing in front of me.

And then they all died.

"Em! Where are you?" Uncle Marvin cried out from downstairs. Frankie and I exchanged a panicked look.

We were going to be caught in my bedroom.

That would not end well.

Chapter 19

We were immediately in panic mode. I could not have Uncle Marvin meeting Frankie. He wasn't even supposed to be here, how on earth did he decide to come home early today of all days? Normally it never would have been a problem.

But today?

My worlds could not be permitted to collide. I'd already somehow managed to fall into a twilight zone with Frankie seeing my lost things. Him having a conversation with my uncle was only going to make everything implode.

Nothing good could come of it.

"What should I do?" Frankie whispered. His blue eyes were now wide open, alert and ready for action. He lost all the softness I had seen in him only moments earlier.

I needed a plan.

We needed a plan.

"Em? Get your ugly butt down here. The door was

unlocked so I know you're here."

"I'll go downstairs and get him into the kitchen. Then you need to sneak out," I quickly replied to Frankie in a whisper. There were a million holes in my plan—I never said it was a good one—but it would have to do. It wasn't like I had a helicopter waiting on the roof for moments like these.

Nobody had ever lost a helicopter.

"Maybe I should just meet him," Frankie said, like it wasn't the most ridiculous idea in the world.

"I'm not playing around, Em. I'm hungry and I want some waffles." Uncle Marvin's tone was getting grumpier with every word he called out.

"No, we stick to my plan. Keep watch, and the moment you see us move, hurry down and leave."

I didn't give him a chance to argue any more. "I'm coming," I called out as I took the stairs two at a time. My body was pumping with adrenalin, making my movement quick and jerky.

Uncle Marvin was standing in the foyer as he took a deep breath and got ready for another bellowing. I reached him just in time. "About time, girl. I want some waffles, go make them for me. What took you so long?"

"I was in the bathroom," I said. "I came as quickly as I could." Hopefully Frankie couldn't overhear my lie. I didn't want him to have visuals of me sitting on the toilet. It wasn't exactly a romantic image. "I thought you said you weren't going to be home until late."

"I wasn't. Plans changed. Get cooking. And I want real

maple syrup, none of that fake shit." He made a shooing movement, corralling me into the kitchen before I could think of a reason not to feed him.

My mind scurried to find a reason for Uncle Marvin to join me. He couldn't sit down on his favorite chair in the living room because then Frankie would never be able to leave. It wasn't like we had an approved fire escape from the second level of the house.

Because, in Uncle Marvin's words, if you were stupid enough to get caught in a fire you were stupid enough to deserve to die. So, therefore, no fire escapes.

Don't blame me for that statement, I didn't share his opinion.

I quickly found the maple syrup—the *real* stuff—and placed it on the highest shelf in the cupboard. "Uncle Marvin, I can't reach the syrup. Would you mind getting it down for me, please?"

"Use a chair."

"I'm mixing the batter. Please?"

I waited with everything crossed, hoping the ruse would get him. He didn't believe in doing work around the house, even if it was just to reach something out of my reach.

Finally, his heavy footsteps padded into the kitchen. I pointed at the syrup and he begrudgingly got it down for me. Over his shoulder I could see Frankie sneaking out. He was holding his shoes in his hand, walking in only socks.

Uncle Marvin plonked the syrup onto the table and then turned to face the archway into the foyer. Frankie only just managed to vanish out the door before he was sprung.

So I thought.

I was wrong.

"Is that the same boy I told you to stay away from?" Uncle Marvin bellowed. He was speaking far louder than our small house needed.

"What boy?"

"You know what boy." His face was starting to redden now as his anger grew. "I told you to stay away from all boys until I said otherwise. What part of this didn't you understand, Em?"

I felt like a deer caught in headlights.

No, scrap that.

A bunny rabbit.

Because my uncle was the size of a car and I felt only a few inches tall. If I could have scurried away, I would have. There was little worse than Uncle Marvin when he was angry. Especially when that anger was directed at me.

"There's nothing going on with any boy," I said, as if it was the most preposterous idea of the century. "Yuck. Seriously, Uncle Marvin, if there was a boy here I would want them to leave just as much as you did."

"Sure. What were you doing? Huh? What were you up to?"

It was getting hot in the kitchen. Even without the warmth of the waffle iron as it heated up, it would have been as hot as an inferno. "I told you, there was nobody here. Maybe you saw Matilda running around."

"I know the difference between a stupid cat and an idiot

boy, Em."

"Would you like ice cream with your waffles?" Deflection, always the last tool in my toolbox. Normally food was the best way to Uncle Marvin's heart.

"Yes," he humphed.

I returned to my task of making the waffles while he stared at me for a while longer. Whatever else he wanted to get out of me didn't last too much longer. He took his grumbling into the living room and turned up the television until it blared in the otherwise quiet house.

His waffles–with ice cream and real maple syrup–was served to him a few minutes later. I retreated to my room afterwards, sitting on my bed and wondering if Frankie had really been in there only that afternoon.

A part of me suspected Frankie wasn't real.

It was very possible that he was merely a figment of my imagination.

An imaginary friend.

It was plausible.

I'd had crazier thoughts.

My cell phone beeped with a message. The odds of it being from Frankie were high. I'd only ever received a text from one other person and that was my stepmother.

I picked up the phone with shaking hands anyway, hopeful that it was from the boy. If I had a message it meant he was real. I couldn't be just making him up.

It was from him:

Are you okay? I'm sorry your uncle went off like that.

If Frankie thought that was as bad as Uncle Marvin got,

he didn't know the man very well. My uncle yelling was an everyday occurrence. It bounced off me by now, completely rolling away as soon as he started.

I texted back:

Yes, all good.

How could I be anything else when I had Frankie in my life? He was beautiful and caring and smart and nice and he always smelled really good. Of course I was okay.

My phone beeped immediately:

Call me if you need me, okay? I'm here for you. xx

Two X's. They were kisses, right? I always got hugs and kisses mixed up. It didn't seem an issue in my life until right now. Nobody had bothered to send them to me before.

My first X's. Maybe I should have taken a photograph and pinned it to my wall. Maybe they would be the first of many. Maybe they would be my last.

I stressed over the message I needed to send back to him. Did I include X's as well? Or was that needy? I wrote it and then deleted the message more times than I wanted to admit.

Finally, I settled on the final one and sent it before I could back out:

I'm happy you're here for me. X

Just one X, one kiss. That was all I could bear to part with for now.

I went to sleep and dreamed of giant X's that chased me around in a dark forest.

I didn't believe in hidden messages in dreams.

Which was just as well.

For the rest of the weekend I remained in quiet solitude. Frankie was busy with his family and Uncle Marvin was still in a foul mood. I spent most of the time in the attic, making sure my new shelves were in perfect condition and ready to take on more lost things.

Monday would have been great–if I didn't have to go to school. I still had to stay on my best behavior, one more strike and the principal was going to come good with his threats to take the matter further.

I kept a special kind of loathing for Principal Moore.

Walking through the school paths, I kept my head low and focused on the ground.

Searching.

Always searching.

But not looking for trouble.

Someone's warm hand slid into mine. My first instinct was to pull away and then use that hand to slap them. But that's not what I did now.

The hand belonged to Frankie.

He didn't say a word about holding my hand. We simply walked, like this was a natural thing. Like our hands were made to always hold each other's.

The warm and fuzzy feeling in my chest was now associated with Frankie. It always appeared within me whenever he was near. Sometimes even when I only thought about him.

Something was happening to me and it was both frightening and exhilarating. I wondered if Frankie was also experiencing the same transformation.

"So school, huh?" Frankie said. "You've got to be cool to go to school, right?" He playfully elbowed me in the ribs to make me laugh at his lame joke.

The giggles flowed freely. Although I suspected it was more from being with Frankie than what he was saying. "Don't get too excited, we have another four days of school after this one. You don't want to peak too early."

"No, wouldn't want that." His face had grown serious in the space of a second. Still, I knew he was only joking. We reached the corridors and stepped inside. Our hand holding was now on display for anyone to see.

As a general rule, I didn't like people looking at me. Looking meant seeing and then they might see me do something I didn't want them to witness. The people looking at me now stirred a mixture of emotions in me.

Frankie walked me all the way to my locker. He squeezed my hand and gave me a small smile. "This is okay, right?" He nodded toward our twined hands.

"It's okay with me if it's okay with you."

He pulled my hand up to his lips and kissed the back of it before releasing me. "It's definitely okay with me. I'll see you in English."

My hand felt cold without him now.

I doubted it would ever feel warm again without him.

To avoid looking at all the people looking at me, I buried my head inside my locker and took extra time gathering my books. It was only when I really needed to get to class did I emerge again.

During my morning classes I formulated a plan. I never

said it was a good one, but it was one nevertheless. In order to make sure Frankie didn't get into trouble, I avoided him at lunch time as I walked as fast as I could without attracting attention to the school gates.

I left.

As long as I returned before my next class and nobody saw me, I wouldn't end up in Principal Moore's office. That was a large part of my plan.

The other part was speaking with my stepsister.

Chapter 20

The little girl was easy to find in the playground of Lakeside Elementary School. Her dark and wavy hair made her stand out amongst all the other children.

Or maybe it was some invisible tether that made me recognize my kin.

Yeah, right.

Most likely it was luck.

I headed straight for April, hoping no teachers would play interference. They probably didn't even know she had a big half-sister.

"Hey, April," I said as I sat on the bench next to her. Her bluest of blue eyes were only startled for a moment before they relaxed again.

"Hi, Em. What are you doing here?" She seemed happy that I was, that was a good start.

"I thought I would visit you and we could have lunch together." I looked around purposefully before leaning closer. "Don't tell anyone but I smuggled in a bar of chocolate. Long live sugar!"

She giggled, her little hand covering her mouth so nobody would realize we were sharing a secret. If I was completely honest, I would say my half-sister was quite adorable. I felt myself being sucked into her little world without a lifejacket.

There were different warm and fuzzy feelings reserved for her.

I pulled my chocolate bar from my backpack and opened it, offering her half. She took it eagerly. "Mom doesn't let me have chocolate until after dinner."

"Good thing this is a secret then." I let her eat for a few minutes before I started with the real reason why I was there. "Speaking of your mom, how is she doing lately?"

"She's sad all the time," April said somberly. I wished I didn't have to take her giggles away.

"Sad because your dad still isn't home?"

Her little head nodded. "Do you know when he's coming back? Mom says it will be soon but she's been saying that for a while now. I miss him."

"I don't know, sorry. I'm trying to find him, if that helps. The police are also searching really hard. We have to keep hopeful that they'll find him soon."

"I heard Mommy say to Auntie Sarah that he might never come home."

It felt like I needed to hug her or something to offer comfort but I wasn't sure. It was safer just sitting there and doing nothing. Words were all I could really offer. "She was probably just worried. If she knew you were listening, I bet she wouldn't have said that. People say things they don't mean all the time, especially when they're sad."

She nodded again, her fringe bouncing with the movement. The chocolate bar was gone now, the only trace was her sticky fingers. "How come I never met you before?" she asked, her eyes alive with innocent curiosity.

"I didn't know I had a half-sister," I replied honestly. There was no point in exposing her to the full story. She didn't need to know about our father walking out and leaving me when I was younger than her.

"Don't say that."

My brow wrinkled with confusion. "Don't say what?"

"Half-sister." Her small arm linked through mine. "We're sisters. I've always wanted a sister and now I have one. You're not going to leave, right, Em?"

There was no way I could break the eight year old's little heart. I wasn't going to be my father. "I'll always be here for you, April. I promise."

She smiled and that was it.

We were sisters.

I didn't get any of the information I went there for. My plans to interrogate her about her parents' relationship completely went out the window after her whole *sisters* speech. From what I could piece together Samantha was distraught over her husband's continued absence. If she was the one responsible for his vanishing act, then April didn't have any inkling.

The only thing I learned from the whole thing was that

I might be able to do the whole sister thing. Maybe I wouldn't mess it up for a while. Until I did, I could be a big sister and know what it was like to be part of a family.

Maybe.

Probably.

The moment the school bell rang I left April and hurried back to my own school. I cleared the front gate with more than five minutes up my sleeve.

Instead of risking being late, I went straight to class instead of finding Frankie like I wanted to. I would see him in class but it wasn't the same as having him all to myself.

Algebra class was first after lunch, the students filed in slowly after the bell rang. I watched the door until Frankie walked in and I gave him a wave. He sat just down the row, the desks surrounding me were already taken by people I didn't care about at all.

Just as Mrs. Keating was about to take a breath and launch into what I was certain would be a fascinating insight into the world of multiplication, a senior student knocked on the door. She was admitted with a sigh. "Principal Moore needs to see Emmeline Gabrielle in his office immediately."

Every single set of eyes in the place turned to me.

Traitors.

The thought of jumping out the window and running did cross my mind.

But I wasn't that fit.

I begrudgingly stood up and gathered my things. There was no point in pretending I would be back again to resume the lesson. In order to leave I had to ignore the questioning glance Frankie gave me.

The moment we were in the corridor, I said, "You can go now, I know the way to the office."

The girl just shrugged. "I have to go back there anyway."

"How's Moore's mood today?"

"He looked like he was going to blow a gasket. Good luck with that."

Great.

She left me at the reception desk and I was told to go straight on in. Apparently Principal Moore was waiting for me. It had to be leaving the school grounds at lunchtime. It was against the rules, but I may have been able to talk him out of throwing the book at me.

My brain hurt as I tried to think of anything else I could possibly be in trouble for. I had been so good, following all the rules like a star pupil. My grades were good, my attendance perfect, and nobody had accused me of stealing for at least a couple of weeks.

I stepped into the office like I was going to the electric chair. "You wanted to see me, Mr. Moore."

The girl was right, he was mad. It roiled off him in waves as he pointed to the seat across the desk from him. "Emmeline. Sit."

I sat.

Ready to jump and run at any moment.

"Do you want to confess anything to me?" he asked. I wasn't stupid enough to fall for that one.

"I'm not sure what you're referring to, sir."

"I think you know perfectly well why you're here."

This was going to be more painful than I first thought. "No, sir, I'm sorry but I don't know. Has someone said something about me?"

He stared at me.

For a long time.

I was immune to all his tricks. He should have known me better by now. I thought we had a good relationship going on, but he didn't really know me at all.

It was disappointing.

I shrugged, trying not to look belligerent but it was difficult. He was wasting both of our time and I couldn't help but notice. I would rather be sitting in Mrs. Keating's class and she spat whenever she was too close.

A sigh filled the silence–his, not mine. I knew better than to sigh when in his company. "Miss Gabrielle, our school mascot has gone missing."

"Bubbles the tuna fish?" I wasn't pretending to be shocked, I really *was* shocked. That ugly statue had been sitting proudly in the courtyard since I could remember. It was far older than I was, probably older than Principal Moore too.

"Yes, Bubbles." He looked at me again as if I should know something about his current missing status. I didn't mind being blamed for things I actually did, but when it came to things I was actually innocent of, it ticked me off.

"Why do you think I did it?" I asked. Because, really, it was just rude making accusations without evidence.

Considering I didn't do it, there was no way he could have any kind of proof.

"Because, Miss Gabrielle, whenever anything goes missing around this place it's usually you that has something to do with it."

"I don't steal things."

"Some would argue otherwise. I just want to know where Bubbles is so he can be returned to his home podium. You've got a one minute window to tell me everything or this matter will have to go to the police."

"I didn't steal Bubbles. As crazy as it may sound, I actually like the damn fish. I have no idea what happened to it but do share your anger at whoever did do it." Only part of my statement was a lie. He didn't have to know that I hated that ugly thing.

"Where were you this lunchtime?" Both of his eyebrows arched upwards, like he had just made the case. Unfortunately, he kind of did. April was my alibi for lunch but I couldn't very well tell him I left campus to visit her. That was also breaking the rules.

Hello, rock. Hello, hard place.

"I was on the big field, eating my lunch." The field was large enough to get lost in. Also one of the few places there were no security cameras.

Don't ask me how I know about the school's security system.

I would only have to lie to you.

"Who can verify that?" Moore continued. Give the man a flashlight to shine in my eyes and he would have been extremely happy.

"Nobody. I ate alone."

"That's convenient."

"In case you haven't noticed, Principal Moore, I don't have any friends. Finding anyone to ever verify my whereabouts would be difficult."

"I've seen you hanging around with Francis Bolero."

Great, the school principal was spying on me. Surely he could only reserve that kind of treatment for me. It occurred to me in that moment that it wasn't going to matter what I said. He would always blame me for stealing the concrete fish.

I had two options. 1. To explain about my life's mission to rescue lost things and risk a trip to the guidance counsellor. And 2. To keep going with my adamant denial and risk a trip to the cop shop.

This meeting wasn't going to end well.

The only thing I was sure of was that Frankie had to stay out of the conversation. He didn't deserve the principal's scrutiny.

"I didn't have lunch with Frankie. I told you I ate alone. And I wasn't anywhere near the courtyard. Don't you have CCTV footage of the area?" Damn it. I wasn't intending to mention the cameras. Nobody was supposed to know they had covertly hidden them.

He didn't deny it. "Someone spray-painted the camera just before the theft occurred."

"Maybe you should be looking for someone with spray paint."

His expression darkened. "I can see we're not going to get any further with this." He started typing furiously on his computer before his printer whirred to life. He grabbed the sheet of paper and sealed it in an envelope before handing it to me. "Give this to your guardian. I want to see him immediately to discuss your behavior further."

Panic alert.

"My uncle is really busy, he won't be able to take time off work," I replied quickly. I tried and failed to keep the horror of that idea out of my head.

"He'll have to find time to deal with this. And before you start plotting ideas of conveniently forgetting to pass on the letter, your guardian needs to sign it. I will know if you forge his signature."

Now who was the liar?

I'd been forging Uncle Marvin's signature since before I could read. The signature they had on file was mine.

"I *will* be meeting with him, Miss Gabrielle."

"What about if I find the fish?" I blurted out, desperate now. "If I solve the whereabouts of Bubbles will you call off the meet and greet?"

"It's done, you're too late. I gave you an opportunity to—"

"I'm not confessing because I didn't do it. But maybe I could ask around, listen to the chatter. Someone must know where it is and I could act as your ears on the ground."

"This isn't up for negotiation. Take that note to your guardian and have him make an appointment for us to discuss your behavior."

"Principal Moore, I really wish you'd—"

"That is all, Miss Gabrielle. We are done here." He stood and pointed at the door, making it clear he wasn't going to discuss the matter any further.

It was his loss, really. I may not be able to locate my missing father but surely a hundred-pound fish would be much easier to find.

I left the office, but not without one more pleading look shot his way.

The man had no heart.

"Make sure you go directly back to your class," he added, just to rub salt into the wound. As if I was planning on making a run for the border.

Actually...

No, not yet.

The missing tuna fish was the talk of the school. The general feeling fell into two parties. The first thought it was an awesome practical joke and they were ready to throw a party for whomever was behind it. The second thought it was the worst thing in the world and only the death penalty was harsh enough for the convicted thief.

I fell into neither category because I couldn't give a damn about the idiot fish (yes, I realized I sounded like Uncle Marvin, but sometimes he wasn't wrong when he called something an idiot). My whole thoughts on the matter was that the damn fish was going to get me into a whole lot of trouble.

As I was leaving school that afternoon, walking

purposefully slow to delay the inevitable, a warm hand slipped into mine. Frankie was starting to make a habit of holding my hand.

"Can you believe it about Bubbles?" he said. He seemed to be more amused than offended. However, the moment he saw my face, he turned serious. "Sorry, I didn't realize you were so upset by it all."

"I don't care about Bubbles. I care that I'm the one being blamed for stealing him."

"Seriously?"

"Yeah, deadly." I could tell he wanted to ask me if I did it but was too polite to actually verbalize it. It was kinder to put him out of his internal dilemma. "I had nothing to do with it. I'm not that stupid. Principal Moore has an unnatural affection for the lump of concrete, everyone knew he'd blow a gasket if it was stolen."

"Someone said it happened during lunch but nobody saw anything. Strange, huh?" Frankie walked alongside me in his happy gait and even strides. He had no idea of the real problems the fish caused.

"Very strange, but I didn't do it. I visited April during lunch but I can't tell the principal that or he'll have me for breaking the school rules."

"Leaving school grounds would be better than theft of the much-loved mascot, right?"

"Doubt it. They think if we leave campus we'll end up kidnapped or committing armed robbery or something. It's probably about on par with fish thievery," I said. Frankie hadn't been at the school long enough to know how paranoid Principal Moore was. He took all the rules very seriously.

With no exceptions.

Frankie twirled around so he was walking in front of me backwards. I took a step forward as I walked and he had to take a step backwards. "How about we do something to take your mind off Bubbles?"

"Like what?" His question and cheeky dimples were enough to at least lesson the panic alarm blaring in my head.

"I have it on good authority that ICM Partners is currently open and will remain that way until five o'clock tonight. What do you say to paying them a visit and seeing if they should remain suspects in your father's case?"

He was so sweet, always thinking of me and my problems. I was sure he had some of his own that he never shared with me. For this afternoon alone, I would remain selfish. "I say that is a really good idea."

Frankie stepped back into stride with me as we walked in the direct opposite direction of school.

Uncle Marvin's wrath could wait a little longer.

Chapter 21

I got to see Frankie in charm mode as we stood in the middle of ICM Partners and spoke with the manager. The boy could talk the scales off a fish.

"Computers and all are just crazy to me," Frankie said to the man. They were the same height and probably only ten years apart. "I want mine fixed but I just don't know who to trust with it. There's some sensitive things on there. Nothing illegal, of course, but I don't want someone to steal my identity."

The man had nodded along with the whole thing. "I know, man. It's hard to hand over your computer system to anyone and give them a list of passwords. You never know what they could get up to."

"Your store here is set up really well, you must have a good IT guy."

"Yeah, we use Computer Mart for all our technology matters. The owner, Marshall, he's fantastic."

Both Frankie and my own ears pricked at hearing my father's name. "Have you been using him long?"

"Yeah, a few years now. He's not exactly cheap but he knows his way around a network," the manager said. He seemed completely at ease speaking about the missing man. He wasn't setting off any of my suspicious sensors.

"That's what I need," Frankie lied. "Do you have his card or contact details so I can give him a call?"

"Sure, no problem. I'll just grab them." Manager Trey walked purposefully to the office and disappeared behind a door.

I spoke quietly to Frankie while we were alone. "It doesn't seem like he knows the news of my father's absence. He's either very good at acting or he hasn't had any computer troubles since before he went missing."

"He seems genuine."

"All the good liars are," I pointed out. You knew you were speaking with an excellent liar when everything seemed genuine. Either Manager Trey was indeed genuine, or he was a better liar than me.

And nobody was a better liar than me.

Trey returned before we could speak any more about him. I wondered if his ears were burning the whole time we were away. "Here's his card. Tell him I sent you and he'll make sure to look after you."

Frankie accepted the card and tucked it into his pocket. "Thanks for that. I appreciate your time."

"Did you want to look at those artworks while you're here?" Trey might have been honest but he was also a salesman about to see a potential sale walk out the door. I had to hand it to him for initiative.

"You know, I think I'll sleep on it," Frankie said. "Thanks for all your advice. Have a great afternoon."

He took my hand and I followed him out of the shop. "I think it's pretty safe to throw him out of the suspect pool," I started. "He wouldn't have given you the card if he'd been responsible for his IT guy going missing."

"Yeah, I agree. He seemed nice."

"Serial killers are also called nice. It's how they get so close to so many victims." Even though Manager Trey did seem innocent, it was still good to remember that we might be wrong. "We seem to be finding a lot of dead ends."

"Then the search continues."

I had to love his optimism.

It wasn't something I was particularly good at.

We went our separate ways after returning to our own neighborhood. There was no point in putting off going home any longer. I still had to cook dinner for Uncle Marvin, Matilda, and myself no matter how late I arrived home.

Many years earlier I had discovered that my uncle took bad news better when he had a stomach full of good, starchy food. With that in mind, I decided to cook pasta with garlic bread on the side. The stench of his breath was worth the potentially quieter yelling.

He groaned as his generous bottom hit the seat and his stubby fingers wrapped around a fork. I placed the bowl of steaming hot pasta in front of him and waited.

My spaghetti was tasteless as I ate it. It was difficult to focus on anything when I had a letter in my pocket that needed his signature. My first thought had been to sign it myself, but then Principal Moore wanted a meeting with him and there was no way I could forge that.

Unless... I *could* have paid an actor to play the part of my uncle.

But he'd already met my real uncle and Uncle Marvin wasn't the kind of person someone forgets easily. He was extraordinarily remarkable in the way he could make an impression on someone.

Mostly he left them with a sense of extreme dislike.

I took after him.

He finished his bowl too soon, slurping up the last piece of spaghetti before it left a ring of tomato sauce around his lips. He wiped it away with the back of his hand.

Delightful.

Luckily I didn't take after him with my table manners.

"Uh, Uncle Marvin," I started. My foot was nervously tapping a beat on the floor. I pressed down hard to try to make it sit still. "I was called to the principal's office today."

"What have you done now, girl?" He pushed back from the table to allow his belly room to spill over his lap.

"Someone stole the giant fish mascot from the school courtyard and he's blaming me for it."

Uncle Marvin was like a boiling kettle. He took a few minutes to brew before he completely blew his top. "Why did you steal the stupid fish, you stupid girl? Didn't you realize you'd get caught for it? How stupid do you have to be?"

"I didn't do it," I said calmly. I had to be a duck and let it roll right off my back. Uncle Marvin yelled a lot, normally at me. I could handle this.

I hoped.

"Yeah, right. Don't lie to me, you idiot. I know what you get up to, you like to take things that don't belong to you. Don't you? I'm not an idiot, I see what goes on around here."

"I don't steal things and I certainly didn't steal the giant fish. I'm not an idiot." It was as far as I could go with defending myself. When my uncle really got going he could have scared a roaring lion. It was better if I just took whatever he threw at me and cried later to myself. "I was given a letter that you have to sign. Principal Moore wants to have a meeting with you."

"What, now I have to deal with your mess? Your idiot principal is a damn idiot. I don't have time for a meeting, and if I did, I wouldn't waste my time with him." Uncle Marvin spat the words at me, his breath laced with garlic.

Funny enough, he was taking it better than I expected.

"I tried to tell him that but he insisted. Will you please sign the letter?" I pushed it across the table with a pen in one hand. All he had to do was squiggle on the line and this conversation could be paused until the meeting. "Please? I'll tell him again how busy you are."

He grumbled under his breath the whole time but Uncle Marvin did eventually sign the letter. He threw the pencil at me and stomped out of the kitchen.

I was shaking all over from the encounter. It was stupid getting upset about what just happened, I'd expected worse and I'd received worse before.

But, somehow, it always hurt when he didn't believe me. It would have been nice to have him in my corner, defending me against the false accusations.

Thank goodness I had Frankie. I had one person in billions who actually believed me.

I only needed one.

I fed Matilda who purred contentedly while she ate. At least someone around the house was grateful for their meal. Washing the dishes and then cleaning the kitchen, I couldn't wait to get back to the sanctity of my bedroom.

Uncle Marvin was engrossed in a football game when I crept behind him and went upstairs. With any luck he would be asleep soon and unable to upset me any further.

Thinking him capable of having something to do with my father's disappearance was beginning to seem more plausible every day that passed. He was angry, not just a little, but a lot. He was revealing his dark side to me piece by piece.

The moment I closed the door to my bedroom, my phone beeped with a message. My heart lifted with anticipation of what Frankie had messaged me.

I looked at the screen, only to find a message from someone unexpected.

The Keeper of Discarded Things.

Hey, Em. Your dad's name is Marshall, right? I think I have something you should see.

Mr. Adison never played around. He also so rarely contacted me that I always forgot he actually had my number and I had his. I stared at the message for a long time while the thoughts and questions whirled around in my head.

What did he have?

Why did I need to see it?

How did he know my dad's name?

What was going on?

No matter how many times I read the message it didn't reveal anything new. I was going to have to speak with him and I was going to have to do it first thing tomorrow.

After the previous encounter with Uncle Marvin, finding my father was now my number one priority. I needed more family in my life, I was no longer satisfied with being my uncle's housemaid.

Maybe Mr. Adison held the key that I needed.

Chapter 22

My choice to skip school the next morning was done with great consideration and thought.

That was a lie.

The moment I woke up I knew I wasn't going to go to school. I'd been on my best behavior forever and all it got me was a false accusation and the dreaded letter home to Uncle Marvin.

What more could they do to me if I skipped one day?

Expulsion would almost be welcomed at this stage.

The only spanner in my works was a boy named Frankie that was waiting for me outside my house. I spotted him too late to sneak out the back door.

"I'm not going to school today," I said by way of greeting. Sometimes I forgot all about the pleasantries that normal people were supposed to begin a conversation with.

I always found it better to get right to the point.

"Is something wrong? Are you sick?" Frankie's brow wrinkled with concern. I fought the sudden urge to smooth it out for him. And to kiss his frowning lips.

"Nothing's wrong, I have something I need to do."

"Where are we going then?" His mood brightened instantly. It was concerning how eager he was to be led astray. It should have been harder to corrupt him.

"I'm going to the tip shop. You are going to school."

"What are we doing at the tip shop?"

"I'm going to see Mr. Adison because he says he has something that I should see. You're not coming with me, Frankie. I don't want to get you into trouble."

He waved away my comments like they were nothing. "What's the point of living if not to get up to mischief with you?"

"Is there any way I can talk you out of this?"

"Absolutely none."

I guessed the decision was made then. We started walking in the opposite direction of school. "I can't guarantee you won't get into trouble for skipping. Principal Moore already knows you're an associate of mine."

"I am proud to be your associate, Em." Frankie puffed out his chest like he was a parading gorilla and made me laugh. No matter how miserable I was determined to be, he always did something to make sure that didn't happen.

Frankie was going to save my life.

It was terrifying how easily he had come to mean so much to me. If I didn't have him now… I don't know what would have happened to me. He was keeping me sane in a very crazy situation.

And I loved him for it.

It was so very difficult to admit that to myself.

Let alone anyone else.

When Frankie asked me what happened when I told Uncle Marvin about the fish situation, I told him a vanilla form of the truth. He didn't have to know how shaken I was by his reaction. He shouldn't worry any more than he always did.

We arrived at the tip shop and found Mr. Adison in his usual place by the front of the store. He grinned a largely toothless grin when he saw me. "Em! I'm glad you're here, but you really should be in school. Did you get my message?"

"I did. You said you had something I needed to see," I replied. His eager gaze travelled to Frankie who gave him an awkward wave. "This is my friend Frankie. He's fine to speak freely in front of."

Because, in our life pursuit, sometimes you had to hide your crazy.

Frankie stepped forward and held out his hand for Mr. Adison to shake. He took it eagerly. "It's nice to meet you, sir. Em has told me great things about you."

Mr. Adison laughed. "I'm sure she did. Our Em here likes to tell all kinds of tales. Much like me. But this news is real, Em. Come with me."

We followed his direction and headed toward his back office. The cynical part of me—which, by now, you should know is quite a big part of me—expected him to have another dancing pug for me to see. But I knew the Keeper of Discarded Things wouldn't have texted me without a good reason.

He lifted a large box from the top of a shelf, swayed a little with the weight, and then placed it on a crowded table in the middle of the room. He had to move a few things before all of it could settle on the table without teetering on other items.

"I was out on the tip site yesterday and found a suitcase. The hipsters love suitcases, they use them for decorations, you see." He paused, making sure we did indeed see. "So I opened it up to leave the contents, because normally it's just real rubbish, and then I saw a book. Who doesn't like a book, I asked myself. So I grabbed it, opened the cover, and then saw the name Marshall Gabrielle written inside. The name sounded familiar and I thought of you. Then I thought I saw your dad's name on the news the other night. That's when I sent you that message."

"I'm glad you did," I said, trying not to get dizzy from the whole story.

"Everything in that suitcase is in this box. You can take it all if you like. But have a look while I go serve this customer. The suitcase is that one over there." He pointed to a single grey suitcase on the shelf. "Call me if you need me, Em. You know you only have to holler."

I thanked him before he shuffled out to deal with a guy looking at some tools in the shop. My whole body was frozen for a moment before I could bear to look in the box.

"It could be nothing," I said, trying to make it seem like this wasn't a big deal. Sure, these items might have belonged to my dad, but so what? They were just more items he lost, threw away like they meant nothing.

I knew how that felt.

"Are you alright?" Frankie asked. "I can look for you, if you want."

I took a deep breath. "No, this is my problem. I'll be okay. It's just lost things, I know how to deal with those."

And I did.

Because that was my thing.

This shouldn't have been any different. My father meant nothing to me, he hadn't since he turned his back on my tear-streaked face and walked away.

At least that's what I told myself.

I dived into the box before I hesitated any longer. I wouldn't allow anyone to see how much it affected me. Not even Frankie. This emotion was mine and mine alone.

The contents of the box:

One men's shirt.

One library card to the Lakeside Community Library belonging to Marshall Gabrielle.

One book—*The Time Seeker's Adventure*—with my father's name inside as Mr. Adison described.

Two used tissues.

A coin purse with various membership cards inside—all printed with the name Marshall Gabrielle.

A sweater vest in several shades of brown.

A blanket with several holes worn into it.

A creased photograph of my father with Samantha and April, taken a few years ago by the looks of it.

It was like he had discarded all the things he wouldn't need anymore. Like he had chosen to start afresh with a new life and he wouldn't have a use for these items anymore.

"Em? You okay?" Frankie prompted. We had both been so quiet, so still in the office.

Was I okay?

That was still up for debate.

"Yeah," I replied. "It seems these do belong to my father. They're just his clothes and cards, plus the book."

"I wonder how they ended up at the dump."

"Me too." Although I did have a vague idea forming. If he wanted to disappear, he could have easily dumped the things he no longer needed into the nearest trash can.

And then run away.

Making sure he would be lost forever.

"Em? You sure you're okay? We can go." Frankie's concerned voice broke through my thoughts, bringing me back to the here and now and not imagining my father lying on a beach and making a new life for himself someplace else.

I shook my head, trying to push all those thoughts away. They weren't helping anyone. "I think I should keep these things. Or maybe I should give them to Samantha. What do you think?"

"Maybe we should tell the police."

"No!" I answered too quickly. "I mean, they probably won't care. It's not like they mean anything or provide some clues about what happened to him."

Really, if the police had these items, they would stop searching for him. They would go through the same thought process I had and conclude he disposed of them intentionally.

Even I was considering stopping the search, but the police should still keep going. They were experts, they had more resources than me, they stood a much better chance of finding Marshall Gabrielle than I did.

Even if he didn't want to be found.

"What's on your mind, Em? There's a lot going on in there and I'm worried," Frankie said. His blue eyes were clouded with concern as he stood so still watching me.

He really was a beautiful boy.

Even when he was sad.

He didn't need to be left in the dark right now. "I'm thinking he might have ditched these things on purpose so he could run away and make a clean break. His wallet was found in the burned down house, and now these are the rest of his personal items. He doesn't have any of them now."

"Do you really think he would do that to his wife and child?"

I shrugged with just one shoulder, it was all I had the energy for. Thinking anything about my father completely drained me, like all the appliances on in the house all at once. "He did it to me." My voice was so small and fragile, I hated hearing it like that. There was only one person in the world that could do that to me.

Of course he could do it to someone else too.

Frankie let out a breath he was holding and then shifted to perch on the edge of the table. His arms crossed over his chest as he stared out the window pensively.

I closed the box and sat beside him, so close our shoulders touched. "When I was talking with April the other day I thought she was talking about some other man. He was such a great dad to her that I thought for sure he must have changed. That sometime in the last ten years something must have happened to him so that he wouldn't think about leaving his daughter again."

"It must have been horrible when he left you."

My head nodded because right then I couldn't speak as the memory threatened to choke me. I didn't want to cry in front of Frankie but it was difficult not to when I remembered that moment. I had worn it as armor for so long that it was starting to wear out.

"He never explained why?" Frankie asked. He was still looking out the window, except this time it was to give me some privacy. He knew I wouldn't want him to see me cry.

"I never heard from him again," I said. "Uncle Marvin wouldn't talk about it. When I asked him when Dad was coming home he would just tell me he wasn't and I had to forget about the idiot. I eventually took his advice."

"That's harsh. I mean, how old were you? Six?"

I wiped away at my wet eyes and sniffled. It was time I

replaced my armor and remember that that moment so long ago made me stronger. And I needed to be strong right now.

"I guess it doesn't matter now, anyway," I said, standing. "If he doesn't want to be found then he never will be. He managed to hide in the same city as me for ten years."

Frankie stood too, stepping closer and taking my shaking hands in his. "What does your gut tell you, Em? Do you really think you should give up on him?"

It was difficult looking into Frankie's kind blue eyes and remembering there were bad people in the world. He was so innocent and sincere. I was changing him, turning him into someone who saw all the monsters in the world like I did.

But what did my gut tell me about my father?

I hated him, that was a given.

More than that, I kept remembering how April's whole face had lit up when she spoke about her dad. She loved him to bits and she made it sound like she was his whole world.

If I hadn't shared lunch with her yesterday, my answer would have been different. But it was too difficult for an eight-year-old to lie believingly.

April was loved by her dad.

"He didn't leave on purpose," I finally replied. With the words out of my mouth, they were free. More surprisingly than anything else was the fact I actually believed them. Still, I could have been wrong. "At least, I don't think so.

But he could have us all fooled."

"That's good enough for me. We have to keep looking."

"You should go to school. I'm going to go home and think about things," I lied. My fingers crossed in the hope he would believe me and do as I said.

"I'm not leaving you alone," Frankie insisted.

"I'm okay, really. I just need some time to think."

He still didn't believe me.

We both knew it.

However, Frankie still carried the box all the way from the tip shop for me. He hauled it all the way home and then up the stairs to the attic where he placed it on a shelf.

He then left me for some time to *think*.

I waited for him to turn the corner at the end of the street before I left the house again. There was no way I was going to sit around and brood all day. Somewhere out there was my father and it was about time someone found him.

There was only one person I knew that could potentially have answers for my questions. Statistics told me it was the spouse that knew the most about their partner's disappearance.

Samantha was on my hit list.

I rode the bus with my head churning over the questions I would throw at her. The time for covertly following her and trying to extract information was over. Today was a day for action and I was going to take it with both hands.

Her minivan was in the driveway, a good sign that she was home. If not, I would sit on her stoop and wait for her arrival. Nothing was going to sway me from the cause today.

I banged on the door and waited. My heart was thrumming like a drum, beating its way out of my chest and lodging itself in my throat where it was going to choke me.

I needed to find my dad.

I needed answers.

Maybe I was going about it the wrong way but I was desperate. There was no point in continuing on with all my leads that only took me to dead ends when she might have information.

Surely someone had to know something.

It angered me to think that I even cared about my father. More than anything I wanted to be immune to any emotions his image conjured up. I wanted to be numb, to feel nothing. He didn't deserve my worry or tears.

He didn't deserve them.

He really didn't.

The door swung open and Samantha's mouth dropped in surprise at seeing my figure there. "Em, I wasn't expecting you. Come in. Is everything okay?"

Why did people keep asking me that?

Everything was not okay.

"I need to speak with you," I said as I followed her into the living room. She tried to offer me something to eat or drink but I refused. This wasn't a social call. I didn't even sit down. "I need to know what you know about my father's disappearance."

"What do you mean, honey?" Her brow might have

wrinkled in confusion but she didn't fool me. Nobody did. You couldn't lie to a liar.

"Did you help him disappear? Were you in on it? Do you know where he is?"

"Honey, no. I'm just as upset about this as you are. What's happened?"

"Don't lie to me. Tell me where he is." My traitorous voice was giving me away. I didn't want her to know how upset I was. I didn't want anyone to know that I was unravelling like a tightly coiled spring.

"Em, sweetie, I don't know. Tell me what's happened, why you're so upset."

"I just need to find him. I need to know why…"

"Why, what?"

"Why…"

"Why?"

"Why he left me," I said. I had been trying so hard to keep it inside but those four words were ripped from me like a gangrenous limb.

I was completely losing it.

Chapter 23

"I know you know something. The statistics say…" I said, trying so hard to stay on track before I completely lost my mind. I wasn't sure I'd be able to get it back again if I did.

"Honey, I don't know anything." Samantha took a tentative step closer to me.

"But you went to the pawnbroker, you were raising cash for something."

"With your father missing, I needed the money fast. Paying our mortgage in his absence was more important to me than hanging onto silly pieces of jewelry." She reached for me and I flinched, expecting her to slap me.

Instead, she *hugged* me.

Samantha pulled me close to her chest, cradling me against her while cooing that everything was going to be okay. I didn't know what to do. Nobody hugged me, nobody touched me. In my entire life I could count on one hand how many people had ever laid a hand on me with compassion.

Five fingers were superfluous.

I only needed two.

My father and Frankie.

Samantha was number three.

She held me so tightly that I couldn't squirm away. I found I didn't have the strength even if I wanted to. My anger seeped away and turned into something I had been avoiding for my entire life–sadness.

Anger made me strong. It protected me from getting too close to anyone. It kept me going when nothing else did. To let it go now was like surrendering, admitting that it was wrong to hold on to it for so long.

But maybe it was okay now to let it go.

Sadness might not make me strong but maybe it would make me into a better person. Someone that didn't have to lie all the time, someone that people didn't instantly hate the moment I opened my mouth.

My eyes were wet again as I cried on Samantha's shoulder. We dissolved onto the floor as she pulled me onto her lap. She held me against her as I let it all out, my body shaking with the effort.

"It's okay, Em," she whispered over and over again in my ear. I had known her for all of a few weeks and already she had torn through my barrier and uncovered the scared little girl within. I'd never known a mother before but I had imagined it was like this many times.

It was just so tiring always being so angry.

Exhausting.

I felt every moment of it in my bones, dragging me down as I carried it through my life with me. I didn't want to carry it like a burden but it had always been there.

I didn't know how to live without it.

But perhaps it was time.

We sat on the floor of her perfectly clean and decorated house, surrounded by pictures of the happy, smiling family. A part of me was guilty for bringing my mess into the pristine space. The other part of me knew it was because of the man in the photographs that I had that mess to begin with.

I pulled back when I was all cried out. "Sorry," I mumbled.

Samantha wiped at my tears, offering me a small smile. "Don't be sorry, sweetie. This is a difficult time for everyone. I can't imagine what you've gone through. Do you want to talk about it some more?"

I did.

It surprised me more than anyone.

However, I never got a chance. The doorbell rang, jerking us both from the moment and stealing the attention away from me. Perhaps that was for the best. Nobody needed to know just how fragile I was.

"Sorry," Samantha said as we stood. I had to climb off her lap before she could go anywhere. While she went to the door, I checked my face in the mirror on the wall. I looked like I'd cried a river.

Tissues helped but could only do so much.

The voices of two men speaking with Samantha quickly

made me forget about my meltdown. She ushered them inside where I could see their police uniforms. They all wore somber looks.

"Have you got news?" Samantha asked them. I stood at her side, trying to be a united front against the fuzz.

The one on the left nodded his head. He was about fifty years old, clearly the senior of the two officers. "I'm afraid it's not good news."

Everything inside of me stopped, gripped with dread. Police officers weren't known for their joking abilities. If they said it wasn't good news, then it wasn't good news. It was probably going to be the worst news someone could possibly hear about their loved ones.

"Shall we take a seat?" the younger of the pair ventured. He gestured to the couch, triggering something in Samantha to bring her back to the conversation again. If she was anything like me, her head was a minefield of spinning thoughts, unable to focus on any one thing in particular.

We all sat on the couches together, the police taking one and us the other. Nobody looked comfortable to be there. We didn't match the homely surroundings, our straight backs and stiff expressions in direct contrast to the soft furnishings and pastel colors.

"So are you going to tell me what you came here to say or are you going to keep me in suspense?" Samantha said, breaking the silence. She smiled, trying to break the tension but she wasn't fooling anyone.

The senior policeman took the lead next. "We have

received a report from the county coroner today. He was investigating the body found on Pearson Street."

The information I heard was that they'd found a wallet belonging to Marshall Gabrielle. The news, online reports, nobody said anything about who the body belonged to. But I hoped jumping to conclusions was the wrong thing to do right now.

My breath hitched in my throat while my heart stopped beating and waited for the next words to escape from the policeman's mouth.

"The body was in bad condition, but I'll spare you the details," he continued. For once I was grateful for his briefness. I normally thrived on the details, needed them like my life depending on them, but not now. Not for this. "There wasn't enough, um, markers for a full identification but the coroner had stated he strongly believes there is enough evidence to support the body belonging to that of your husband."

Samantha gasped and made a whelping sound like a little puppy that had been kicked.

No matter how long I lived I was never going to be able to forget that noise.

She broke down in tears, great sobbing rolls of weeping that wracked through her whole body. I returned the compassion she had shown me just minutes before and hugged her against me while she let the tears flow.

The police officers didn't know what to do. I could tell they still had information to unload on her but they didn't want to seem callous and continue on when Samantha was in such a state.

Maybe I was all cried out.

Maybe I'd already cried for the loss of my father many years ago.

Whatever it was, for now my eyes were dry.

"Mrs. Gabrielle, I'm very sorry for your loss," the officer started again after a reasonable pause. "There will be some formalities that we will need to go over but they can wait for another time. If you like, we can leave you for now and come back when you're ready to discuss them."

Samantha nodded. "Yes, please."

They awkwardly stood and I accompanied them to the door, feeling like it was something I should do so Samantha didn't have to. She would have wanted someone to remember their manners in the situation, I got the feeling she wouldn't have wanted to be rude even in the horrible situation.

We stood on the stoop in silence. I couldn't keep quiet any longer. "Do you really think it's him?" I blurted out.

They gave me the look. The one that said they had sympathy for me because I was so stupid I couldn't accept the truth. I didn't like that look.

I'd received it too many times before.

"The evidence is pointing that way," the officer said softly, like I was fragile and only moments away from breaking down like my stepmother.

I couldn't reply, just in case they were right. I nodded instead and they mirrored my actions before leaving. Nothing more was said as they backed down the driveway and sped off down the road.

Back to their lives.

Back to their families.

Away from the grief.

They were lucky.

I returned back inside and sat with Samantha for a very long time. We didn't speak, just held each other and thought of all ways that the news could not be true.

The longer I sat there, the more I truly didn't believe it. The coroner wasn't entirely sure it had been the body of Marshall Gabrielle. It was only the evidence that had led him to believe that.

What if someone had made it seem that way?

What if it was my father himself that did it?

Or someone else, so the police stopped looking?

There were a million reasons why someone could fake someone's death. If there was a fire involved it made it even easier. If a flame burned hot enough it could destroy a multitude of identity markers.

I didn't share any of my outlandish ideas with Samantha. There was still a good chance I was completely wrong and only grasping at straws. She didn't need that kind of false hope in the midst of her grief.

At close to three o'clock, Samantha's phone beeped with a reminder. She didn't need to check it to know what it meant. Neither did I–school was almost over. "What do I tell April? How do I tell her that her daddy is dead?"

"I honestly don't know," I replied. For once I wished I could come up with a convincing lie for the purposes of doing good instead of evil. "Maybe you shouldn't tell her yet. Maybe wait for a bit longer."

"He's not coming back, Em. The coroner was certain, otherwise they wouldn't make a report. He's gone." Her tears started to well up all over again. They were already red, raw and puffy. "He's really gone."

"Do you want me to pick her up?"

She took a deep breath. "No, I need to do it myself. Thank you, sweetie. For everything. Are you going to be okay?"

"I lost him a long time ago."

She hugged me again before we walked to the door and parted ways. I wouldn't accept a lift home, mainly because I wasn't planning on going home.

Many people had called me stubborn before, mainly teachers and occasionally Principal Moore. They always made it seem like a bad thing but I always took it as a compliment.

Right now, I was being stubborn once more.

I didn't believe the coroner or his stupid report. They didn't have a body, they didn't have a real identification, and that meant it wasn't time to give up just yet.

Frankie asked me what my gut thought earlier that day. When I asked myself the same question now all I could think about was that my father couldn't be dead.

He was alive.

Somewhere out there.

I wasn't ready to bury him like Samantha was. I wasn't ready to accept that he was gone and call a few pieces of burned bones his remains.

Yes, I was stubborn.

But I also might have been right, too.

I didn't have any leads, I didn't have any clues, all I had was my gut and itchy feet. They led me to my father's office, a place I had only been once before.

Breaking in a second time was easier. I had no idea what more I could find there or what I was looking for but I was desperate and it was the closest connection to my dad I could find.

The moment I stepped inside I knew something was wrong.

It was more than a feeling in my gut.

Chapter 24

My first thought as I walked through my father's messy office was that the police would have gone through his things. They would have had people go through with a fine toothed comb, searching for clues of his whereabouts.

I'd seen the TV cop shows, I knew the deal.

I knew things would look different to my first visit because of the police and their thoroughness. Or coffee stains and donut crumbs, whatever.

But I knew the difference between a search and targeted thieving of items. The stack of contracts for IT services to be provided by my father was in neat pile. The police had done that, because Frankie and I had left it in the mess we had found it in.

All the contracts were no longer there.

One was missing.

Just one.

It was memorable only because the name made me

think of a giant shining sun. It was with Julia Golden Design, the business belonging to the mean lady that had all but thrown me out of the shop.

If it was the police that had taken it, then why? Why that one and none of the others? I counted them again, just to make sure I hadn't missed one or two on my way through. I hadn't. There was definitely only one missing.

After making that discovery, I surveyed the room with a more suspicious eye. I trudged my memory, trying to remember everything as it was the first time I saw it.

My memory was a pretty good one. Uncle Marvin told me dozens of times growing up that I needed to forget more than I remembered otherwise I was going to get myself into trouble.

Good thing I never listened to Uncle Marvin.

I looked at everything, comparing it to my recollection and tried to find anything else out of place or missing. It was pretty dark the first time I'd been there so it wasn't exactly an easy or accurate process.

As far as I could tell, everything else looked about the same. A round circle of missing dust told me there was probably a coffee mug next to the main computer at one stage but that was about it. And who knew how long that mug had been gone. Someone might have just taken pity on it and cleaned it.

It still felt like my dad could step back into the office at any minute and start working. Even though it had been so long since I'd seen him, I could imagine him crouched over at the computer. His face would be all scrunched up with concentration as he glared at the screen.

I wished he would breeze on in and sit down.

It sure would make our lives much easier.

But I got the feeling that wasn't going to happen. Not anytime soon, anyway. And probably not without help. If the police were so certain he was dead, they weren't going to be looking for him any longer.

That only left me.

My poor father, having me as his last hope.

I couldn't stand to be there a moment longer. I needed to get out of the office or it was going to suffocate me with the force of a thousand paper cuts.

Running to catch the bus, I didn't know where I was going until I got there. It was almost dark by that stage and I should have been thinking about Uncle Marvin's dinner instead of missing parental figures.

However, I knocked on Frankie's front door anyway and hoped he was home. I also hoped I wasn't interrupting his perfect family dinner. I didn't want to be the dark shadow that took him away from that.

His sister answered the door. I couldn't remember which one, but it was the smaller of the lot. "Are you Frankie's girlfriend?"

"I, uh," I stammered, just managing to get out vowel sounds instead of actual words.

The kid turned into the hallway and yelled. "Frankie, it's your girlfriend! She wants to kiss you! Oooh!"

At least the kid got a chuckle out of it.

My face burned with embarrassment the entire time it

took for Frankie to relieve her from greeter duties and close the door behind him. "Sorry about Mary. Just be grateful she didn't start singing about sitting in a tree."

I rolled my eyes. "I hate that song."

"Me too." Even though Frankie said it like he agreed, he was still smiling with amusement at my embarrassment. He was taking none of it seriously.

I couldn't find it in me to hate him for it.

He shuffled down the few steps to the sidewalk and sat on the bottom step. I plonked down next to him and he took in my disheveled appearance for the first time. "Something happened today, didn't it? And here I was joking and all. God, I'm so sorry, Em. What happened?"

I swallowed to try to get some moisture back into my mouth. "The police told Samantha they found a body in that house fire. They're saying it's my father."

"Oh my god. I'm so sorry."

"I don't think it's him." Saying the words out loud made me sound like a crazy person. Maybe I was, it wouldn't have surprise me. But the words still needed to be said. If I walked away from this now I would never forgive myself.

And I would never have answers.

Samantha might have been able to bury the charcoal pieces and mourn for the loss of Marshall Gabrielle but I wasn't prepared to yet.

Not until I was certain.

"What makes you think they're wrong?" Frankie asked. I launched into the full explanation, using the opportunity to not only fill him in but to also gather my thoughts and put them into some kind of order.

Things I knew for sure:

My father was missing.

Some of his personal items had shown up, including his wallet.

A contract for one of his clients was missing from his business.

Nobody knew where he was.

Nobody else was looking for him.

The police considered Uncle Marvin a person of interest in the case.

Anything I had stumbled over was just conjecture or my own personal opinion. The facts were so little to go off that they seemed pitiful.

But cases had been solved with less, I'm sure.

"I think my dad's customer has something to do with it all," I finished the story with my suspicions. If other service contracts were taken I wouldn't have thought twice about it. But just one? It couldn't have just been a coincidence.

I was the Keeper of Lost Things, it was my duty to find this missing contract.

Right?

"So what's the plan?" It lifted my heart to know he had my back, no matter how insane I sounded. After all, when someone of authority told you your father was dead, you were supposed to believe them. You weren't supposed to call them liars.

I filled Frankie in on the vague, sketchy plan I had and he grabbed a coat before coming with me. While we walked I sent Uncle Marvin a text message, telling him I was caught up with a Recycle Club meeting and couldn't get away. Hopefully he wouldn't think about it too hard.

It wasn't even Wednesday.

While I was texting, Frankie was also on his phone. He knew all the places to look up online to get people's addresses. Companies had to be registered and they had to have directors. Those directors had to have residential addresses. Apparently for a small fee, anyone could look up these details if they knew where to look.

Lucky for me, Frankie did.

In little more than a few minutes, we had the home address of the owners of Julia Golden Design. Privacy did not exist in this world anymore. Clearly, it was a thing of the past. It was scary the amount of personal information so freely available to just anyone.

After working out the bus routes we'd need to take to get into the Moorborough district of Lakeside, Frankie decided it was going to be easier to go back for his bike and hike it into the neighborhood. I went with him so I didn't have to stand around and look like a weirdo by myself.

Another twenty minutes and we were on our way again. Frankie was on the pedals of his neon green bike while I rode shotgun on the handlebars. It wasn't entirely safe but that never really stopped me from doing anything before.

The Moorborough part of Lakeside was occupied by

the more affluent members of our society. The streets were neatly kept with even the leaves not daring to fall where they weren't supposed to. High fences ringed every generous boundary and barely managed to hide the mansions behind them.

Not to mention the Bentleys and Mercedes parked in the driveways.

Claudine and Derrick Bowden lived at number forty-nine Twiningdale Drive. Their house was one of the smaller ones on the street, probably only containing about eight bedrooms instead of ten.

Only a few lights were on in their house. At least they were thrifty with their fossil fuels. The streets were lined with large trees, heavy with their leafy foliage. They provided us with some cover from anyone who dared to venture a look out their window too hard.

Frankie leaned his bike against one of those trees and we stayed close to it. Hopefully if anyone did glimpse us, they would assume we were just taking a quick rest.

Instead of staking out the place.

Not that I was planning on breaking into number forty-nine or anything. I didn't really have a plan. All I knew was that I had to keep a close eye on them because nobody else was. The moment the word got out that Marshall Gabrielle was pronounced dead, it would have a ripple effect.

Those responsible for his disappearance would also hear the news.

And react.

In what way, I couldn't say. But I was expecting

something to happen and I wanted to be there when it did.

"I'm sorry to be taking you away from your family tonight," I said, breaking the silence as it hung in the air as prominent as the full moon in the sky.

"You're doing me a favor. My house can be chaotic at times. This is like a holiday." I could see his white teeth as he flashed me a quick smile. "I'm more worried about you. Do you think you should be with your family tonight? Maybe Samantha or your uncle Marvin?"

"He's not dead. I'm not going to mourn for him."

"But they'll be mourning, right?"

"I don't know if anyone has told Uncle Marvin yet." Reflectively, I checked my cell phone. There was no message from my uncle, neither in response to mine about dinner or a warning message about some bad news he had to tell me.

Uncle Marvin wasn't exactly a cell phone type of guy.

On the odd occasion he did message me, he always wrote in all caps.

OF COURSE.

"You probably never guessed what a messed up family you were getting involved with when you first talked to me," I said, remembering the first time Frankie had spoken to me. He shouldn't have walked away from me then, he should have *run*.

"Everyone has weirdness in their families," Frankie replied. "It just varies in degrees."

"Come on, you have the most normal family in the world."

"That's so not true. I have an uncle in jail, an aunt in the Amazon jungle researching worms, and one of my grandmothers has been on the TV show *Extreme Hoarders*. Not just *Hoarders*, but *Extreme Hoarders*."

"You're kidding."

"I'm serious."

"Really?" My eyebrows both arched in disbelief but he really was telling the truth.

Huh.

I guess what was the point of having skeletons in your closet if they didn't dance a little and have some fun?

"Oh, and Mary? My sister that answered the door? She has to see a therapist once a month because she thinks she can remember a past life where she was a cat."

"Now you're joking."

"Nope." He was trying to keep the smile from his face but I got the feeling he was again speaking only the truth. His family looked so picture perfect on the outside. I guess anything could be interpreted from the outside in.

I pushed him playfully. "Wow, Frankie. You make my family seem normal. Thanks for that. I feel so much better now. You've saved me a lifetime's worth of therapy."

"Glad I could help." He chuckled back and I felt good for the first time all day. What I was going through really sucked but Frankie made it bearable. I couldn't even imagine what I would have done if I'd had to deal with it all alone.

Being a basket case sprung to mind.

We caught our breath again before we continued the

conversation. Frankie placed his arm around me and pulled me close. "Remember, Em, our families don't define who we are. No matter what happens, we are still our own people. You're still going to be awesome no matter what your dad does."

He pulled me into a hug and it was the best place in the world to be. I could have snuggled up against his chest for the rest of my life. Breathing in his scent, listening to his steady heartbeat, feeling the strength of his arms.

It would never have been my choice to leave his embrace.

But I had to.

Because there was movement at number forty-nine.

Chapter 25

The steel grey gate opened first. It pulled back on itself and allowed a sleek black BMW to pass through. The car pulled onto the street and moved slowly down the road, barely making a noise in the quiet neighborhood.

We instantly moved.

Frankie was on his bike and I was on the handlebars so quickly we were blurred like in a cartoon. The poor guy peddled so fast I thought he was going to give himself a coronary heart attack.

The BMW had to stop at several red lights, allowing us to catch up with it every time. The traffic was still pretty bad from rush hour while people were still making their way home from work for the day. The darkness of the night made it seem like later than it actually was.

I hung on the bike so hard my knuckles turned white. I trusted Frankie with my life but we had to be going forty kilometers an hour and neither of us had any protective gear on. Some knee pads or helmets wouldn't have gone astray. As much as I liked to live life on the edge, this was a bit close to the cusp for my comfort.

The black BMW went around a corner in the distance and we lost sight of it. By the time we rounded the same bend, it was completely gone. Frankie refused to give up, he peddled faster. His poor legs had to be killing him by now.

"Frankie, it's okay," I said. The air was rushing against my face as we raced along the sidewalk. I risked gripping my hair in one hand so it didn't flick in his face and cause some sight issues. It made my balance a bit more vicarious. "He's probably not going anywhere exciting anyway."

Frankie spoke through gritted teeth. "We've come this far. He's not getting away."

His breaths were short and gasping, his limbs burning, I'm sure. Still, Frankie did not give up. He peddled that bicycle like his life depended on it and there was a million dollars at the end of our journey.

We went around another corner.

The black BMW was there.

He had slowed down to pull into a driveway. Frankie had to slow his pace so we didn't run straight into the side of it. We came to a halt about a hundred meters away and waited for the BMW to make the next move.

The car slid into the driveway and we could then see the signage on the other side of the drive. It was Pack, Stack, & Store, a storage facility for the long and short term customers. For a weekly or monthly fee, they could purchase a storage locker and dump all their junk there.

As the car went deeper into the row of lockers, we walked up to the gate to get a better look. The darkness of the evening was shielding us pretty well. Plus, we faced each other so it looked like we were having a conversation instead of loitering and watching the storage facility.

Which, of course, we were.

The BMW stopped about a third of the way down. The headlights went off before the driver stepped out. Judging by the silhouette, it was a man with the beginnings of a pot belly. He unlocked a padlock on the storage locker door and then heaved it open.

We moved positions to the other side of the driveway so we could get a better view inside the locker. It was still hard to see but if I stood on my tiptoes I could get a glimpse inside when the guy moved to the side.

I wasn't sure if I was seeing right.

"Do you see what I see?" I asked. It was a stupid question but my brain wasn't really functioning correctly by that stage. It felt like I was seeing things and now I didn't know anything.

"I think I see a lot of money," Frankie replied. So it wasn't just me then.

The man rifled around in the storage locker for a few minutes. He moved thick wads of money from one shelf to another as if it was in his way. I mean, if it was really that much of a hassle to him I'm sure there were plenty of people willing to help him out with that particular problem.

You didn't hear people complaining too often of having

too much money to store.

Hadn't he ever heard of a place called a bank? It was a really handy place, they looked after all your money for you. All you had to do was use a little plastic card instead of carrying around all that burdensome cash.

Behind the dough was the white stuff.

And then it all made sense.

Drugs.

The money was still in cash form because it came from the sale of illegal drugs. I was no substance expert but I would put my money on it being heroin or cocaine or something similar. It was white and it looked powdery.

Every little piece I had tried to put together to form a picture suddenly fell into place. They fell into a pattern like little mosaic tiles, floating onto the ground and forming the most intricate of patterns I had ever seen.

It was beautiful, really.

The way they all worked together. It was like they were snowing around me. Falling together and locking as if the facts and details always belonged with one another.

I wished Frankie could see them. I wished everyone could see them like I did. All around me the whispery pieces spoke the words I had tried to form into a story all along but couldn't get to work.

Now they spoke.

And the story they told wasn't one I liked.

But I did know what happened.

The realization made me stumble backwards as I fell off my tiptoes. I also fell right into the snowflakes of facts where I felt certain I would be able to make angels out of the details.

"We need to go back to Samantha's house," I said as I started walking. To make sure Frankie followed I took his bike with me. He wouldn't stay there without it.

It took a few moments for him to catch up to me.

I was walking that fast.

"Why? What's there?" he asked. His confusion was written in every wrinkle on his wonderful face. "Did you see all the drugs and money in that storage locker? These people are dangerous. We should go to the police and tell them what we saw. We need to report them."

"We need to go to Samantha's house."

"Why?"

"Because I need to be sure."

"Of what?" He took the bike from my hands and stopped, like he was going to be fueled by answers and wouldn't go any further without any.

He deserved them but there was no time. I needed answers of my own and I would have more to share after I had been to Samantha's and saw what I needed to see.

"I promise I will explain everything once I'm there," I offered. It was all I had. If Frankie was even a fraction of the boy I thought he was it would be enough for him.

We had a standoff that was only seconds long but seemed to stretch out into hours when measured in the heartbeats echoing frantically in my chest.

They thudded in warped speed.

Frankie nodded as he came to a decision in his head. He

273

climbed onto his bike and patted the handlebars. "You'd better get on if we're going to hurry. The Bolero Express is about to leave the station."

His smile lit up the night.

It was my beacon of hope.

I jumped on and gripped the cold steel of his bike as if my life depended on it.

Because someone's did.

Chapter 26

Samantha was in a messy state when I roused her from in front of the television. She was already in her pajamas even though it was only seven o'clock.

April was already in bed, sent earlier so Mommy could have some alone time because she was tired. The news of our father's so-called death had not reached her young ears yet, apparently.

All that information was given to me in one long stream of information about two seconds after I was through the front door. I swore to Samantha I was only going to be there for a minute and no longer, I wasn't there to cause her any problems. I just wanted to see a photo.

"A photo? What for?" she asked. Frankie's ears perked up too, wanting to know the answer just as eagerly at my side. He was still puffing from his heroic cycling efforts. Getting us across Lakeside in record time was like preparing for the Olympics.

"I don't have time to explain right now, I just need to see it. Please?" I said. It wasn't true, of course. There was no real urgency and all the time in the world.

It was only my father's life at stake.

He may still have been alive or he may have been killed already.

A few minutes of explanation could have been factored into the time budget. But, still, why risk it?

While Samantha still buzzed with confusion, I pushed past her and went to the photograph in question. It was a habit I had learned over my life, I scanned locations. Normally it was to look for lost things. However it also came in handy to really see my surroundings.

When I looked at things, I actually *saw* things.

The shoddy paint job my father probably did one weekend himself instead of hiring a professional, the skirting board that had been replaced in one area where the paint work didn't quite match up, the piece of Lego hidden underneath the drawers, the fact there wasn't one piece of dust on the countertop, and the perfectly aligned photographs that all pointed frontwards in a row.

In one of those pictures was my father. He was standing outside a log cabin with a man. They were shaking hands and smiling, rugged up and surrounded by snow. The lake in the background was frozen over and it was obviously taken in the middle of winter.

It had taken me a while to place the man. At first I had no idea who he was because I'd never seen him before.

Then I met him.

It took a few days after that for me to place him as the man in the picture.

It happened tonight.

He lived at number forty-nine Twiningdale Drive.

His name was Derrick Bowden.

And he had a stash of drugs and money in a storage locker.

I picked up the photograph and traced my father's face with my finger, wishing I could reach inside and ask him what had happened between them. Were they really friends? Were they still, even now?

At least there was one person in the room that still might be able to provide an answer. I held the photograph up to Samantha so she could see it clearly. "Do you know the man in this picture?"

She took it from me and replaced it on the counter, making sure it was perfectly straight once more. My stepmother had a touch of OCD in her. "Yes, he's a friend of your father's. Or, at least, was."

"They're not friends anymore?"

"I mean, while he was alive."

"That man is still alive," I pointed out, remembering how he was living and breathing only minutes earlier. I had seen him with my own two eyes.

"I was referring to your father," Samantha said sadly with a whimper. I wanted to kick myself. I had to remember that she thought Marshall Gabrielle was dead. She didn't share my thoughts and I wasn't about to convince her otherwise without any proof.

"Oh, sorry."

"It's okay. It's going to take a while for the news to sink in. I still don't know how I'm going to tell April." Fresh tears started to prick her red eyes and I felt like the worst person on the planet for putting her through this.

I forced myself to continue on before I chickened out. This was for the greater good. The end had to justify the means, I would make sure of it.

"The other man," I started again, "they were good friends?"

The tiniest of smiles graced her lips as she recalled a memory. "Very good friends. They went on a fishing trip every winter. Derrick would insist on Marshall staying at his cabin in the woods for the week. They'd have their male bonding time and come home smelling like fish. Marshall loved it."

"Where is this cabin?" I asked.

Samantha shrugged, staring at the photograph with misty eyes. "Marshall said it was out on Highway Eleven, just past the turnoff with the Hanging Tree. We drove past it a few times on our way to my mother's house. It's so isolated out there, always kind of gave me the creeps, if I was being honest. But Marshall loved it. Men." She laughed a little under her breath but it was a half-sob at the same time.

I gave her an awkward hug in goodbye. "Thanks, Samantha. I'll talk to you tomorrow, okay? Try to get some sleep."

"That's all you want to know?"

"That's all for now."

She still looked confused when she closed the door on us.

The moment we were outside, I pulled my cell phone out of my pocket and pulled up the bus schedule. Frankie hovered around me, a thousand questions just burning on the tip of his tongue.

Surprisingly, the first thing he said wasn't one of them. "You think this Derrick guy has your father in the cabin, don't you?"

"Yep."

"Are you going to tell me who he is?"

"I am going to tell you everything. Just as soon as I figure out a way to get to Highway Eleven using the Lakeside Bus Service." I searched with lightning speed through all the different routes. Throughout my sixteen years I thought I'd just about mastered the system but there were places even I'd learned were black holes of the system.

Frankie sighed and pulled out his cell phone, tapping on the screen before giving up and calling information instead. While he waited on hold, I continued to search and scroll through all the various routes.

The best I could do was get to the roadhouse that was still twenty miles from the highway. I would still have to hitch a ride from there to the cabin and I wasn't prepared to make myself into a victim in the process. I valued my life, I didn't want to end up as a True Crime Story in the process.

Frankie thanked the operator and ended the call. "Well?" I asked eagerly, hoping he'd had more luck speaking with a real person.

"She laughed at me. Told me good luck," he said, ruining all my optimism.

"Damn it."

"I could ask my parents but they're going to want a full explanation about what's going on."

"No. I don't want them dragged into this. It could be dangerous out there," I said. There was absolutely no way the good Bolero family was going to get wrapped up in this mess.

No freaking way.

I had three options.

Steal a car and learn how to drive.

Walk.

Beg and plead with Uncle Marvin, and by some sheer miracle, he agreed to take me out there.

Each seemed just as unlikely as the previous option. But only one seemed like the quickest option. I was going to have to go home and speak to my nearest and dearest.

"I have to get Uncle Marvin to take me," I said.

"Do you think he will?"

"Crazier things have happened."

"True that," Frankie said. And just like that, I burst out laughing. Because, surely, Frankie going gangster was much crazier than anything else that was going to happen that night.

Suddenly my chances with Uncle Marvin didn't seem so

bad.

We made the pilgrimage back home with an urgency that didn't seem misplaced. I had nothing but a hunch but I felt closer to my father than I had in ten years. He was out there somewhere and for the first time it was quite possible I knew where.

It seemed ridiculous that it took a kidnapping for me to finally work out where he was. I'd wasted so many seconds, minutes, hours, days, and even months of my life wondering where he was and now I knew. All I had to do was convince an overweight, cynical, and oftentimes grumpy man to take me to him.

Simple.

Not.

Frankie was very quiet as he peddled the bicycle like a boss all the way across Lakeside. He was puffed by the time the brakes squealed to a stop outside the door to our house but he never complained once.

Even though his legs had to be hurting.

And his lungs burning.

And his butt sore.

"Maybe you should wait here," I said as I jumped off the handlebars.

"Will you be okay?"

"It's Uncle Marvin, I think I can handle him."

Frankie nodded. "Call me if you need me and I'll come running inside. Just say the word."

I couldn't resist the urge to give him a quick hug before I hurried inside. He was so huggable that it was impossible to avoid or ignore those urges when they occurred.

It felt like I was going into a battlefield when I walked through the front door. Uncle Marvin was in front of the television, slumped in his favorite chair and holding a beer in one hand, the remote control in the other. I hoped the beer was the first of the evening and not the fifth—otherwise the entire plan was shot to pieces before it got a chance to begin.

"You didn't make dinner," Uncle Marvin greeted me. He often used such delightful words that I was taken aback by how lucky I was to have such wonderful family members.

"I was busy, I'm sorry."

"What was more important than making my dinner?"

"I think I know where Dad is. I need you to drive me there, the buses don't go out on that route."

I could have been mistaken but it appeared to me that Uncle Marvin sat up a little straighter, maybe a little more interested in what I had to say. Maybe his dinner was a little less more important now. "What makes you all knowledgeable all of a sudden?"

"I found out some information about him," I replied. We didn't have time to go through the whole story. Every nerve in my body wanted to get to the cabin in the woods before it was too late. Surely there was an expiry date on my father's life and it had to be getting close to reaching that time soon. "You're going to have to trust me on this, Uncle Marvin."

"Girl, I haven't trusted you a moment since your mama

pushed you out sixteen years ago."

"I know. But... please?"

"Why should I?"

"Because this time I think I'm right." Admittedly, it was a shaky argument and I didn't have a leg to stand on but surely if there was a moment in my life when I needed his blind trust, it was now.

We waited in silence while I willed Uncle Marvin to believe in miracles. I was a liar, I had lied my entire life and never much cared if people trusted me. If they believed me or if they didn't, it wasn't my problem.

Now, I really needed Uncle Marvin to believe me.

We stood in the middle of the living room, waiting for one of us to make the next move in our silent game of chess. I could feel my heart beating out the moments as it counted down the seconds.

Thump thump.

Thump thump.

If I was a bomb I would have already exploded. Sweat beaded on my brow, trickled down my temples before I could wipe it away with the back of my hand.

The ground started shaking.

From the reverberations from Uncle Marvin's foot as he placed it on the ground and stood up. He heaved his bulky frame from the comfortable armchair and stood.

"Let's go then."

I didn't question whether he was serious or not. I didn't dare say a word or give him the opportunity to change his mind. All I did was watch as Uncle Marvin collected his car keys from the bowl by the door and walked the few steps outside.

"Are you coming or not?" he asked brusquely as he paused with one hand on the screen door.

"Of course I am," I replied as I hurried to catch up. "Frankie's coming too." I took his grumbling as a sign of acquiescence rather than disapproval.

The three of us were in the car a few minutes later. We were on the road and heading down highway eleven while my mind was in a panicked haze. If I was wrong we were embarking on a complete wild goose chase that Uncle Marvin would never let me live down.

If I was right then we could be heading straight into a viper's nest. If Derrick Bowden was dangerous enough to kidnap his best friend, there was no telling how far he would go to protect the secret of his illegal operations. I was certain he wouldn't have any scruples about doing away with a few teenagers and an obnoxious middle aged man.

Hell, even I'd had thoughts about getting rid of Uncle Marvin before.

Just a little arsenic in his morning coffee would have done it.

But that would have been wrong. Even I had my limits. I was a liar, not a murderer.

There was a difference.

My stomach churned with a gazillion butterflies and not in a good way. All I could think about were the drugs and cash in the storage locker back in Lakeside. To make that kind of cash there must have been some serious business involved and to think my father was somehow involved in it all was horrible.

Whatever was waiting for us out at the cabin was not going to be pretty.

I just hoped we weren't too late.

Chapter 27

The winding roads leading to the cabin were making me nauseous. Street lights were a foreign concept out there, moonbeams and the car's headlights the only thing leading our way.

Uncle Marvin wasn't the best driver in good conditions. Out here it was like he had transformed into a rally car driver and didn't place any value on his life. He was living each moment like it was his last and I was expecting each moment to be the last one for us all.

My knuckles were as ghostly pale as my face.

At least it was dark so nobody noticed.

I swallowed down the urge to ask 'are we there yet?' because nobody would have the answer to that question. Uncle Marvin would only tell me we would be there when we got there. He was good at being obvious like that. Plus, I didn't want to take away any of his concentration from the road.

A glance into the backseat told me Frankie was having similar thoughts as he held on looking sufficiently concerned. Perhaps my father's life wasn't the only one in danger tonight.

The cabin finally loomed in the distance as we rounded a bend and skidded to a stop. The brakes locked as the wheels screeched and kicked up stones behind us.

There was chaos at the scene in front of us and not the kind I had been expecting. We climbed out of the car quietly, kind of a little redundant with the kind of noise the car had made with our grand arrival.

Still, the men we could see inside the cabin hadn't seemed to notice. They were engaged in a loud argument, too busy with their own drama to notice ours.

We crept to the window and crouched down, listening through the open screens with a clear view of what was happening.

There were three of them, including Derrick Bowden. He had beaten us to the cabin, he must have left as soon as he had checked on his storage locker. Without having to beg Uncle Marvin for a ride first, he would have easily made it with plenty of time to spare.

I recognized one of the other men from the shop. His nametag had identified him as Malcolm and he was *Ready to Assist*. That was probably a bigger lie than anything I had ever said.

"The police are declaring him dead. I'm telling you, they are calling off the search," Malcom said. I exchanged a look with Frankie.

They were talking about my dad.

Derrick shook his head. "It's not that simple, Mal. There is a process, they need a body. Just because some simple cops say someone is dead, doesn't mean they close the case. We can't dump the body and consider the whole mess over and done with. It's not that easy."

The body?

That didn't sound good.

Everything inside me froze.

"Why can't we make it that easy? I'll make a fire out back and we'll burn him. Nobody will ever find a thing."

The way they were talking so blasé about the death of my father was sickening. I couldn't process the fact he was gone yet or the fact we were too late. The option to walk away wasn't there, not when we'd come this way.

If I couldn't walk away with him alive then I would walk away with his body. At least he would have a proper burial. At least I would be able to have a proper goodbye and April would have a grave to visit when she wanted somewhere to grieve when she grew up.

That was something I could do.

It was something I had to do.

I could cry later. While there was still work to be done I would hold myself together and do it.

That was what I'd been doing my entire life.

"Smoke will get everywhere," Derrick complained.

"I'll close the windows first."

He still wasn't convinced. There was no telling what the third guy was thinking. He stood as still as a statue with his arms crossed. He was blonde-headed and built like a brick wall. I got the feeling in a showdown with a tornado, it would be the tornado that would go around him.

"Fine," Derrick said. "If you want to kill him so badly, then you go do it. I'm going to have a beer."

Wait.

He wasn't dead yet.

That meant he still had a chance.

It meant *I* still a chance. There was something I still could do. I wasn't sure what it was yet but that had never stopped me before.

I stood up.

And waved my hands in front of the window.

"Em!" Frankie angry-whispered at me.

I ignored him and walked to the door, hoping the boy and my uncle would catch onto my plan soon enough. If I could distract the men for just a few moments, hopefully it would give them enough time to look for my dad. He had to be in the house somewhere if they were going to kill him.

The door to the cabin was unlocked. I walked straight on in. "You know, for criminals, you aren't very smart on security measures," I said. The trio stared at me like they couldn't believe what they were seeing. It would have been funny if they weren't within reaching distance of guns.

The tornado killer was holding one in his right hand already.

Talk about quick as lightning.

He was the one to watch.

"Who are you?" Malcolm asked. Clearly he wasn't as eagle-eyed as me.

"I'm Marshall Gabrielle's daughter. You can call me Em."

They exchanged a glance. They were hardly panicked about my presence. Considering they were all much larger than I was and there were three of them, I wouldn't have been worried either if the tables were turned. If anyone should have been terrified, it was me.

And I was, seriously.

I just prayed Uncle Marvin and Frankie had my back somewhere close by.

And for once in my life the lucky stars were shining favorably on me.

"What are you doing here?" Derrick asked. He seemed perplexed more than anything. I could run with that emotion, it seemed better than the option of violence.

"I'm here to rescue my father. I heard he was in a bit of a sticky situation and I was hoping you could find it in your hearts to let him go," I said. "But I'm guessing that's probably not going to happen, right?"

"Uh, yeah, you guessed right."

"So you're planning on killing me too? At least you'll have a bigger fire in the backyard now, right?"

Malcolm grinned like a fool but it quickly turned into a scowl when he looked at his boss for confirmation. "You shouldn't have come here, girlie. You've made everything that much messier. Your father would not be pleased to see you."

"Oh, I don't know about that. I think he'd be proud of his firstborn, coming to the rescue, riding in to save the day. There's got to be something good in that story, one would think," I said. Behind him, Frankie came into view. He was carrying a stick above his head, poising it ready to hit Derrick with. It didn't look heavy enough to do enough damage to his thick skull. I tried not to look and give away his presence. "Wouldn't you be proud of your children if the situation were reversed?"

"My kids know better than to get into situations that are well over their heads."

"Maybe you need to feed them concrete, make them tougher."

Malcolm chuckled, I thought he was warming to me. I stole a glance his way and regretted it. Uncle Marvin's large form loomed behind him with nothing more than a potted plant to use as a weapon against him. We were mice taking on elephants–clumsy, ill-equipped mice.

Derrick almost looked around and my heart practically stopped. "I called the police, did I mention that?" I said quickly. "Yeah, on my way here. I called them and told them everything I know, which is actually a lot. I told them about the drugs and the fact you kidnapped my father, who is alive in this cabin. They are on the way here. I had to fill in some blanks, though. I'm assuming you took my father because he uncovered some things about your illegal activities that he shouldn't have. But you needed someone to do your computer work so you brought Marshall into the fold. When he found out too much you had no choice except to threaten his life. When he didn't comply you were going to kill him. Am I close?"

"This isn't *Scooby Doo*, I'm not going to confess everything to you," Derrick replied.

"But I'm right, aren't I?"

The look on Malcolm's face all but confirmed it.

So I just kept on lying while I was on a roll. "The police believed everything, we'll be hearing their sirens any second now. You'll all be arrested and your entire world will come down all around you. That's what you get for messing with a Gabrielle."

All of a sudden Frankie took a swing and the stick collided with the back of Derrick's head. It made a sickening crack at the same time Uncle Marvin threw his potted plant at Malcolm's head. I lunged for the tornado killer, taking him by surprise and managing to sidestep him at the last minute to grab his gun. I used the butt of it to slam into his ribcage. While he was clutching it I took the opportunity to slap the gun across his face which caused blood to instantly gush from his forehead.

Frankie ended the job with the stick, bringing it over the back of his head and bringing him down to the floor. The three of the men sprawled on the carpet, unconscious–for now.

We didn't have much time before they regained their senses.

I quickly scoped out the cabin, running from room to room. There were only a few and my father was in none of them. The last room was a set of stairs that led down a set of stairs.

"Downstairs!" I shouted, already taking two steps at a time. It was dark and I couldn't see what I was running into. It was so quiet all I could hear was my own ragged breaths.

The steps seemed to go on forever as it grew colder and colder. At least I knew I was going into the depths of hell. My foot suddenly hit concrete, the jolt shuddering through my body sharply. I felt around the walls for a light switch, wishing for even a flickering of light in the absolute darkness.

Finally, I found one and flicked it.

I closed my eyes and turned around slowly, terrified about what I was going to see when I opened them again.

It took every inch of my resolve to open them again. Once I saw what I was about to see there was no going back again. I couldn't un-see what I was about to view.

I opened one eye first.

Then the other.

And then I saw what I would never be able to un-see.

My father.

Chapter 28

He was sitting only four feet from me.

Marshall Gabrielle.

The man I had not seen since I was six years old.

My father.

The man whom I had had many imaginary conversations with over my lifetime. The one I missed, blamed, loved, hated, and a plethora more of emotions I couldn't even begin to describe in the few seconds I stood there staring at him.

He was tied up, bound with rope with a rag tied around his mouth. He couldn't move, all he could do was stare at me with the same surprised expression as the one I wore across my face. Considering we were related we probably looked like mirror images of one another.

I wasn't entirely sure who was more shocked to see each other.

Him or me.

A fleeting thought wondered if he even recognized me.

It had been a long time since my father saw me and I had grown up a lot since he left me standing in the middle of Uncle Marvin's house with a tear in my eye and confusion written across my face.

But we didn't have time to go into that right now.

Not for the first time in my life, I shoved all those emotions into a teeny tiny little box in the back of my head and suppressed it into the depths of my mind. Maybe I would save it for another day, maybe I would leave it there forever.

Just getting through the remainder of the night would be good.

The rest would have to wait and see.

"Em, you got him?" Frankie yelled down from the top of the staircase.

"Yeah," I called back. "Should be up soon."

"You might want to hurry. Need a hand?"

"All good."

"Okay."

Like a spell had been broken, the lid was placed on the box and I came to my senses. I got to work with my father's ropes. I untied them with shaking hands. I almost forgot the gag around his mouth, he pulled that one loose himself.

"Emmeline?" he asked with wonderment lacing the word.

"It's Em." He would have known that if he hadn't lost me all those years ago.

Those that loved me knew it.

Even those that tolerated me knew it.

"How did you find me? What are you doing here?"

"You can ask questions later. Right now we have to get out of here," I said. Besides, if anyone had a right to answers it was me. He had no business in asking questions here. Not when there were years' worth festering inside of me.

Dad opened his mouth to protest but a loud crash from above closed it again. He pulled the remains of his ropes from around his body and threw them to the ground. Standing, he didn't tower so far above me anymore like he used to. We were almost eye level now. In the years that had passed I had grown. Somehow it was a change I hadn't been expecting.

"You're so big now," Dad muttered.

Apparently the surprise wasn't owned entirely by me.

It annoyed me more than anything.

"If you didn't leave me it wouldn't be so much of a shock," I replied, not bothering to stick around and wait to hear whatever else he wanted to say.

I charged for the stairs and headed upwards, now more concerned about how Frankie and Uncle Marvin were fairing than my father. I knew he was safe now but the others were a different story.

The moment my head peeked into the next floor, my panic levels went into overdrive. Not only were the terrible duo upright and kicking, they had backup in the form of another five men who were packing more heat than a blanket factory.

We were going to lose that fight.

Not only because we were sadly outnumbered but because we weren't fighters. We had no training, we had no weapons, and we actually had scruples. We cared about the law, we cared about not inflicting pain upon another human being.

"Emmeline, get out of here," Marshall Gabrielle urged from behind me. He pushed me toward the front door but my feet didn't budge. I wasn't going to leave Frankie and Uncle Marvin when they were still there. Nor was I going to take an order from a man who called me Emmeline.

My name was not Emmeline.

Maybe legally, fine. But that name belonged to my dead mother, it would never belong to me.

I was Em.

Only Em.

Frankie picked up a vase and threw it at Malcolm's head, he ducked to the side and it hit the wall. The vase smashed into a million pieces and made Malcolm so angry he immediately lunged at Frankie and pinned him to the wall. I screamed and leaped for him, trying to drag the muscled man away from the boy I loved.

Uncle Marvin was losing his own battle, locked in a triangle of doom with the tornado killer and one of the new guys. They were all struggling, trying to get my uncle to the floor where they could take him out for good. Uncle Marvin was trying to use his weight to his advantage, it was the only thing he had, but he was losing.

"Get off me, you bitch," Malcolm hissed at me.

I replied by trying to gouge his eyes out. He didn't appreciate it but he did let Frankie go. He slumped to the ground, taking only a few quick moments to recover before making it to his feet again.

Malcolm shook me off so violently I fell against the wall. My arm felt the impact, promising a serious bruise I would be sporting for a few days afterwards. If that was the extent of my injuries after all this I would consider myself lucky.

Uncle Marvin lost his battle and tumbled to the floor. He was like a bug, his arms and legs flailing in the air while he couldn't stand up again. "Uncle Marvin!" I called out. Frankie and I exchanged a quick glance before running to his aid.

We barged past the men and stood guard over my uncle. There was no way he could get up without assistance and we didn't have a chance of being able to give it to him while we were under attack.

"Pick on someone your own size," I snarled at them.

"Move aside, little girl," Derrick growled. "You're gonna get hurt. Don't think we won't touch you because you're a girl."

"I'm sure you'll do whatever it takes."

"Then let us do what we need to."

"That's not going to happen," I said. I might have had all the words but I was terrified inside. There didn't seem to be a way out of the situation and my father had disappeared once again. It was just the eight of them against the three of us.

We were cornered.

Uncle Marvin was on his back like a cockroach.

Frankie was by my side, his hand in mine.

It wouldn't be long before Malcolm would be starting the fire in the backyard.

I hope he had some marshmallows to toast.

It was going to be a heck of a bonfire.

Chapter 29

The darkness of the night outside suddenly flashed with colors.

For a moment I thought I was having an honest to goodness heart attack. The room lit up with the lights, shining as brightly as if we were being swarmed by UFOs and aliens were about to join us for some late night snacks.

Everyone froze as the seconds ticked by the room.

The criminals were momentarily stunned by the flashing lights before they jumped into action. They recognized the implications before I did, instantly understanding the police were outside.

"Lay down your weapons and place your hands on your head," boomed the voice from outside. They were speaking on a megaphone with a slight echo.

The guys scoffed, trying to put on bravado in front of one another. Either that or they really were just stupidly brave. Sure, they had guns and knives, but so did the police.

Considering the police were permitted to use theirs, I know which side I would be more afraid of.

"Nobody needs to get hurt tonight," the police negotiator continued.

Derrick whispered to his men, so quietly I couldn't hear them. We were momentarily forgotten while they consulted between themselves. Surely they had to understand they were outnumbered. With the police outside their door, and probably surrounding the property, their chances of getting out of there were zero to none.

Or were they crazy enough to believe they could get away?

I'd seen crazier.

I remained quiet, too scared to say a word. It was up to the police now. Plus, I didn't want to remind them that they had three hostage candidates with them. We had red targets blazoned across our chests which I hoped they didn't notice.

"We have you surrounded. There is no way out."

More whispering.

"We all want a peaceful resolution tonight."

All of a sudden the group broke up and Malcolm raised his gun, shooting out the back window without warning. An involuntary scream escaped my throat. Frankie held me against him as I buried my face against his chest. I couldn't look any more, I didn't want to see what else they were about to shoot.

The window at the front of the cabin suddenly exploded as a can was thrown through from the other side. After a few seconds it started leaking with smoke, filling the entire room with a thick fog. It choked my lungs and made breathing difficult as I coughed and spluttered.

My eyes started watering, making everything blurry through the grey smog. I held onto Frankie tighter as I struggled to see what was going on around me.

The noise of doors opening, slamming, closing, and then footsteps, shouting, guns, cries, orders surrounded me. If I could have seen anything I probably would have been terrified. As it was, all I could do was stay completely still and hold onto Frankie with a silent prayer on my lips that we were invisible and therefore safe.

"This is the police, you're okay. Come with me," a woman said softly into my ear. For a moment I wondered if she was lying to me but there were no females in Derrick's gang so I opened my watering eyes and followed her.

"We need to help Uncle Marvin," I said.

"We have an officer assisting him," she replied.

I held onto Frankie like my life depended on it. There was no way I was letting him out of my sight.

Outside the house I blinked and reveled in the fresh air. Wiping my eyes on my sleeve, I pushed all the grit and smoke out of them. They had to blink several times before they would entertain the idea of staying open for a long length of time.

The policewoman guided us to the bank of several vehicles. She sat us at the back of an SUV, handing us some water and telling us to drink and wash our eyes out. We followed directions like robots. Uncle Marvin joined us a few minutes later.

Honestly, I don't think I've ever been that excited to see my uncle before. I wrapped my arms around him and buried my face in the folds of his stomach before sitting back down again.

He perched on the edge of the vehicle with us. "About time you showed up. You sure took your time," he grumbled.

"We came as soon as we could, sir," the policewoman replied. Uncle Marvin grumbled in response, his usual demeanor returning. Clearly his near-death experience hadn't given him a new outlook on life.

I turned to my uncle. "You called the police?"

"Yeah."

"When?"

"Just before we left home."

"Why?" I asked as I replayed the moments just after I convinced him to give me a ride out to the cabin. There had been a few moments I left him alone while I got Frankie and told him we had a lift. I never expected him to call the police in that time, though.

"Because you said your father was out here," Uncle Marvin replied, like it should have been obvious.

"But you think I lie about everything," I said.

"You do. Most things, anyway. I trusted you on this so I thought I'd save us all some trouble and call the police." I could have been mistaken but his cheeks blushed just a little while he spoke. Maybe Uncle Marvin didn't loathe me as much as I thought he did. Maybe he had a teeny, tiny soft spot for me somewhere inside. "Stop looking at me like that. I only did it because I knew you were leading us into something dangerous and I need you to keep making my dinner."

"Right, of course," I said.

At least I didn't lie when I told Derrick Bowden and his friends that the police were on the way. That had to be a first. Maybe I was turning over a new leaf. Maybe I would start telling the truth from now on.

Like that was ever going to happen.

I loved lying.

It was a part of me.

The policewoman's walkie-talkie crackled. "All suspects have been apprehended. No casualties. The place is clear. Crime Scene Unit can move in and start to process."

All the fear left my body with a sigh. Frankie squeezed my hand in silent communication. We had done it. We survived and succeeded in rescuing my dad. Everyone important to me was safe and sound.

Even if my dad had disappeared again.

At least I'd got to see him.

For a few moments.

I had a new image of him to add to my image bank. Maybe all I needed was a few minutes every decade and that would tide me over until the next encounter. I'd done fine without him all this time, it wasn't like I needed him in my life, after all.

Still, it stung.

To know he just took off like that. He couldn't even stick around to see if we were all right?

I was his daughter, Uncle Marvin was his brother. He should have been fighting alongside us, helping us, we were there because of him. We saved his life, risked ours for his. He should have had the decency to stick around.

Frankie pulled me closer to him as if he could read everything that was going on inside my mind. I felt safe snuggled up next to him. He had shown me how brave he was tonight.

And how stupid he was by coming with me.

I thought he was smarter than that.

He was my hero. The boy that knew better than to take on a guy twice his size and did it anyway. He could have died several times tonight but he fought alongside me anyway.

I loved him.

With every piece of my broken heart.

I'd given so many pieces of myself to those that just threw them away. Those pieces were laying in dumps all over Lakeside. I hoped someone like Mr. Adison would find them and give them a home.

I would never get them back again.

But maybe they could regenerate. Perhaps it would take people like Frankie and Samantha and April to shape new pieces and place them in the gaping holes left by those of the past.

My heart might be whole again one day.

Perhaps, one day.

Miracles had proven themselves to occur so I wasn't about to dismiss anything too quickly.

A long shadow took away the light from all the cars, stealing my attention away from my thoughts. I looked up, expecting to see Uncle Marvin waiting impatiently so we could leave—he was probably hungry or ready for bed.

Instead I saw someone that looked similar but was half his weight. Someone that shared the same nose but his was straight and hadn't been broken at some stage. A man that shared the same surname but didn't raise me from a child.

My father.

Marshall Gabrielle.

I guessed he didn't take off after all.

Chapter 30

"Can I talk to you?" Dad asked. His eyes didn't stay on me, they flicked between all of us. Me, Uncle Marvin, Frankie, the police officers surrounding us.

Frankie squeezed my hand. "Do you want us to stay?"

I both wanted to speak with my father and I didn't. There were things I wanted to say and things I didn't want to hear. Inside me was a war raging on while everybody looked at me and expected an answer.

It was difficult catching my thoughts as they flew around my brain and then sorted them into some sort of order. The best I could come up with was knowing that if I didn't speak now, I would regret it later.

There were things I needed to say to him.

I pushed to my feet and unraveled the blanket from around my shoulders that the policewoman had given to me. I could do this. I needed to speak with my father but I couldn't do it with so many eyes watching me. "We'll be right back," I assured them.

My father and I found a quiet spot by a police van a few cars over. Everyone else was busy with their tasks while we stood in silence looking at each other expectantly. Apparently we'd forgotten how to speak with one another.

The silence was killing me. "I thought you ran away."

"I heard the sirens. I ran outside to wave down the police, it's difficult to find the cabins sometimes," he explained. I wanted to believe him so I chose to. It seemed easy enough. "Did you really think I would just run away when you were still in there?"

I shrugged. It seemed the appropriate response.

He slumped against the vehicle as his face turned up toward the sky. His profile made him look exactly like Uncle Marvin. I hadn't noticed that when I was six years old. He was always just my dad, I never thought of him as my uncle's brother.

He sighed out a long breath. "I really stuffed everything up. I'm so sorry, Emmeline."

"Please don't call me that. I'm Em. Everybody calls me Em."

"Why's that?" He seemed genuinely interested, like perhaps I was an enigma he was trying to figure out.

"Because it was her name, it belonged to Mom. I'm Em, that name belongs to me."

My father stared at me for a long time, his eyes grazing over my features like a razor blade. I refused to look away, stuck in his gaze like a deer caught in headlights. In all the hundreds of ways I'd imagined this reunion, I'd never pictured it to be like this.

There were no slow motion scenes with inspirational music playing in the background.

No tears and smiles with outstretched arms that we ran into, spinning around until we were both dizzy and giggling when we finally collided in the middle.

A montage of our lives didn't play in the sky, showing our lives as we made our way back to each other.

It was just the two us standing in the shadows, awkwardly trying to work out what we were supposed to do and say to one another. The years that had passed seemed to tear apart our relationship brick by brick, scattering the pieces in the wind.

I wondered if we would ever be able to rebuild that relationship.

Did I want to?

Did *he?*

"You look just like her, you know that?" Dad said. It took me a moment to realize he was talking about my mother again. Emmeline Gabrielle.

The *original* Emmeline Gabrielle.

The *only* Emmeline Gabrielle, as far as I was concerned.

"Uncle Marvin doesn't have any pictures of her," I replied honestly. I had no idea what my mother looked like. I'd wondered many times but it was a pointless exercise. Her image was lost and I couldn't find it no matter how often I searched.

"I do, at home. I can give them to you, if you like."

"I would like that, thank you."

He nodded, again reminding me of Uncle Marvin. His brother might have grumbled about him mercilessly but they sure had a lot in common. I remembered the photograph I'd seen of them in Uncle Marvin's closet, of the two boys up to mischief together, I could see it now. I bet they got up to so much trouble they gave their parents more headaches than not.

"Why'd you leave?" I asked before I lost the nerve. The question popped out before I could have second thoughts about it. It was, after all, the question I really wanted to know the answer to.

My father's eyes snapped to mine, sadness turning them darker. "I wasn't coping. Your mother was the love of my life. I thought we were going to be together forever, grow old together and the whole deal. When she died I just lost it. I fell apart and I didn't know how to put myself back together again."

"It wasn't my fault she died."

"No, it wasn't. It wasn't anyone's fault. But I wasn't a good father. I couldn't look after you, I couldn't even look after myself. I didn't know what to do so I just left. I didn't think it through, all I could think of was getting away from everything that reminded me of her."

"You could have taken me with you," I pointed out.

"I couldn't look after you, honey. I was a mess. You were too young to understand, but I was barely functioning. I knew Marvin would provide for you, he would look after you when I couldn't. You were safe with him."

"He wasn't you, he wasn't my father." Tears started to prick my eyes, making them sting. I didn't want to turn into a blubbering mess right now but it didn't seem like I had much of a choice in the matter.

Ten years of holding it all inside tended to make you an emotional time bomb.

Yeah, me.

"I'm so sorry, Em. I thought I was making the right decision at the time. I've regretted it ever since."

"You were living in Lakeside, only a few streets from my house," I said, my voice got louder as I forced the shakiness from it. "You could have visited me any time but you didn't. You just let me stay lost all this time. I have a sister, for crying out loud! Would you ever have found me? Ever?"

"I didn't want to disrupt your life. I know that sounds like an excuse or me taking the easy way out, but it's not. Em, I've thought about you every day since I last saw you. I've dreamed about having you back in my life but I've feared this moment too. I've been so scared you wouldn't want me that I'd convinced myself it was better this way." He stopped, taking a deep breath and staring back up at the stars again. "I want us to be a family, Em. Please give me a second chance. I'm not perfect, I know I made a huge mistake, but please let me make it up to you."

"How do I know you won't do it again? How do I know you won't leave again one day if it all gets too hard?"

"I've changed. I've grown up. I'm not that same man anymore. I have a wife, and you obviously know about your sister…"

"I've met Samantha and April."

"We could be a family," Dad said hopefully.

My heart tugged and I wanted to believe him. A part of me already did. I wasn't so hard that I didn't give second chances when they were due. Perhaps Marshall Gabrielle didn't deserve one but maybe my dad did. I was only sixteen years old, I had a whole life ahead of me. Carrying a grudge was hard work, forgiveness was lighter and far less strenuous.

"We can go for ice cream as a start," I said, putting up a hand to stop him when it seemed like he was about to go in for a hug. "But I already have a family. Uncle Marvin is part of my life and he has to be included in everything. He's part of the deal or there is no deal."

Dad stuck out his hand in lieu of the hug, I shook it. "We have a deal."

"You also need to meet Frankie. If I get my way, he's going to be around for a long time too."

"Can I give him a hard time?"

"Only when he deserves it." I smiled and it felt good as my dad smiled back at me. We had the same one, just slightly crooked but not in a way that other people would notice.

We returned to the others, exhausted. It wasn't so much the physical fight that had taken its toll on me but the emotional showdown with my father that had had the biggest impact.

I still couldn't believe my father was back.

We piled into the back of a police vehicle and were taken to the Lakeside Police Station. All I wanted to do was climb into bed and sleep for a thousand years but apparently that had to wait until we'd given a full statement.

Each of us were given a blank piece of paper and pen, told to write out everything we knew. Typing would have been a million times quicker but the police budget didn't extend that far.

I checked.

And was shot down quickly.

My hand was aching and sore by the time I squiggled the last few words on the yellow legal pad. The poor person who had to decipher the last few parts was really going to struggle with my slipping penmanship. They would reconsider the budget position afterwards.

A commotion caught my attention as I twirled my pen through my fingers and waited for the others to finish. The door to the otherwise quiet room burst open, startling me for a few panic-filled seconds.

Samantha and April ran into the room. My father was across the floor in no time, sweeping them up in his arms and hugging them tight to his chest. It was beautiful watching their reunion, I couldn't stop the lump forming in my throat and the new round of tears stinging my eyes.

If I needed any more confirmation that my father was sticking around for good this time, it was right in front of my eyes. He wouldn't voluntarily leave his wife and kid. Samantha and April were his entire life, they filled his soul with love and life. There was no conceivable way he would lose them like he had lost me.

Maybe there was something poetic in the way he had left me, after all. He had loved my mother so much he couldn't bear to be reminded of her. I was the ultimate memory keeper, the kid born from their affections. There *was* romance in that concept, just the realistic implications of it were ugly.

At least I knew my parents loved each other once.

I was sure my father once wrapped my mother and me in the same bear hug he now held Samantha and April in now. If I filled my head with thoughts like that, I could only smile.

Maybe, in time, the image I had burning in my mind of his back as he left would slowly dissolve.

He would turn around and I would only see him entering.

My father broke his hug with Samantha and April, freeing up one arm to beckon me over. I actually looked behind me to make sure he was speaking with me.

There was nobody behind me.

Slowly, I pushed my seat back and stood. Everything swayed around me for a moment as all the blood rushed to my head. More than anything I needed to sleep, but it would have to be on pause for a few minutes more.

A hug was awaiting me.

Shyness suddenly overwhelmed me when I reached the trio. They were a family and it still felt odd that they wanted me to be a part of it. Frankie gave me a thumbs up when I looked for some reassurance over my shoulder.

Uncle Marvin rolled his eyes.

Dad didn't give me any more time to hesitate. His arm wrapped around my back and pulled me into the group. We hugged, all four of us together.

It felt warm.

It felt safe.

It felt like something was starting.

Something good.

It was the police officer that eventually broke us up, collecting our statements like it was homework and telling us we were free to leave. I assured my father I would be fine to go home with Uncle Marvin and I would catch up with him sometime soon.

He assured me he wouldn't leave again.

Ninety-nine percent of me believed him.

The remaining one percent would stay with me forever, a scar carved into my being that would never fully fade.

"Let's go home, girl," Uncle Marvin said. Even he looked tired, all the wrinkles on his face just that much deeper. He had been reunited with his brother tonight but they hadn't said much. His scars were going to take time to heal too.

Maybe they were deeper than mine.

The bond of brotherhood was a sin to sever and my father had done just that. An impassioned speech and an apology wouldn't be sufficient for Uncle Marvin.

I would have to tell my father to invite his brother for dinner, that was the way to his forgiveness. A few lamb shanks cooked just the right way and Uncle Marvin would forgive anything.

Frankie rode with us, sitting in the back seat while I rode shotgun. "Thank you for believing in me," I said to my uncle. It was easier talking in the car, we didn't have to look at each other while the road demanded his attention.

He sighed and shifted in his seat, adjusting the seatbelt. "I always believe in you, Em. I might not say it, but I always know it. I'm glad you got to see your idiot dad tonight."

"I am too."

"You'll always have a home with me, though. Don't be thinking you have to leave me just because he's back. Okay?"

"I won't. Thank you." I knew what his offer cost him because Uncle Marvin was not one for talking about his feelings. This was about the most touchy-feely conversation we'd ever had.

And I think I preferred it that way.

"I know Recycle Club is a sham," Uncle Marvin suddenly blurted out. He risked a quick glance my way, seeing the shocked expression on my face. "You go to the mall every Wednesday, I've seen you there. You don't have to lie about it anymore."

"Why didn't you tell me?" I wasn't sure whether I should have been relieved or horrified. It wasn't like I enjoyed people knowing I was a liar. Especially my family.

My uncle shrugged one heavy shoulder. "Thought you had your reasons. You have your secrets, I have mine."

I remembered all the times I had seen Uncle Marvin

acting a little odd recently. He did have secrets, ones I wasn't sure I wanted to know about. If he could give me Recycle Club, I could give him his secret meetings.

Our awkward conversation came to a stop when we pulled up at our house. Uncle Marvin was quick to get inside, shooting me a final pointed look before leaving.

He still didn't like Frankie.

Now I had two fatherly figures to hassle me about my boyfriend.

Great.

Actually, it kind of was.

Frankie and I climbed out of the car and into the still night air. The sun was just starting to peek over the horizon, we'd been up all night long. The grass was dewy at our feet, just wet enough to permeate the air with a crisp sweet scent.

"I'm sorry he wouldn't drop you at home," I apologized.

"It's no problem. I don't mind the walk," Frankie replied. Even with his fatigue he could still flash me that brilliant smile of his. He was worth every piece of gold in the entire world.

"Maybe things can start to resemble normal around here."

"Where would the fun be in that?" He gave me a warm hug and it was more wonderful than seeing the sun rise at the end of the street. Things seemed so much shinier in Lakeside that morning.

It was a new dawn.

A new day.

A new era.

Frankie loosened his grip on me as I stood back so I could see his beautiful blue eyes. I was lost in them momentarily as I fought the urge to drown in them.

And then a noise caught my attention.

"Hey, someone's moving in down the road," I said, pointing to a removals truck as it pulled up. It was followed by a small car. A family piled out—a man, woman, and teenage girl.

"Looks like a nice family," Frankie replied, always the optimist. "The girl looks to be about our age. I wonder if she's going to be attending our school?"

"I don't know." Until I knew more about her, I also didn't know if I wanted her to attend the same school. New people made me wary, even if they did look like a nice family, as Frankie said.

"So maybe a trip to the mall on Saturday?" Frankie suggested.

"I don't think so. Maybe we should do something different. How about going to the movies? Or we could go swimming if the weather's nice," I said.

Two things I wouldn't have done before.

You couldn't find lost things at the movies or in the water.

"Sounds good," Frankie said, giving me a gentle kiss on the lips. "I'll talk to you later after we get some sleep. Sweet dreams, Em."

"Sweet dreams, Frankie."

I watched the boy I love as he walked with a slight limp down the sun-streaked street. My heart beat excessively just because of him. He was gorgeous and wonderful, even seeing just the back of him as he left.

Seeing him go didn't fill me with panic.

I knew Frankie would come back.

Knew it like I knew my own name.

There were some people in your life you knew wouldn't hurt you and others you always suspected would. Frankie was in the former category while everyone else was in the latter. Slowly, over time, maybe they would shift into the first category.

I hoped so.

I staggered back inside and pulled myself up to my bedroom. Taking one last look at my shelves containing all the lost things, I knew I didn't need the shelves in the attic anymore.

The urge I always held to seek out and find those items that had been lost didn't beat within me anymore. It had been silenced, quelled, and stilled. I felt at peace for the first time since I could remember.

Maybe I didn't have the compulsion anymore for one simple reason.

I wasn't lost anymore.

I had been found.

* * *

Little did Em or Frankie realize at the time but what

they had witnessed outside the house with the removals truck was also a new beginning. Very soon, days in fact, they would meet The Keeper of Secret Things.

Her story was completely unlike Ems.

She had a family, a nice one just as Frankie had correctly guessed. They had a happy home, warmth lived in every room, and love flowed freely.

But the Keeper of Secret Things had secrets herself.

Secrets that had the potential to turn the city of Lakeside completely on its head.

CONTINUE THE STORY

The keeper of secret Things

THE BIGGEST SECRET SHE KEEPS IS
HER OWN.

OUT NOW

About the Author

Jamie Campbell grew up in the New South Wales town of Port Macquarie as the youngest of six children. She now resides on the Gold Coast in Queensland, Australia.

Writing since she could hold a pencil, Jamie's passion for storytelling and wild imagination were often a cause for concern with her school teachers. Now that imagination is used for good instead of mischief.

Visit www.jamiecampbell.com.au now for exclusive website only content.

Jamie loves hearing from her readers, send her an email at Jamie@jamiecampbell.com.au

Made in the USA
Middletown, DE
12 February 2021